**Date: 2/3/12**

**FIC ROHMER
Rohmer, Sax,
The Golden Scorpion /**

# "YOU ARE EITHER A FIEND OR A MADMAN!"

# THE GOLDEN SCORPION

## Sax Rohmer

## The American Reprint Company
MATTITUCK

Reprinted 1984


International Standard Book Number 0-89190-806-4

**To the Reader**

It is our pleasure to keep available uncommon
fiction and to this end, at the time of publication,
we have used the best available sources. To aid
catalogers and collectors, this title is printed in
an edition limited to 300 copies. ――― **Enjoy!**

To order contact
AMERICAN REPRINT COMPANY, a division of
American Reprint Co./Rivercity Press
PO Box 1200
Mattituck, New York 11952


*Manufactured in the United States of America*

# Contents

## PART III

### AT THE HOUSE OF AH-FANG-FU

## PART IV

### THE LAIR OF THE SCORPION

# PART I

## Chapter 1

## THE SHADOW OF A COWL

KEPPEL STUART, M.D., F.R.S., awoke with a start and discovered himself to be bathed in cold perspiration. The moonlight shone in at his window, but did not touch the bed, therefore his awakening could not be due to this cause. He lay for some time listening for any unfamiliar noise which might account for the sudden disturbance of his usually sound slumbers. In the house below nothing stirred. His windows were widely open and he could detect that vague drumming which is characteristic of midnight London; sometimes, too, the clashing of buffers upon some siding of the Brighton railway where shunting was in progress and occasional siren notes from the Thames. Otherwise—nothing.

He glanced at the luminous disk of his watch. The hour was half-past two. Dawn was not far off. The night seemed to have become almost intolerably hot, and to this heat Stuart felt disposed to ascribe both his awakening and also a feeling of uncomfortable tension of which he now became aware. He continued to listen, and, listening and hearing nothing, recognised with anger that he was frightened. A sense of some presence oppressed him. Someone or something evil was near him—perhaps in the room, veiled by the shadows. This uncanny sensation grew more and more marked.

Stuart sat up in bed, slowly and cautiously, looking all about him. He remembered to have awakened once thus in India—and to have found a great cobra coiled at his feet. His inspection revealed the presence of nothing unfamiliar, and he stepped out on to the floor.

A faint clicking sound reached his ears. He stood quite still. The clicking was repeated.

"There is someone downstairs in my study!" muttered Stuart.

He became aware that the fear which held him was such that unless he acted and acted swiftly he should become incapable of action, but he remembered that whereas the moonlight poured into the bedroom, the staircase would be in complete darkness. He walked barefooted across to the dressing-table and took up an electric torch which lay there. He had not used it for some time, and he pressed the button to learn if the torch was charged. A beam of white light shone out across the room, and at the same instant came another sound.

If it came from below or above, from the adjoining room or from outside in the road, Stuart knew not. But following hard upon the mysterious disturbance which had aroused him it seemed to pour ice into his veins, it added the complementary touch to his panic. For it was a kind of low wail—a ghostly minor wail in falling cadences —unlike any sound he had heard. It was so excessively horrible that it produced a curious effect.

Discovering from the dancing of the torch-ray that his hand was trembling, Stuart concluded that he had awakened from a nightmare and that this fiendish wailing was no more than an unusually delayed aftermath of the imaginary horrors which had bathed him in cold perspiration.

He walked resolutely to the door, threw it open and cast the beam of light on to the staircase. Softly he began to descend. Before the study door he paused. There was no sound. He threw open the door, directing the torch-ray into the room.

Cutting a white lane through the blackness, it shone fully upon his writing-table, which was a rather fine Jacobean piece having a sort of quaint bureau superstructure containing cabinets and drawers. He could detect nothing unusual in the appearance of the littered table. A tobacco jar stood there, a pipe resting in the lid. Papers and books were scattered untidily as he had left them, surrounding a tray full of pipe and cigarette ash. Then, suddenly, he saw something else.

One of the bureau drawers was half opened.

Stuart stood quite still, staring at the table. There was no sound in the room. He crossed slowly, moving the light from right to left. His papers had been overhauled methodically. The drawers had been replaced, but he felt assured that all had been examined. The light switch was immediately beside the outer door, and Stuart walked over to it and switched on both lamps. Turning, he surveyed the brilliantly illuminated room. Save for himself, it was empty. He looked out into the hallway again. There was no one there. No sound broke the stillness. But that consciousness of some near presence asserted itself persistently and uncannily.

"My nerves are out of order!" he muttered. "No one has touched my papers. I must have left the drawer open myself."

He switched off the light and walked across to the door. He had actually passed out intending to return to his room, when he became aware of a slight draught. He stopped.

Someone or something, evil and watchful, seemed to be very near again. Stuart turned and found himself gazing fearfully in the direction of the open study door. He became persuaded anew that someone was hiding there, and snatching up an ash stick which lay upon a chair in the hall he returned to the door. One step into the room he took and paused—palsied with a sudden fear which exceeded anything he had known.

A white casement curtain was drawn across the French windows . . . and outlined upon this moon-bright screen he saw a tall figure. It was that of a *cowled man!*

Such an apparition would have been sufficiently alarming had the cowl been that of a monk, but the outline of this phantom being suggested that of one of the Miseri-

cordia brethren or the costume worn of old by the famil-
iars of the Inquisition!

His heart leapt wildly, and seemed to grow still. He
sought to cry out in in his terror, but only emitted a dry
gasping sound.

The psychology of panic is obscure and has been but
imperfectly explored. The presence of the terrible cowled
figure afforded confirmation of Stuart's theory that he was
the victim of a species of waking nightmare.

Even as he looked, the shadow of the cowled man moved
—and was gone.

Stuart ran across the room, jerked open the curtains
and stared out across the moon-bathed lawn, its prospect
terminated by high privet hedges. One of the French
windows was wide open. There was no one on the lawn;
there was no sound.

"Mrs. M'Gregor swears that I always forget to shut
these windows at night!" he muttered.

He closed and bolted the window, stood for a moment
looking out across the empty lawn, then turned and went
out of the room.

## Chapter 2

## THE PIBROCH OF THE M'GREGORS

DR. STUART awoke in the morning and tried to recall
what had occurred during the night. He consulted his
watch and found the hour to be six a.m. No one was stirring in the house, and he rose and put on a bath robe. He
felt perfectly well and could detect no symptoms of nervous disorder. Bright sunlight was streaming into the
room, and he went out on to the landing, fastening the
cord of his gown as he descended the stairs.

His study door was locked, with the key outside. He
remembered having locked it. Opening it, he entered and
looked about him. He was vaguely disappointed. Save for
the untidy litter of papers upon the table, the study was
as he had left it on retiring. If he could believe the evidence of his senses, nothing had been disturbed.

Not content with a casual inspection, he particularly examined those papers which, in his dream adventure, he had believed to have been submitted to mysterious inspection. They showed no signs of having been touched. The casement curtains were drawn across the recess formed by the French windows, and sunlight streamed in where, silhouetted against the pallid illumination of the moon, he had seen the man in the cowl. Drawing back the curtains, he examined the window fastenings. They were secure. If the window had really been open in the night, he must have left it so himself.

"Well," muttered Stuart—"of all the amazing nightmares!"

He determined, immediately he had bathed and completed his toilet, to write an account of the dream for the Psychical Research Society, in whose work he was interested. Half an hour later, as the movements of an awakened household began to proclaim themselves, he sat down at his writing-table and commenced to write.

Keppel Stuart was a dark, good-looking man of about thirty-two, an easy-going bachelor who, whilst not over ambitious, was nevertheless a brilliant physician. He had worked for the Liverpool School of Tropical Medicine and had spent several years in India studying snake poisons. His purchase of this humdrum suburban practice had been dictated by a desire to make a home for a girl who at the eleventh hour had declined to share it. Two years had elapsed since then, but the shadow still lay upon Stuart's life, its influence being revealed in a certain apathy, almost indifference, which characterised his professional conduct.

His account of the dream completed, he put the paper into a pigeon-hole and forgot all about the matter. That day seemed to be more than usually dull and the hours to drag wearily on. He was conscious of a sort of suspense. He was waiting for something, or for someone. He did not choose to analyse this mental condition. Had he done so, the explanation was simple—and one that he dared not face.

At about ten o'clock that night, having been called out to a case, he returned to his house, walking straight into the study as was his custom and casting a light Burberry with a soft hat upon the sofa beside his stick and bag. The lamps were lighted, and the book-lined room, indicative of a studious and not over-wealthy bachelor, looked cheerful enough with the firelight dancing on the furniture.

Mrs. M'Gregor, a grey-haired Scotch lady, attired with scrupulous neatness, was tending the fire at the moment, and hearing Stuart come in she turned and glanced at him.

"A fire is rather superfluous to-night, Mrs. M'Gregor," he said. "I found it unpleasantly warm walking."

"May is a fearsome treacherous month, Mr. Keppel," replied the old housekeeper, who from long association with the struggling practitioner had come to regard him as a son. "An' a wheen o' dry logs is worth a barrel o' pheesic. To which I would add that if ye're hintin' it's time ye shed ye're woolsies for ye're summer wear, all I have to reply is that I hope sincerely ye're patients are more prudent than yoursel'."

She placed his slippers in the fender and took up the hat, stick and coat from the sofa. Stuart laughed.

"Most of the neighbors exhibit their wisdom by refraining from becoming patients of mine, Mrs. M'Gregor."

"That's no weesdom; it's just preejudice."

"Prejudice!" cried Stuart, dropping down upon the sofa.

"Aye," replied Mrs. M'Gregor firmly—"preejudice! They're no' that daft but they're well aware o' who's the cleverest physeecian in the deestrict, an' they come to nane other than Dr. Keppel Stuart when they're sair sick and think they're dying; but ye'll never establish the practice you desairve, Mr. Keppel—never—until——"

"Until when, Mrs. M'Gregor?"

"Until ye take heed of an auld wife's advice and find a new housekeeper."

"Mrs. M'Gregor!" exclaimed Stuart with concern. "You don't mean that you want to desert me? After—let me see—how many years is it, Mrs. M'Gregor?"

"Thirty years come last Shrove Tuseday; I dandled ye on my knee, and eh! but ye were bonny! God forbid, but I'd like to see ye thriving as ye desairve, and that ye'll never do whilst ye're a bachelor."

"Oh!" cried Stuart, laughing again—"oh, that's it, is it? So you would like me to find some poor inoffensive girl to share my struggles?"

Mrs. M'Gregor nodded wisely. "She'd have nane so many to share. I know ye think I'm old-fashioned, Mr. Keppel, and it may be I am; but I do assure you I would be sair harassed, if stricken to my bed—which, please God,

I won't be—to receive the veesits of a pairsonable young bachelor—"

"Er—Mrs. M'Gregor!" interrupted Stuart, coughing in mock rebuke—"quite so! I fancy we have discussed this point before, and as you say your ideas are a wee bit, just a wee bit, behind the times. On this particular point I mean. But I am very grateful to you, very sincerely grateful, for your disinterested kindness; and if ever I should follow your advice———"

Mrs. M'Gregor interrupted him, pointing to his boots. "Ye're no' that daft as to sit in wet boots?"

"Really they are perfectly dry. Except for a light shower this evening, there has been no rain for several days. However, I may as well, since I shall not be going out again."

He began to unlace his boots as Mrs. M'Gregor pulled the white casement curtains across the windows and then prepared to retire. Her hand upon the door knob, she turned again to Stuart.

"The foreign lady called half an hour since, Mr. Keppel."

Stuart desisted from unlacing his boots and looked up with lively interest. "Mlle. Dorian! Did she leave any message?"

"She obsairved that she might repeat her veesit later," replied Mrs. M'Gregor, and, after a moment's hesitation: "she awaited ye're return with exemplary patience."

"Really, I am sorry I was detained," declared Stuart, replacing his boot. "How long has she been gone, then?"

"Just the now. No more than two or three minutes. I trust she is no worse."

"Worse!"

"The lass seemed o'er anxious to see you."

"Well, you know, Mrs. M'Gregor, she comes a considerable distance."

"So I am given to understand, Mr. Keppel," replied the old lady; "and in a grand luxurious car."

Stuart assumed an expression of perplexity to hide his embarrassment. "Mrs. M'Gregor," he said rather ruefully, "you watch over me as tenderly as my own mother would have done. I have observed a certain restraint in your manner whenever you have had occasion to refer to Mlle. Dorian. In what way does she differ from my other lady patients?" And even as he spoke the words he knew in his heart that she differed from every other woman in the world.

Mrs. M'Gregor sniffed. "Do your other lady patients wear furs that your airnings for six months could never pay for, Mr. Keppel?" she inquired.

"No, unfortunately they pin their faith, for the most part, to gaily coloured shawls. All the more reason why I should bless the accident which led Mlle. Dorian to my door."

Mrs. M'Gregor, betraying, in her interest, real suspicion, murmured *sotto voce*: "Then she *is* a patient?"

"What's that?" asked Stuart, regarding her surprisedly. "A patient? Certainly. She suffers from insomnia."

"I'm no' surprised to hear it."

"What do you mean, Mrs. McGregor?"

"Now, Mr. Keppel, laddie, ye're angry with me, and like enough I am a meddlesome auld woman. But I know what a man will do for shining een and a winsome face—nane better to my sorrow—and twa times have I heard the Warning."

Stuart stood up in real perplexity. "Pardon my density, Mrs. M'Gregor, but—er—the Warning? To what 'warning' do you refer?"

Seating herself in the chair before the writing-table, Mrs. M'Gregor shook her head pensively. "What would it be," she said softly, "but the Pibroch o' the M'Gregors?"

Stuart came across and leaned upon a corner of the table. "The Pibroch of the M'Gregors?" he repeated.

"Nane other. 'Tis said to be Rob Roy's ain piper that gives warning when danger threatens ane o' the M'Gregors or any they love."

Stuart restrained a smile, and, "A well-meaning but melancholy retainer!" he commented.

"As well as I hear you now, laddie, I heard the pibroch on the day a certain woman first crossed my threshold, nigh thirty years ago, in Inverary. And as plainly as I heard it wailing then, I heard it the first evening that Miss Dorian came to this house!"

Torn between good-humoured amusement and real interest, "If I remember rightly," said Stuart, "Mlle. Dorian first called here just a week ago, and immediately before I returned from an Infirmary case?"

"Your memory is guid, Mr. Keppel."

"And when, exactly, did you hear this Warning?"

"Twa minutes before you entered the house; and I heard it again the now."

"What! you heard it to-night?"

"I heard it again just the now and I lookit out the window."

"Did you obtain a glimpse of Rob Roy's piper?"

"Ye're laughing at an auld wife, laddie. No, but I saw Miss Dorian away in her car and twa minutes later I saw yourself coming round the corner."

"If she had only waited another two minutes," murmured Stuart. "No matter; she may return. And are these the only occasions upon which you have heard this mysterious sound, Mrs. M'Gregor?"

"No, Master Keppel, they are not. I assure ye something threatens. It wakened me up in the wee sma' hours last night—the piping—an' I lay awake shaking for long eno'."

"How extraordinary. Are you sure your imagination is not playing you tricks?"

"Ah, ye're no' takin' me seriously, laddie."

"Mrs. M'Gregor"—he leaned across the table and rested his hands upon her shoulders—"you are a second mother to me, your care makes me feel like a boy again; and in these grey days it's good to feel like a boy again. You think I am laughing at you, but I'm not. The strange tradition of your family is associated with a tragedy in your life; therefore I respect it. But have no fear with regard to Mlle. Dorian. In the first place she is a patient; in the second—I am merely a penniless suburban practitioner. Good-night, Mrs. M'Gregor. Don't think of waiting up. Tell Mary to show Mademoiselle in here directly she arrives—that is if she really returns."

Mrs. M'Gregor stood up and walked slowly to the door. "I'll show Mademoiselle in mysel', Mr. Keppel," she said—"and show her out."

She closed the door very quietly.

## Chapter 3

## THE SCORPION'S TAIL

SEATING himself at the writing-table, Stuart began mechanically to arrange his papers. Then from the tobacco jar he loaded his pipe, but his manner remained abstracted. Yet he was not thinking of the phantom piper but of Mlle. Dorian.

Until he had met this bewilderingly pretty woman he had thought that his heart was for evermore proof against the glances of bright eyes. Mademoiselle had disillusioned him. She was the most fragrantly lovely creature he had ever met, and never for one waking moment since her first visit, had he succeeded in driving her bewitching image from his mind. He had tried to laugh at his own folly, then had grown angry with himself, but finally had settled down to a dismayed acceptance of a wild infatuation.

He had no idea who Mlle. Dorian was; he did not even know her exact nationality, but he strongly suspected that there was a strain of Eastern blood in her veins. Although she was quite young, apparently little more than twenty years of age, she dressed like a woman of unlimited means, and although all her visits had been at night he had had glimpses of the big car which had aroused Mrs. M'Gregor's displeasure.

Yes—so ran his musings, as, pipe in mouth, he rested his chin in his hands and stared grimly into the fire—she had always come at night and always alone. He had supposed her to be a Frenchwoman, but an unmarried French girl of good family does not make late calls, even upon a medical man, unattended. Had he perchance unwittingly made himself a party to the escapade of some unruly member of a noble family? From the first he had shrewdly suspected the ailments of Mlle. Dorian to be imaginery—Mlle. Dorian? It was an odd name.

"I shall be imagining she is a disguised princess if I wonder about her any more!" he muttered angrily.

Detecting himself in the act of heaving a weary sigh, he coughed in self-reproval and reached into a pigeonhole for the MS. of his unfinished paper on "Snake Poisons and Their Antidotes." By chance he pulled out the brief account, written the same morning, of his uncanny experience during the night. He read it through reflectively.

It was incomplete. A certain mental haziness which he had noted upon awakening had in some way obscured the facts. His memory of the dream had been imperfect. Even now, whilst recognizing that some feature of the experience was missing from his written account, he could not identify the omission. But one memory arose starkly before him—that of the cowled man who had stood behind the curtains. It had power to chill him yet. The old incredulity returned and methodically he reexamined the contents of some of the table drawers. Ere long, however, he desisted impatiently.

"What the devil could a penniless doctor have hidden in his desk that was worth stealing!" he said aloud. "I must avoid cold salmon and cucumber in future."

He tossed the statement aside and turned to his scientific paper.

There came a knock at the door.

"Come in!" snapped Stuart irritably; but the next moment he had turned, eager-eyed, to the servant who had entered.

"Inspector Dunbar has called, sir."

"Oh, all right," said Stuart, repressing another sigh. "Show him in here."

There entered, shortly, a man of unusual height, a man gaunt and square both of figure and face. He wore his clothes and his hair untidily. He was iron grey and a grim mouth was ill concealed by the wiry moustache. The most notable features of a striking face were the tawny leonine eyes, which could be fierce, which could be pensive and which were often kindly.

"Good-evening, doctor," he said—and his voice was pleasant and unexpectedly light in tone. "Hope I don't intrude."

"Not at all, Inspector," Stuart assured him. "Make yourself comfortable in the armchair and fill your pipe."

"Thanks," said Dunbar. "I will." He took out his pipe and reached out a long arm for the tobacco jar. "I came to see if you could give me a tip on a matter that has cropped up."

"Something in my line?" asked Stuart, a keen professional look coming momentarily into his eyes.

"It's supposed to be a poison case, although I can't see it myself," answered the detective—to whom Keppel Stuart's unusual knowledge of poisons had been of service in the past; "but if what I suspect is true, it's a very big case all the same."

Laying down his pipe, which he had filled but not lighted, Inspector Dunbar pulled out from the inside pocket of his tweed coat a bulging note-book and extracted therefrom some small object wrapped up in tissue paper. Unwrapping this object, he laid it upon the table.

"Tell me what that is, doctor," he said, "and I shall be obliged."

Stuart peered closely at that which lay before him. It was a piece of curiously shaped gold, cunningly engraved in a most unusual way. Rather less than an inch in length, it formed a crescent made up of six oval segments joined one to another, the sixth terminating in a curled point. The first and largest segment ended jaggedly where it had evidently been snapped off from the rest of the ornament —if the thing had formed part of an ornament. Stuart looked up, frowning in a puzzled way.

"It is a most curious fragment of jewellery—possibly of Indian origin," he said.

Inspector Dunbar lighted his pipe and tossed the match-end into the fire. "But what does it represent?" he asked.

"Oh, as to that—I said a *curious* fragment advisedly, because I cannot imagine any woman wearing such a beastly thing. It is the *tail of a scorpion.*"

"Ah!" cried Dunbar, the tawny eyes glittering with excitement. "The tail of a scorpion! I thought so! And Sowerby would have it that it represented the stem of a Cactus or Prickley Pear!"

"Not so bad a guess," replied Stuart. "There *are* resemblances—not in the originals but in such a miniature reproduction as this. He was wrong, however. May I ask where you obtained the fragment?"

"I'm here to tell you, doctor, for now that I know it's a scorpion's tail I know that I'm out of my depth as well. You've travelled in the East and lived in the East—two very different things. Now, while you were out there, in India, China, Burma and so on, did you ever come across a religion or a cult that worshipped scorpions?"

Stuart frowned thoughtfully, rubbing his chin with the mouthpiece of his pipe. Dunbar watched him expectantly.

"Help yourself to whiskey-and-soda, Inspector," said Stuart absently. "You'll find everything on the side-table yonder. I'm thinking."

Inspector Dunbar nodded, stood up and crossed the room, where he busied himself with syphon and decanter. Presently he returned, carrying two full glasses, one of which he set before Stuart. "What's the answer, doctor?" he asked.

"The answer is *no*. I am not acquainted with any sect of scorpion-worshippers, Inspector. But I once met with a curious experience at Sû-Chow in China, which I have never been able to explain, but which may interest you. It wanted but a few minutes to sunset, and I was anxious to get back to my quarters before dusk fell. Therefore I hurried up my boy, who was drawing the rickshaw, telling him to cross the Canal by the Wû-Men Bridge. He ran fleetly in that direction, and we were actually come to the steep acclivity of the bridge, when suddenly the boy dropped the shafts and fell down on his knees, hiding his face in his hands.

" 'Shut your eyes tightly, master!' he whispered. 'The Scorpion is coming!'

"I stared down at him in amazement, as was natural, and not a little angrily; for his sudden action had almost pitched me on my head. But there he crouched, immovable, and staring up the slope I saw that it was entirely deserted except for one strange figure at that moment crossing the crown of the bridge and approaching. It was the figure of a tall and dignified Chinaman, or of one who wore the dress of a Chinaman. For the extraordinary thing about the stranger's appearance was this: he also wore a thick green veil!"

"Covering his face?"

"So as to cover his face completely. I was staring at him in wonder, when the boy, seeming to divine the other's approach, whispered, 'Turn your head away! Turn your head away!'"

"He was referring to the man with the veil?"

"Undoubtedly. Of course I did nothing of the kind, but it was impossible to discern the stranger's features through the thick gauze, although he passed quite close to me. He had not proceeded another three paces, I should think, before my boy had snatched up the shafts and darted across the bridge as though all hell were after him! Here's the odd thing, though: I could never induce him to speak a word on the subject afterwards! I bullied him and bribed him, but all to no purpose. And although I must have asked more than a hundred Chinamen in every station of society from mandarin to mendicant, 'Who or what is *The Scorpion?*' one and all looked stupid, blandly assuring me that they did not know what I meant."

"H'm!" said Dunbar, "it's a queer yarn, certainly. How long ago would that be, doctor?"

"Roughly—five years."

"It sounds as though it might belong to the case. Some months back, early in the winter, we received instructions at the Yard to look out everywhere in the press, in buffets, theatres, but particularly in criminal quarters, for any reference (of any kind whatever) to a scorpion. I was so puzzled that I saw the Commissioner about it, and he could tell me next to nothing. He said the word had come through from Paris, but that Paris seemed to know no more about it than we did. It was associated in some way with the sudden deaths of several notable public men about that time; but as there was no evidence of foul play in any of the cases, I couldn't see what it meant at all. Then, six weeks ago, Sir Frank Narcombe, the surgeon, fell dead in the foyer of a West-End theatre —you remember?"

"Perfectly—an extraordinary case. There should have been an autopsy."

"It's curious you should say so, doctor, because we had the tip to press for one; but Sir Frank's people had big influence, and we lost. This is the point, though. I was working day and night for a week or more, cross-questioning Tom, Dick and Harry and examining shoals of papers to try and find some connection between Sir Frank Narcombe and a scorpion! Paris information again! Of course I found no trace of such a thing. It was a devil of a job, because I didn't really know what I was looking for. I had begun to think that the scorpion-hunt had gone the way of a good many other giant gooseberries, when last night the River Police got the grapnel on a man off Hanover Hole —a rich spot for 'finds.' He was frightfully battered about; he seemed to have got mixed up with a steamer's propeller blades. The only two things by which he may ultimately be identified are a metal disk which he wore on a

chain around his wrist and which bore thé initials G.M.
and the number 49685, and—that."

"What?" said Stuart.

"The scorpion's tail. It was stuck in the torn lining of
his jacket pocket."

## Chapter 4

## MADEMOISELLE DORIAN

THE telephone bell rang.

Stuart reached across for the instrument and raised
the receiver. "Yes," he said—"Dr. Stuart speaking. Inspector Dunbar is here. Hold on."

He passed the instrument to Dunbar, who had stood up
on hearing his name mentioned. "Sergeant Sowerby at
Scotland Yard wishes to speak to you, Inspector."

"Hullo," said Dunbar—"that you, Sowerby. Yes—but I
arrived here only a short time ago. What's that?—Max! Did
you say Max? Good God! what does it all mean! Are you
sure of the number—49685? Poor chap—he should have
worked with us instead of going off alone like that. But he
was always given to that sort of thing. Wait for me. I'll
be with you in a few minutes. I can get a taxi. And, Sowerby—listen! It's 'The Scorpion' case right enough. That
bit of gold found on the dead man is not a cactus stem; it's
a scorpion's tail!"

He put down the telephone and turned to Stuart, who
had been listening to the words with growing concern.
Dunbar struck his open palm down on to the table with a
violent gesture.

"We have been asleep!" he exclaimed. "Gaston Max
of the Paris Service has been at work in London for a
month, and we didn't know it!"

"Gaston Max!" cried Stuart—"then it must be a big case
indeed."

As a student of criminology the name of the celebrated
Frenchman was familiar to him as that of the foremost
criminal investigator in Europe, and he found himself

staring at the fragment of gold with a new and keener interest.

"Poor chap," continued Dunbar—"it was his last. The body brought in from Hanover Hole has been identified as his."

"What! it is the body of Gaston Max!"

"Paris has just wired that Max's reports ceased over a week ago. He was working on the case of Sir Frank Narcombe, it seems, and I never knew! But I predicted a long time ago that Max would play the lone-hand game once too often. They sent particulars. The identification disk is his. Oh! there's no doubt about it, unfortunately. The dead man's face is unrecognizable, but it's not likely there are two disks of that sort bearing the initials G.M. and the number 49685. I'm going along now. Should you care to come, doctor?"

"I am expecting a patient, Inspector," replied Stuart —"er—a special case. But I hope you will keep me in touch with this affair?"

"Well, I shouldn't have suggested your coming to the Yard if I hadn't wanted to do that. As a matter of fact, this scorpion job seems to resolve itself into a case of elaborate assassination by means of some unknown poison; and although I should have come to see you in any event, because you have helped me more than once, I came to-night at the suggestion of the Commissioner. He instructed me to retain your services if they were available."

"I am honoured," replied Stuart. "But after all, Inspector, I am merely an ordinary suburban practitioner. My reputation has yet to be made. What's the matter with Halesowen of Upper Wimpole Street? He's the big man."

"And if Sir Frank Narcombe was really poisoned—as Paris seems to think he was—he's also a big fool," retorted Dunbar bluntly. "He agreed that death was due to heart trouble."

"I know he did; unsuspected ulcerative endocarditis. Perhaps he was right."

"If he was right," said Dunbar, taking up the piece of gold from the table, "what was Gaston Max doing with this thing in his possession?"

"There may be no earthly connection between Max's inquiries and the death of Sir Frank."

"On the other hand—there may! Leaving Dr. Halesowen

out of the question, are you open to act as expert adviser in this case?"

"Certainly; delighted."

"Your fee is your own affair, doctor. I will communicate with you later, if you wish, or call again in the morning."

Dunbar wrapped up the scorpion's tail in the piece of tissue paper and was about to replace it in his note-case. Then:

"I'll leave this with you, doctor," he said. "I know it will be safe enough, and you might like to examine it at greater leisure."

"Very well," replied Stuart. "Some of the engraving is very minute. I will have a look at it through a glass later."

He took the fragment from Dunbar, who had again unwrapped it, and, opening a drawer of the writing-table in which he kept his cheque-book and some few other personal valuables, he placed the curious piece of gold-work within and relocked the drawer.

"I will walk as far as the cab-rank with you," he said, finding himself to be possessed of a spirit of unrest. Whereupon the two went out of the room, Stuart extinguishing the lamps as he came to the door.

They had not left the study for more than two minutes ere a car drew up outside the house, and Mrs. M'Gregor ushered a lady into the room but lately quitted by Stuart and Dunbar, turning up the lights as she entered.

"The doctor has gone out but just now, Miss Dorian," she said stiffly. "I am sorry that ye are so unfortunate in your veesits. But I know he'll be no more than a few minutes."

The girl addressed was of a type fully to account for the misgivings of the shrewd old Scotswoman. She had the slim beauty of the East allied to the elegance of the West. Her features, whilst cast in a charming European mould, at the same time suggested in some subtle way the Oriental. She had the long, almond-shaped eyes of the Egyptian, and her hair, which she wore unconventionally in a picturesque fashion reminiscent of the *harêm,* was inclined to be "fuzzy," but gleamed with coppery tints where the light touched its waves.

She wore a cloak of purple velvet having a hooded collar of white fox fur; it fastened with golden cords. Beneath it was a white and gold robe, cut with classic simplicity of line and confined at the waist by an ornate Eastern girdle. White stockings and dull gold shoes exhibited to advantage her charming little feet and slim ankles, and she carried a handbag of Indian beadwork. Mlle. Dorian was a figure calculated to fire the imagination of any man and to linger long and sweetly in the memory.

Mrs. M'Gregor, palpably ill at ease, conducted her to an armchair.

"You are very good," said the visitor, speaking with a certain hesitancy and with a slight accent most musical and fascinating. "I wait a while if I may."

"Dear, dear," muttered Mrs. M'Gregor, beginning to poke the fire, "he has let the fire down, of course! Is it out? No . . . I see a wee sparkie!"

She set the poker upright before the nearly extinguished fire and turned triumphantly to Mlle. Dorian, who was watching her with a slight smile.

"That will be a comforting blaze in a few minutes, Miss Dorian," she said, and went towards the door.

"If you please," called the girl, detaining her—"do you permit me to speak on the telephone a moment? As Dr. Stuart is not at home, I must explain that I wait for him."

"Certainly, Miss Dorian," replied Mrs. M'Gregor; "use the telephone by all means. But I think the doctor will be back any moment now."

"Thank you so much."

Mrs. M'Gregor went out, not without a final backward glance at the elegant figure in the armchair. Mlle. Dorian was seated, her chin resting in her hand and her elbow upon the arm of the chair, gazing into the smoke arising from the nearly extinguished embers of the fire. The door closed, and Mrs. M'Gregor's footsteps could be heard receding along the corridor.

Mlle. Dorian sprang from the chair and took out of her handbag a number of small keys attached to a ring. Furtively she crossed the room, all the time listening intently, and cast her cloak over the back of the chair which was placed before the writing-table. Her robe of white and gold clung to her shapely figure as she bent over the table and tried three of the keys in the lock of the drawer which contained Stuart's cheque-book and in which he had recently placed the mysterious gold ornament. The third key fitted the lock, and Mlle. Dorian pulled open the drawer. She discovered first the cheque-book and next a private account-book; then from under the latter she drew out a foolscap envelope sealed with red wax and bearing, in Stuart's handwriting, the address:

Lost Property Office,
Metropolitan Police,
New Scotland Yard, S. W. I.

She uttered a subdued exclamation; then, as a spark of light gleamed within the open drawer, she gazed as if stupefied at the little ornament which she had suddenly perceived lying near the cheque-book. She picked it up and stared at it aghast. A moment she hesitated; then, laying down the fragment of gold and also the long envelope upon the table, she took up the telephone. Keeping her eyes fixed upon the closed door of the study, she asked for the number East 89512, and whilst she waited for the connection continued that nervous watching and listening. Suddenly she began to speak, in a low voice.

"Yes! . . . Miska speaks. Listen! One of the new keys —it fits. I have the envelope. But, also in the same drawer, I find a part of a broken gold *'agrab* (scorpion). Yes, it is broken. It must be they find it, on him." Her manner grew more and more agitated. "Shall I bring it? The envelope it is very large. I do not know if——"

From somewhere outside the house came a low, wailing cry—a cry which Stuart, if he had heard it, must have recognized to be identical with that which he had heard in the night—but which he had forgotten to record in his written account.

"Ah!" whispered the girl—"there is the signal! It is the doctor who returns." She listened eagerly, fearfully, to the voice which spoke over the wires. "Yes—yes!"

Always glancing toward the door, she put down the instrument, took up the long envelope and paused for a moment, thinking that she had heard the sound of approaching footsteps. She exhibited signs of nervous indecision, tried to thrust the envelope into her little bag and realized that even folded it would not fit so as to escape observation. She ran across the the grate and dropped the envelope upon the smouldering fire. As she did so, the nicely balanced poker fell with a clatter upon the tiled hearth.

She started wildly, ran back to the table, took up the broken ornament and was about to thrust it into the open drawer, when the study door was flung open and Stuart came in.

# Chapter 5

## THE SEALED ENVELOPE

"MADEMOISELLE DORIAN!" cried Stuart joyously, advancing with outstretched hand. She leaned back against the table watching him—and suddenly he perceived the open drawer. He stopped. His expression changed to one of surprise and anger, and the girl's slim fingers convulsively clutched the table edge as she confronted him. Her exquisite colour fled and left her pallid, dark-eyed and dismayed.

"So," he said bitterly—"I returned none too soon, Mlle. —Dorian!"

"Oh!" she whispered, and shrank from him as he approached nearer.

"Your object in selecting an obscure practitioner for your medical adviser becomes painfully evident to me. Diagnosis of your case would have been much more easy if I had associated your symptoms with the presence in my table drawer of"—he hesitated—"of something which you have taken out. Give me whatever you have stolen and compose yourself to await the arrival of the police."

He was cruel in his disillusionment. Here lay the explanation of his romance; here was his disguised princess —a common thief! She stared at him wildly.

"I take nothing!" she cried. "Oh, let me go! Please, please let me go!"

"Pleading is useless. What have you stolen?"

"Nothing—see." She cast the little gold ornament on the table. "I look at this, but I do not mean to steal it."

She raised her beautiful eyes to his face again, and he found himself wavering. That she had made his acquaintance in order to steal the fragment of the golden scorpion was impossible, for he had not possessed it at the time of her first visit. He was hopelessly mystified and utterly miserable.

"How did you open the drawer?" he asked sternly.

She took up the bunch of keys which lay upon the table

and naïvely exhibited that which fitted the lock of the drawer. Her hands were shaking.

"Where did you obtain this key; and why?"

She watched him intently, her lips trembling and her eyes wells of sorrow into which he could not gaze unmoved.

"If I tell you—will you let me go?"

"I shall make no promises, for I can believe nothing that you may tell me. You gained my confidence by a lie—and now, by another lie, you seem to think that you can induce me to overlook a deliberate attempt at burglary—common burglary." He clenched his hands. "Heavens! I could never have believed it of you!"

She flinched as though from a blow and regarded him pitifully as he stood, head averted.

"Oh, please listen to me," she whispered. "At first I tell you a lie, yes."

"And now?"

"Now—I tell you the truth."

"That you are a petty thief?"

"Ah! you are cruel—you have no pity! You judge me as you judge—one of your Englishwomen. Perhaps I cannot help what I do. In the East a woman is a chattel and has no will of her own."

"A chattel!" cried Stuart scornfully. "Your resemblance to the 'chattels' of the East is a remote one. There is Eastern blood in your veins, no doubt, but you are educated, you are a linguist, you know the world. Right and wrong are recognizable to the lowest savage."

"And if they recognize, but are helpless?"

Stuart made a gesture of impatience.

"You are simply seeking to enlist my sympathy," he said bitterly. "But you have said nothing which inclines me to listen to you any longer. Apart from the shock of finding you to be—what you are, I am utterly mystified as to your object. I am a poor man. The entire contents of my house would fetch only a few hundred pounds if sold to-morrow. Yet you risk your liberty to rifle my bureau. For the last time what have you taken from that drawer?"

She leaned back against the table, toying with the broken piece of gold and glancing down at it as she did so. Her long lashes cast shadows below her eyes, and a hint of colour was returning to her cheeks. Stuart studied her attentively—even delightedly, for all her shortcomings, and knew in his heart that he could never give her in charge of the police. More and more the wonder of it all grew upon him, and now he suddenly found himself thinking of the unexplained incident of the previous night.

"You do not answer," he said. "I will ask you another question: have you attempted to open that drawer prior to this evening?"

Mlle. Dorian looked up rapidly, and her cheeks, which had been pale, now flushed rosily.

"I try twice before," she confessed, "and cannot open it."

"Ah! And—has *someone else* tried also?"

Instantly her colour fled again, and she stared at him wide-eyed, fearful.

"Someone else?" she whispered.

"Yes—someone else. A man . . . wearing a sort of cowl ——"

"Oh?" she cried and threw out her hands in entreaty. "Do not ask me of *him*! I dare not answer—I dare not!"

"You *have* answered," said Stuart, in a voice unlike his own; for a horrified amazement was creeping upon him and supplanting the contemptuous anger which the discovery of this beautiful girl engaged in pilfering his poor belongings had at first aroused.

The mystery of her operations was explained—explained by a deeper and a darker mystery. The horror of the night had been no dream but an almost incredible reality. He now saw before him an agent of the man in the cowl; he perceived that he was in some way entangled in an affair vastly more complex and sinister than a case of petty larceny.

"Has the golden scorpion anything to do with the matter?" he demanded abruptly.

And in the eyes of his beautiful captive he read the answer. She flinched again as she had done when he had taunted her with being a thief; but he pressed his advantage remorselessly.

"So you were concerned in the death of Sir Frank Narcombe!" he said.

"I was not!" she cried at him fiercely, and her widely opened eyes were magnificent. "Sir Frank Narcombe is ——"

She faltered—and ceased speaking, biting her lip which had become tremulous again.

"Sir Frank Narcombe is?" prompted Stuart, feeling himself to stand upon the brink of a revelation.

"I know nothing of him—this Sir Frank Narcombe."
Stuart laughed unmirthfully.

"Am I, by any chance, in danger of sharing the fate of that distinguished surgeon?" he asked.

His question produced an unforeseen effect. Mlle. Dorian suddenly rested her jewelled hands upon his shoulders, and he found himself looking hungrily into those wonderful Eastern eyes.

"If I swear that I speak the truth, will you believe me?" she whispered, and her fingers closed convulsively upon his shoulders.

He was shaken. Her near presence was intoxicating. "Perhaps," he said unsteadily.

"Listen, then. *Now* you are in danger, yes. Before, you were not, but now you must be very careful. Oh! indeed, indeed, I tell you true! I tell you for your own sake. Do with me what you please. I do not care. It does not matter. You ask me why I come here. I tell you that also. I come for what is in the long envelope—look, I cannot hide it. It is on the fire!"

Stuart turned and glanced toward the grate. A faint wisp of brown smoke was arising from a long white envelope which lay there. Had the fire been actually burning, it must long ago have been destroyed. More than ever mystified, for the significance of the envelope was not evident to him, he ran to the grate and plucked the smouldering paper from the embers.

As he did so, the girl, with one quick glance in his direction, snatched her cloak, keys and bag and ran from the room. Stuart heard the door close, and racing back to the table he placed the slightly charred envelope there beside the fragment of gold and leapt to the door.

"Damn!" he said.

His escaped prisoner had turned the key on the outside. He was locked in his own study!

Momentarily nonplussed, he stood looking at the closed door. The sound of a restarted motor from outside the house spurred him to action. He switched off the lamps, crossed the darkened room and drew back the curtain, throwing open the French windows. Brilliant moonlight bathed the little lawn with its bordering of high privet hedges. Stuart ran out as the sound of the receding car reached his ears. By the time that he had reached the front of the house the street was vacant from end to end. He walked up the steps to the front door, which he unfastened with his latch-key. As he entered the hall, Mrs. M'Gregor appeared from her room.

"I did no' hear ye go out with Miss Dorian," she said.

"That's quite possible, Mrs. M'Gregor, but she has gone, you see."

"Now tell me, Mr. Keppel, did ye or did ye no' hear the wail o' the pibroch the night?"

"No—I am afraid I cannot say that I did, Mrs. M'Gregor," replied Stuart patiently. "I feel sure you must be very tired and you can justifiably turn in now. I am expecting no other visitor. Good-night."

Palpably dissatisfied and ill at ease, Mrs. M'Gregor turned away.

"Good-night, Mr. Keppel," she said.

Stuart, no longer able to control his impatience, hurried to the study door, unlocked it and entered. Turning on the light, he crossed and hastily drew the curtains over the window recess, but without troubling to close the window which he had opened. Then he returned to the writing-table and took up the sealed envelope whose presence in his bureau was clearly responsible for the singular visitation of the cowled man and for the coming of the lovely Mlle. Dorian.

The "pibroch of the M'Gregors": He remembered something—something which, unaccountably, he hitherto had failed to recall: that fearful wailing in the night—which had heralded the coming of the cowled man!—or had it been a *signal* of some kind?

He stared at the envelope blankly, then laid it down and stood looking for some time at the golden scorpion's tail. Finally, his hands resting upon the table, he found that almost unconsciously he had been listening—listening to the dim night sounds of London and to the vague stirrings within the house.

. . "*Now*, you are in danger. Before, you were not. . . ."

Could he believe her? If in naught else, in this at least surely she had been sincere? Stuart started—then laughed grimly.

A clock on the mantel-piece had chimed the half-hour.

## Chapter 6

## THE ASSISTANT COMMISSIONER

DETECTIVE INSPECTOR DUNBAR arrived at New Scotland Yard in a veritable fever of excitement. Jumping out of the cab he ran into the building and without troubling the man in charge of the lift went straight on upstairs to his room. He found it to be in darkness and switched on the green-shaded lamp which was suspended above the table. Its light revealed a bare apartment having distempered walls severely decorated by an etching of a former and unbeautiful Commissioner. The blinds were drawn. A plain, heavy deal table (bearing a blotting-pad, a pewter ink-pot, several pens and a telephone), together with three uncomfortable chairs, alone broke the expanse of highly polished floor. Dunbar glanced at the table and then stood undecided in the middle of the bare room, tapping his small, widely separated teeth with a pencil which he had absently drawn from his waistcoat pocket. He rang the bell.

A constable came in almost immediately and stood waiting just inside the door.

"When did Sergeant Sowerby leave?" asked Dunbar.

"About three hours ago, sir."

"What!" cried Dunbar. "Three hours ago! But I have been here myself within that time—in the Commissioner's office."

"Sergeant Sowerby left before then. I saw him go."

"But, my good fellow, he has been back again. He spoke to me on the telephone less than a quarter of an hour ago."

"Not from here, sir."

"But I say it *was* from here!" shouted Dunbar fiercely; "and I told him to wait for me."

"Very good, sir. Shall I make inquiries?"

"Yes. Wait a minute. Is the Commissioner here?"

"Yes, sir, I believe so. At least I have not seen him go."

"Find Sergeant Sowerby and tell him to wait here for me," snapped Dunbar.

He walked out into the bare corridor and along to the room of the Assistant Commissioner. Knocking upon the door, he opened it immediately, and entered an apartment which afforded a striking contrast to his own. For whereas the room of Inspector Dunbar was practically unfurnished, that of his superior was so filled with tables, cupboards, desks, bureaux, files, telephones, bookshelves and stacks of documents that one only discovered the Assistant Commissioner sunk deep in a padded armchair and a cloud of tobacco smoke by dint of close scrutiny. The Assistant Commissioner was small, sallow and satanic. His black moustache was very black and his eyes were of so dark a brown as to appear black also. When he smiled he revealed a row of very large white teeth, and his smile was correctly Mephistophelean. He smoked a hundred and twenty Egyptian cigarettes per diem, and the first and second fingers of either hand were coffee-coloured.

"Good-evening, Inspector," he said courteously. "You come at an opportune moment." He lighted a fresh cigarette. "I was detained here unusually late to-night or this news would not have reached us till the morning." He laid his finger upon a yellow form. "There is an unpleasant development in 'The Scorpion' case."

"So I gather, sir. That is what brought me back to the Yard."

The Assistant Commissioner glanced up sharply.

"*What* brought you back to the Yard?" he asked.

"The news about Max."

The Assistant Commissioner leaned back in his chair. "Might I ask, Inspector," he said, "what news you have learned and how you have learned it?"

Dunbar stared uncomprehendingly.

"Sowerby 'phoned me about half an hour ago, sir. Did he do so without your instructions?"

"Most decidedly. What was his message?"

"He told me," replied Dunbar, in ever-growing amazement, "that the body brought in by the River Police last night had been identified as that of Gaston Max."

The Assistant Commissioner handed a pencilled slip to Dunbar. It read as follows:—

"Gaston Max in London. Scorpion, Narcombe. No report since 30th ult. Fear trouble. Identity-disk G.M. 49685."

"But, sir," said Dunbar—"this is exactly what Sowerby told me!"

"Quite so. That is the really extraordinary feature of

the affair. Because, you see, Inspector, I only finished decoding this message at the very moment that you knocked at my door!"

"But——"

"There is no room for a 'but,' Inspector. This confidential message from Paris reached me ten minutes ago. You know as well as I know that there is no possibility of leakage. No one has entered my room in the interval, yet you tell me that Seargeant Sowerby communicated this information to you, by telephone, half an hour ago."

Dunbar was tapping his teeth with the pencil. His amazement was too great for words.

"Had the message been a false one," continued the Commissioner, "the matter would have been resolved into a meaningless hoax, but the message having been what it was, we find ourselves face to face with no ordinary problem. Remember, Inspector, that voices on the telephone are deceptive. Sergeant Sowerby has marked vocal mannerisms——"

"Which would be fairly easy to imitate? Yes, sir—that's so."

"But it brings us no nearer to the real problems; viz., first, the sender of the message; and, second, his purpose."

There was a dull purring sound and the Assistant Commissioner raised the telephone.

"Yes. Who is it that wishes to speak to him? Dr. Keppel Stuart? Connect with my office."

He turned again to Dunbar.

"Dr. Stuart has a matter of the utmost urgency to communicate, Inspector. It was at the house of Dr. Stuart, I take it, that you received the unexplained message?"

"It was—yes."

"Did you submit to Dr. Stuart the broken gold ornament?"

"Yes. It's a scorpion's tail."

"Ah!" The Assistant Commissioner smiled satanically and lighted a fresh cigarette. "And is Dr. Stuart agreeable to placing his unusual knowledge at our disposal for the purposes of this case?"

"He is, sir."

The purring sound was repeated.

"You are through to Dr. Stuart," said the Assistant Commissioner.

"Hullo!" cried Dunbar, taking up the receiver—"is that Dr. Stuart? Dunbar speaking."

He stood silent for a while, listening to the voice over the wires. Then: "You want me to come around now, doctor? Very well. I'll be with you in less than half an hour."

He put down the instrument.

"Something extraordinary seems to have taken place at Dr. Stuart's house a few minutes after I left, sir," he said. "I'm going back there, now, for particulars. It sounds as though the 'phone message might have been intended to get me away." He stared down at the pencilled slip which the Assistant Commissioner had handed to him, but stared vacantly, and: "Do you mind if I call someone up, sir?" he asked. "It should be done at once."

"Call by all means, Inspector."

Dunbar again took up the telephone.

"Battersea 0996?" he asked. "Is Dr. Stuart there? He is speaking? Oh, this is Inspector Dunbar. You called me up here at the Yard a few moments ago, did you not? Correct, doctor; that's all I wanted to know. I am coming now."

"Good," said the Assistant Commissioner, nodding his approval. "You will have to check 'phone messages in that way until you have run your mimic to earth, Inspector. I don't believe for a moment that it was Sergeant Sowerby who rang you up at Dr. Stuart's."

"Neither do I," said Dunbar grimly. "But I begin to have a glimmer of a notion who it was. I'll be saying good-night, sir. Dr. Stuart seems to have something very important to tell me."

As a mere matter of form he waited for the report of the constable who had gone in quest of Sowerby, but it merely confirmed the fact that Sowerby had left Scotland Yard over three hours earlier. Dunbar summoned a taxicab and proceeded to the house of Dr. Stuart.

## Chapter 7

## CONTENTS OF THE SEALED ENVELOPE

STUART personally admitted Dunbar, and once more the Inspector found himself in the armchair in the study. The fire was almost out and the room seemed to be chilly. Stuart was labouring under the influence of suppressed excitement and was pacing restlessly up and down the floor.

"Inspector," he began. "I find it difficult to tell you the facts which have recently come to my knowledge bearing upon this most mysterious 'Scorpion' case. I clearly perceive, now, that without being aware of the fact I have nevertheless been concerned in the case for at least a week."

Dunbar stared surprisedly, but offered no comment.

"A fortnight ago," Stuart continued, "I found myself in the neighbourhood of the West India Docks. I had been spending the evening with a very old friend, chief officer of a liner in dock. I had intended to leave the ship at about ten o'clock and to walk to the railway station, but, as it fell out, the party did not break up until after midnight. Declining the offer of a berth on board, I came ashore determined to make my way home by tram and afoot. I should probably have done so and have been spared— much; but rain began to fall suddenly and I found myself, foolishly unprovided with a top-coat, in those grey East End streets without hope of getting a lift.

"It was just as I was crossing Limehouse Causeway that I observed, to my astonishment, the headlamps of a cab or car shining out from a dark and forbidding thoroughfare which led down to the river. The sight was so utterly unexpected that I paused, looking through the rainy mist in the direction of the stationary vehicle. I was still unable to make out if it were a cab or a car, and accordingly I walked along to where it stood and found that it was a taxicab and apparently for hire.

" 'Are you disengaged?' I said to the man.

" 'Well, sir, I suppose I am,' was his curious reply. 'Where do you want to go?'

"I gave him this address and he drove me home. On arriving, so grateful did I feel that I took pity upon the man, for it had settled down into a brute of a night, and asked him to come in and take a glass of grog. He was only too glad to do so. He turned out to be quite an intelligent sort of fellow, and we chatted together for ten minutes or so.

"I had forgotten all about him when, I believe on the following night, he reappeared in the character of a patient. He had a badly damaged skull, and I gathered that he had had an accident with his cab and had been pitched out into the road.

"When I had fixed him up, he asked me to do him a small favour. From inside his tunic he pulled out a long stiff envelope, bearing no address but the number 30 in big red letters. It was secured at both ends with black wax bearing the imprint of a curious and complicated seal.

" 'A gentleman left this behind in the cab to-day, sir,' said the man—'perhaps the one who was with me when I had the spill, and I've got no means of tracing him; but he may be able to trace *me* if he happened to notice my number, or he may advertise. It evidently contains something valuable.'

" 'Then why not take it to Scotland Yard?' I asked. 'Isn't that the proper course?'

" 'It is,' he admitted; 'but here's the point: if the owner reclaims it from Scotland Yard he's less likely to dub up handsome than if he gets it direct from me!'

"I laughed at that, for the soundness of the argument was beyond dispute. 'But what on earth do you want to leave it with *me* for?' I asked.

" 'Self-protection,' was the reply. 'They can't say I meant to pinch it! Whereas, directly there's any inquiry I can come and collect it and get the reward; and your word will back me up if any questions are asked; that's if you don't mind, sir.'

"I told him I didn't mind in the least, and accordingly I sealed the envelope in a yet larger one which I addressed to the Lost Property Office and put into a private drawer of my bureau. 'You will have no objection,' I said, 'to this being posted if it isn't reclaimed within a reasonable time?'

"He said that would be all right and departed—since

which moment I have not set eyes upon him. I now come to the sequel, or what I have just recognized to be the sequel."

Stuart's agitation grew more marked and it was only by dint of a palpable effort that he forced himself to resume.

"On the evening of the following day a lady called professionally. She was young, pretty, and dressed with extraordinary elegance. My housekeeper admitted her, as I was out at the time but momentarily expected. She awaited my return here, in this room. She came again two days later. The name she gave was an odd one: Mademoiselle Dorian. There is her card,"—Stuart opened a drawer and laid a visiting-card before Dunbar—"no initials and no address. She travelled in a large and handsome car. That is to say, according to my housekeeper's account it is a large and handsome car. I personally, have had but an imperfect glimpse of it. It does not await her in front of the house, for some reason, but just around the corner in the side turning. Beyond wondering why Mademoiselle Dorian had selected me as her medical adviser I had detected nothing suspicious in her behaviour up to the time of which I am about to speak.

"Last night there was a singular development, and to-night matters came to a head."

Thereupon Stuart related as briefly as possible the mysterious episode of the cowled man, and finally gave an account of the last visit of Mlle. Dorian. Inspector Dunbar did not interrupt him, but listened attentively to the singular story.

"And there," concluded Stuart, "on the blotting-pad, lies the sealed envelope!"

Dunbar took it up eagerly. A small hole had been burned in one end of the envelope and much of the surrounding paper was charred. The wax with which Stuart had sealed it had lain uppermost, and although it had been partly melted, the mark of his signet-ring was still discernible upon it. Dunbar stood staring at it.

"In the circumstances, Inspector, I think you would be justified in opening both envelopes," said Stuart.

"I am inclined to agree. But let me just be clear on one or two points." He took out the bulging note-book and also a fountain-pen with which he prepared to make entries. "About this cabman, now. You didn't by any chance note the number of his cab?"

"I did not."

"What build of a man was he?"

"Over medium height and muscular. Somewhat inclined to flesh and past his youth, but active all the same."

"Dark or fair?"

"Dark and streaked with grey. I noted this particularly in dressing his skull. He wore his hair cropped close to the scalp. He had a short beard and moustache and heavily marked eyebrows. He seemed to be very short-sighted and kept his eyes so screwed up that it was impossible to detect their colour, by night at any rate."

"What sort of wound had he on his skull?"

"A short ugly gash. He had caught his head on the foot-board in falling. I may add that on the occasion of his professional visit his breath smelled strongly of spirits, and I rather suspected that his accident might have been traceable to his condition."

"But he wasn't actually drunk?"

"By no means. He was perfectly sober, but he had recently been drinking—possibly because his fall had shaken him, of course."

"His hands?"

"Small and very muscular. Quite steady. Also very dirty."

"What part of the country should you say he hailed from?"

"London. He had a marked cockney accent."

"What make of cab was it?"

"I couldn't say."

"An old cab?"

"Yes. The fittings were dilapidated, I remember, and the cab had a very musty smell."

"Ah," said Dunbar, making several notes. "And now—the lady: about what would be her age?"

"Difficult to say, Inspector. She had Eastern blood and may have been much younger than she appeared to be. Judged from a European standpoint and from her appearance and manner of dress, she might be about twenty-three or twenty-four."

"Complexion?"

"Wonderful. Fresh as a flower."

"Eyes?"

"Dark. They looked black as night."

"Hair?"

"Brown and 'fuzzy' with copper tints."

"Tall?"

"No; slight but beautifully shaped."

"Now—from her accent what should you judge her nationality to be?"

Stuart paced up and down the room, his head lowered in reflection, then:

"She pronounced both English and French words with an intonation which suggested familiarity with Arabic."

"Arabic? That still leaves a fairly wide field."

"It does, Inspector, but I had no means of learning more. She had certainly lived for a long time somewhere in the Near East."

"Her jewellery?"

"Some of it was European and some of it Oriental, but not characteristic of any particular country of the Orient."

"Did she use perfume?"

"Yes, but it was scarcely discernible. Jasmine—probably the Eastern preparation."

"Her ailment was imaginary?"

"I fear so."

"H'm—and now you say that Mrs. M'Gregor saw the car?"

"Yes, but she has retired."

"Her evidence will do to-morrow. We come to the man in the hood. Can you give me any kind of a description of him?"

"He appeared to be tall, but a shadow is deceptive, and his extraordinary costume would produce that effect, too. I can tell you absolutely nothing further about him. Remember, I thought I was dreaming. I could not credit my senses."

Inspector Dunbar glanced over the notes which he had made, then returning the note-book and pen to his pocket, he took up the long smoke-discoloured envelope and with a paper-knife which lay upon the table slit one end open. Inserting two fingers, he drew out the second envelope which the first enclosed. It was an ordinary commercial envelope only notable by reason of the number, 30, appearing in large red figures upon it and because it was sealed with black wax bearing a weird-looking device.

Stuart bent over him intently as he slit this envelope in turn. Again, he inserted two fingers—and brought forth the sole contents . . . a plain piece of cardboard, roughly rectangular and obviously cut in haste from the lid of a common cardboard box!

## Chapter 8

## THE ASSISTANT COMMISSIONER'S THEORY

On the following morning Inspector Dunbar, having questioned Mrs. M'Gregor respecting the car in which Mlle. Dorian had visited the house and having elicited no other evidence than that it was "a fine luxurious concern," the Inspector and Dr. Stuart prepared to set out upon gruesome business. Mrs. M'Gregor was very favourably impressed with the Inspector. "A grand, pairsonable body," she confided to Stuart. "He'd look bonny in the kilt."

To an East-End mortuary the cab bore them, and they were led by a constable in attendance to a stone-paved, ill-lighted apartment in which a swathed form lay upon a long deal table. The spectacle presented, when the covering was removed, was one to have shocked less hardened nerves than those of Stuart and Dunbar; but the duties of a police officer, like those of a medical man, not infrequently necessitate such inspections. The two bent over the tragic flotsam of the Thames unmoved and critical.

"H'm," said Stuart—"he's about the build, certainly. Hair iron-grey and close cropped and he seems to have worn a beard. Now, let us see."

He bent, making a close inspection of the skull; then turned and shook his head.

"No, Inspector," he said definitely. "This is not the cabman. There is no wound corresponding to the one which I dressed."

"Right," answered Dunbar, covering up the ghastly face. "That's settled."

"You were wrong, Inspector. It was not Gaston Max who left the envelope with me."

"No," mused Dunbar, "so it seems."

"Your theory that Max, jealously working alone, had left particulars of his inquiries, and clues, in my hands, knowing that they would reach Scotland Yard in the event of his death, surely collapsed when the envelope proved to contain nothing but a bit of cardboard?"

40

"Yes—I suppose it did. But it sounded so much like Max's round-about methods. Anyway I wanted to make sure that the dead man from Hanover Hole and your mysterious cabman were not one and the same."

Stuart entertained a lively suspicion that Inspector Dunbar was keeping something up his sleeve, but with this very proper reticence he had no quarrel, and followed by the constable, who relocked the mortuary behind them, they came out into the yard where the cab waited which was to take them to Scotland Yard. Dunbar, standing with one foot upon the step of the cab, turned to the constable.

"Has anyone else viewed the body?" he asked.

"No, sir."

"No one is to be allowed to do so—you understand?— *no one*, unless he has written permission from the Commissioner."

"Very good, sir."

Half an hour later they arrived at New Scotland Yard and went up to Dunbar's room. A thick-set, florid man of genial appearance, having a dark moustache, a breezy manner and a head of hair resembling a very hard-worked blacking-brush, awaited them. This was Detective-Sergeant Sowerby with whom Stuart was already acquainted.

"Good-morning, Sergeant Sowerby," he said.

"Good-morning, sir. I hear that someone was pulling your leg last night."

"What do you mean exactly, Sowerby?" inquired Dunbar, fixing his fierce eyes upon his subordinate.

Sergeant Sowerby exhibited confusion.

"I mean nothing offensive, Inspector. I was referring to the joker who gave so good an imitation of my voice that even *you* were deceived."

The subtle flattery was apparently effective.

"Ah," replied Dunbar—"I see. Yes—he did it well. He spoke just like you. I could hardly make out a word he said."

With this Caledonian shaft and a side-glance at Stuart, Inspector Dunbar sat down at the table.

"Here's Dr. Stuart's description of the missing cabman," he continued, taking out his note-book. "Dr. Stuart has viewed the body and it is not the man. You had better take a proper copy of this."

"Then the cabman wasn't Max?" cried Sowerby eagerly. "I thought not."

"I believe you told me so before," said Dunbar sourly. "I also seem to recall that you thought a scorpion's tail was a Prickly Pear. However—here, on the page numbered twenty-six, is a description of the woman known as Mlle. Dorian. It should be a fairly easy matter to trace the car through the usual channels, and she ought to be easy to find, too."

He glanced at his watch. Stuart was standing by the lofty window looking out across the Embankment.

"Ten o'clock," said Dunbar. "The Commissioner will be expecting us."

"I am ready," responded Stuart.

Leaving Sergeant Sowerby seated at the table studying the note-book, Stuart and Dunbar proceeded to the smoke-laden room of the Assistant Commissioner. The great man, suavely satanic, greeted Stuart with that polished courtesy for which he was notable.

"You have been of inestimable assistance to us in the past, Dr. Stuart," he said, "and I feel happy to know that we are to enjoy the aid of your special knowledge in the present case. Will you smoke one of my cigarettes? They are some which a friend is kind enough to supply to me direct from Cairo, and are really quite good."

"Thanks," replied Stuart. "May I ask in what direction my services are likely to prove available?"

The Commissioner lighted a fresh cigarette. Then from a heap of correspondence he selected a long report typed upon blue foolscap.

"I have here," he said, "confirmation of the telegraphic report received last night. The name of M. Gaston Max will no doubt be familiar to you?"

Stuart nodded.

"Well," continued the Commissioner, "it appears that he has been engaged in England for the past month endeavouring to trace the connection which he claims to exist between the sudden deaths of various notable people, recently—a list is appended—and some person or organisation represented by, or associated with, a scorpion. His personal theory not being available—poor fellow, you have heard of his tragic death—I have this morning consulted such particulars as I could obtain respecting these cases. If they were really cases of assassination, some obscure poison was the only mode of death that could possibly have been employed. Do you follow me?"

"Perfectly."

"Now, the death of Gaston Max under circumstances not yet explained, would seem to indicate that his theory was a sound one. In other words, I am disposed to believe that he himself represents the most recent outrage of what we will call 'The Scorpion.' Even at the time that the body of the man found by the River Police had not been identified, the presence upon his person of a fragment of gold strongly resembling the tail of a scorpion prompted me to instruct Inspector Dunbar to consult you. I had determined upon a certain course. The identification of the dead man with Gaston Max merely strengthens my determination and enhances the likelihood of my idea being a sound one."

He flicked the ash from his cigarette and resumed:

"Without mentioning names, the experts consulted in the other cases which—according to the late Gaston Max —were victims of 'The Scorpion,' do not seem to have justified their titles. I am arranging that you shall be present at the autopsy upon the body of Gaston Max. And now, permit me to ask you a question: are you acquainted with any poison which would produce the symptoms noted in the case of Sir Frank Narcombe, for instance?"

Stuart shook his head slowly.

"All that I know of the case," he said, "is that he was taken suddenly ill in the foyer of a West-End theatre, immediately removed to his house in Half Moon Street, and died shortly afterwards. Can you give me copies of the specialists' reports and other particulars? I may then be able to form an opinion."

"I will get them for you," replied the Commissioner, the exact nature of whose theory was by no means evident to Stuart. He opened a drawer. "I have here," he continued, "the piece of cardboard and the envelope left with you by the missing cabman. Do you think there is any possibility of invisible writing?"

"None," said Stuart confidently. "I have tested in three or four places as you will see by the spots, but my experiments will in no way interfere with those which no doubt your own people will want to make. I have also submitted both surfaces to a microscopic examination. I am prepared to state definitely that there is no writing upon the cardboard, and except for the number, 30, none upon the envelope."

"It is only reasonable to suppose," continued the Commissioner, "that the telephone message which led Inspector Dunbar to leave your house last night was originated by that unseen intelligence against which we find ourselves pitted. In the first place, no one in London, myself and, presumably, 'The Scorpion' excepted, knew at that time that M. Gaston Max was in England or that M. Gaston Max was dead. I say, presumably 'The Scorpion' because it is fair to assume that the person whom Max pursued was responsible for his death.

"Of course"—the Commissioner reached for the box of cigarettes—"were it not for the telephone message, we should be unjustified in assuming that Mlle. Dorian and this"—he laid his finger upon the piece of cardboard—"had any connection with the case of M. Max. But the message was so obviously designed to facilitate the purloining of the sealed envelope and so obviously emanated from one already aware of the murder of M. Max, that the sender is identified at once with—'The Scorpion'."

The Assistant Commissioner complacently lighted a fresh cigarette.

"Finally," he said, "the mode of death in the case of M. Max may not have been the same as in the other cases. Therefore, Dr. Stuart"—he paused impressively—"if you fail to detect anything suspicious at the post mortem examination I propose to apply to the Home Secretary for power to exhume the body of the late Sir Frank Narcombe!"

## Chapter 9

### THE CHINESE COIN

DEEP in reflection, Stuart walked alone along the Embankment. The full facts contained in the report from Paris the Commissioner had not divulged, but Stuart concluded that this sudden activity was directly due, not to the death of M. Max, but to the fact that he (Max) had left behind him some more or less tangible clue. Stuart fully recognized that the Commissioner had accorded him an opportunity to establish his reputation—or to wreck it.

Yet, upon closer consideration, it became apparent that it was to Fate and not to the Commissioner that he was indebted. Strictly speaking, his association with the matter dated from the night of his meeting with the mysterious cabman in West India Dock Road. Or had the curtain first been lifted upon this occult drama that evening, five years ago, as the setting sun reddened the waters of the Imperial Canal and a veiled figure passed him on the Wû-Men Bridge?

"Shut your eyes tightly, master—the Scorpion is coming!"

He seemed to hear the boy's words now, as he passed along the Embankment; he seemed to see again the tall figure. And suddenly he stopped, stood still and stared with unseeing eyes across the muddy waters of the Thames. He was thinking of the cowled man who had stood behind the curtains in his study—of that figure so wildly bizarre that even now he could scarcely believe that he had ever actually seen it. He walked on.

Automatically his reflections led him to Mlle. Dorian, and he remembered that even as he paced along there beside the river the wonderful mechanism of New Scotland Yard was in motion, its many tentacles seeking—seeking tirelessly—for the girl, whose dark eyes haunted his sleeping and waking hours. *He* was responsible, and if she were arrested *he* would be called upon to identify her. He condemned himself bitterly.

After all, what crime had she committed? She had tried to purloin a letter—which did not belong to Stuart in the first place. And she had failed. Now—the police were looking for her. His reflections took a new form.

What of Gaston Max, foremost criminologist in Europe, who now lay dead and mutilated in an East-End mortuary? The telephone message which had summoned Dunbar away had been too opportune to be regarded as a mere coincidence. Mlle. Dorian was, therefore, an accomplice of a murderer.

Stuart sighed. He would have given much—more than he was prepared to admit to himself—to have known her to be guiltless.

The identity of the missing cabman now engaged his mind. It was quite possible, of course, that the man had actually found the envelope in his cab and was in no other way concerned in the matter. But how had Mlle. Dorian, or the person instructing her, traced the envelope to his study? And why, if they could establish a claim to it, had they preferred to attempt to steal it? Finally, why all this disturbance about a blank piece of cardboard?

A mental picture of the envelope arose before him, the number, 30, written upon it and the two black seals securing the lapels. He paused again in his walk. His reflections had led him to a second definite point and he fumbled in his waistcoat pocket for a time, seeking a certain brass coin about the size of a halfpenny, having a square hole in the middle and peculiar characters engraved around the square, one on each of the four sides.

He failed to find the coin in his pocket, however, but he walked briskly up a side street until he came to the entrance to a tube station. Entering a public telephone call-box, he asked for the number, City 400. Being put through and having deposited the necessary fee in the box:

"Is that the Commissioner's Office, New Scotland Yard?" he asked. "Yes! My name is Dr. Keppel Stuart. If Inspector Dunbar is there, would you kindly allow me to speak to him."

There was a short interval, then:

"Hullo!" came—"is that Dr. Stuart?"

"Yes. That you, Inspector? I have just remembered something which I should have observed in the first place if I had been really wide-awake. The envelope—you know the one I mean?—the one bearing the number, 30, has been sealed with a Chinese coin, known as *cash*. I have just recognized the fact and thought it wise to let you know at once."

"Are you sure?" asked Dunbar.

"Certain. If you care to call at my place later to-day I can show you some *cash*. Bring the envelope with you and you will see that the coins correspond to the impression in the wax. The inscriptions vary in different provinces, but the form of all *cash* is the same."

"Very good. Thanks for letting me know at once. It seems to establish a link with China, don't you think?"

"It does, but it merely adds to the mystery."

Coming out of the call-box, Stuart proceeded home, but made one or two professional visits before he actually returned to the house. He now remembered having left this particular *cash* piece (which he usually carried) in his dispensary, which satisfactorily accounted for his failure to find the coin in his waistcoat pocket. He had broken the cork of a flask, and in the absence of another of correct size had manufactured a temporary stopper with a small cork to the top of which he had fixed the Chinese coin with a drawing-pin. His purpose served he had left the extemporised stopper lying somewhere in the dispensary.

Stuart's dispensary was merely a curtained recess at one end of the waiting-room and shortly after entering the house he had occasion to visit it. Lying upon a shelf among flasks and bottles was the Chinese coin with the cork still attached. He took it up in order to study the inscription. Then:

"Have I cultivated somnambulism!" he muttered.

Fragments of black sealing-wax adhered to the coin!

Incredulous and half fearful he peered at it closely. He remembered that the impression upon the wax sealing the mysterious envelope had had a circular depression in the centre. It had been made by the head of the drawing-pin!

He found himself staring at the shelf immediately above that upon which the coin had lain. A stick of black sealing-wax used for sealing medicine was thrust in beside a bundle of long envelopes in which he was accustomed to post his Infirmary reports!

One hand raised to his head, Stuart stood endeavouring to marshal his ideas into some sane order. Then, knowing what he should find, he raised the green baize curtain hanging from the lower shelf which concealed a sort of cupboard containing miscellaneous stores and not a little rubbish, including a number of empty cardboard boxes.

A rectangular strip had been roughly cut from the lid of the topmost box!

The mysterious envelope and its contents, the wax and the seal—all had come from his own dispensary!

## Chapter 10

### "CLOSE YOUR SHUTTERS AT NIGHT"

INSPECTOR DUNBAR stood in the little dispensary tapping his teeth with the end of a fountain-pen.

"The last time he visited you, doctor—the time when he gave you the envelope—did the cabman wait here in the waiting-room?"

"He did—yes. He came after my ordinary consulting hours and I was at supper, I remember, as I am compelled to dine early."

"He would be in here alone?"

"Yes. No one else was in the room."

"Would he have had time to find the box, cut out the piece of cardboard from the lid, put it in the envelope and seal it?"

"Ample time. But what could be his object? And why mark the envelope 30?"

"It was in your consulting-room that he asked you to take charge of the envelope?"

"Yes."

"Might I take a peep at the consulting room?"

"Certainly, Inspector."

From the waiting-room they went up a short flight of stairs into the small apartment in which Stuart saw his patients. Dunbar looked slowly about him, standing in the middle of the room, then crossed and stared out of the window into the narrow lane below.

"Where were you when he gave you the envelope?" he snapped suddenly.

"At the table," replied Stuart with surprise.

"Was the table-lamp alight?"

"Yes. I always light it when seeing patients."

"Did you take the letter into the study to seal it in the other envelope?"

"I did, and he came along and witnessed me do it."

"Ah," said Dunbar, and scribbled busily in his note-book. "We are badly tied at Scotland Yard, doctor, and this case looks like being another for which somebody else will reap the credit. I am going to make a request that will surprise you."

He tore a leaf out of the book and folded it carefully.

"I am going to ask you to seal up something and lock it away! But I don't think you'll be troubled by cowled burglars or beautiful women because of it. On this piece of paper I have written—*a*"—he ticked off the points on his fingers: "what I believe to be the name of the man who cut out the cardboard and sealed it in an envelope; *b*: the name of the cabman; and, *c*: the name of the man who rang me up here last night and gave me information which had only just reached the Commissioner. I'll ask you to lock it away until it's wanted, doctor."

"Certainly, if you wish it," replied Stuart. "Come into the study and you shall see me do as you direct. I may add that the object to be served is not apparent to me."

Entering the study, he took an envelope, enclosed the piece of paper, sealed the lapel and locked the envelope in the same drawer of the bureau which once had contained that marked 30.

"Mlle. Dorian has a duplicate key to this drawer," he said. "Are you prepared to take the chance?"

"Quite," replied Dunbar, smiling; "although my information is worth more than that which she risked so much to steal."

"It's most astounding. At every step the darkness increases. Why should *anyone* have asked me to lock up a blank piece of cardboard?"

"Why, indeed," murmured Dunbar. "Well, I may as well get back. I am expecting a report from Sowerby. Look after yourself, sir. I'm inclined to think your pretty patient was talking square when she told you there might be danger."

Stuart met the glance of the tawny eyes.

"What d'you mean, Inspector? Why should *I* be in danger."

"Because," replied Inspector Dunbar, "if 'The Scorpion' is a poisoner, as the chief seems to think, there's really only one man in England he has to fear, and that man is Dr. Keppel Stuart."

When the Inspector had taken his departure Stuart stood for a long time staring out of the study window at the little lawn with its bordering of high neatly-trimmed privet above which at intervals arose the mop crowns of dwarf acacias. A spell of warm weather seemed at last to have begun, and clouds of gnats floated over the grass, their minute wings glittering in the sunshine. Despite the nearness of teeming streets, this was a backwater of London's stream.

He sighed and returned to some work which the visit of the Scotland Yard man had interrupted.

Later in the afternoon he had occasion to visit the institution to which he had recently been appointed as medical officer, and in contemplation of the squalor through which his steps led him he sought forgetfulness of the Scorpion problem—and of the dark eyes of Mlle. Dorian. He was not entirely successful, and returning by a different route he lost himself in memories which were sweetly mournful.

A taxicab passed him, moving slowly very close to the pavement. He scarcely noted it until it had proceeded some distance ahead of him. Then its slow progress so near to the pavement at last attracted his attention, and he stared vacantly towards the closed vehicle.

Mlle. Dorian was leaning out of the window and looking back at him!

Stuart's heart leapt high. For an instant he paused, then began to walk rapidly after the retreating vehicle. Perceiving that she had attracted his attention, the girl extended a white-gloved hand from the window and dropped a note upon the edge of the pavement. Immediately she withdrew into the vehicle—which moved away at accelerated speed, swung around the next corner and was gone.

Stuart ran forward and picked up the note. Without pausing to read it, he pressed on to the corner. The cab was already two hundred yards away, and he recognized pursuit to be out of the question. The streets were almost deserted at the moment, and no one apparently had witnessed the episode. He unfolded the sheet of plain notepaper, faintly perfumed with jasmine, and read the following, written in an uneven feminine hand:

"Close your shutters at night. Do not think too bad of me."

## Chapter 11

## THE BLUE RAY

DUSK found Stuart in a singular frame of mind. He was torn between duty—or what he conceived to be his duty —to the community, and . . . something else. A messenger from New Scotland Yard had brought him a bundle of documents relating to the case of Sir Frank Narcombe, and a smaller packet touching upon the sudden end of Henrik Ericksen, the Norwegian electrician, and the equally unexpected death of the Grand Duke Ivan. There were medical certificates, proceedings of coroners, reports of detectives, evidence of specialists and statements of friends, relatives and servants of the deceased. A proper examination of all the documents represented many hours of close study.

Stuart was flattered by the opinion held of his ability by the Assistant Commissioner, but dubious of his chance of detecting any flaw in the evidence which had escaped the scrutiny of so many highly trained observers.

He paced the study restlessly. Although more than six hours had elapsed, he had not communicated to Scotland Yard the fact of his having seen Mlle. Dorian that afternoon. A hundred times he had read the message, although he knew it by heart, knew the form of every letter, the odd crossing of the *t*'s and the splashy dotting of the *i*'s.

If only he could have taken counsel with someone—with someone not bound to act upon such information—it would have relieved his mental stress. His ideas were so chaotic that he felt himself to be incapable of approaching the task presented by the pile of papers lying upon his table.

The night was pleasantly warm and the sky cloudless. Often enough he found himself glancing toward the opened French windows, and once he had peered closely across into the belt of shadow below the hedge, thinking that he had detected something which moved there. Stepping to the window, the slinking shape had emerged into the moonlight—and had proclaimed itself to be that of a black cat!

Yet he had been sorely tempted to act upon the advice so strangely offered. He refrained from doing so, however, reflecting that to spend his evenings with closed and barred shutters now that a spell of hot weather seemed to be imminent would be insufferable. Up and down the room he paced tirelessly, always confronted by the eternal problem.

Forcing himself at last to begin work if only as a sedative, he filled and lighted his pipe, turned off the centre lamp and lighted the reading lamp upon his table. He sat down to consider the papers bearing upon the death of Ericksen. For half an hour he read on steadily and made a number of pencil notes. Then he desisted and sat staring straight before him.

What possible motive could there be in assassinating these people? The case of the Grand Duke might be susceptible of explanation, but those of Henrik Ericksen and Sir Frank Narcombe were not. Furthermore he could perceive no links connecting the three, and no reason why they should have engaged the attention of a common enemy. Such crimes would seem to be purposeless. Assuming that "The Scorpion" was an individual, that individual apparently was a dangerous homicidal maniac.

But, throughout the documents, he could discover no clue pointing to the existence of such an entity. "The Scorpion" might be an invention of the fertile brain of M. Gaston Max; for it had become more and more evident, as he had read, that the attempt to trace these deaths to an identical source had originated at the Service de Sûréte, and it was from Paris that the name "The Scorpion" had come. The fate of Max was significant, of course. The chances of his death proving to have been due to accident were almost negligible and the fact that a fragment of a golden scorpion had actually been found upon his body was certainly curious.

"Close your shutters at night. . . ."

How the words haunted him and how hotly he despised himself for a growing apprehension which refused to be ignored. It was more mental than physical, this dread which grew with the approach of midnight, and it resembled that which had robbed him of individuality and all but stricken him inert when he had seen upon the moonbright screen of the curtains the shadow of a cowled man.

Dark forces seemed to be stirring, and some unseen menace crept near to him out of the darkness.

The house was of early Victorian fashion and massive folding shutters were provided to close the French windows. He never used them, as a matter of fact, but now he tested the fastenings which kept them in place against the inner wall and even moved them in order to learn if they were still serviceable.

Of all the mysteries which baffled him, that of the piece of cardboard in the envelope sealed with a Chinese coin was the most irritating. It seemed like the purposeless trick of a child, yet it had led to the presence of the cowled man—and to the presence of Mlle. Dorian. Why?

He sat down at his table again.

"Damn the whole business!" he said. "It is sending me crazy."

Selecting from the heap of documents a large sheet of note-paper bearing a blue diagram of a human bust, marked with figures and marginal notes, he began to read the report to which it was appended—that of Dr. Halesowen. It stated that the late Sir Frank Narcombe had a "horizontal" heart, slightly misplaced and dilatated, with other details which really threw no light whatever upon the cause of his death.

"*I* have a horizontal heart," growled Stuart—"and considering my consumption of tobacco it is certainly dilatated. But I don't expect to drop dead in a theatre nevertheless."

He read on, striving to escape from that shadowy apprehension, but as he read he was listening to the night sounds of London, to the whirring of distant motors, the whistling of engines upon the railway and dim hooting of sirens from the Thames. A slight breeze had arisen and it rustled in the feathery foliage of the acacias and made a whispering sound as it stirred the leaves of the privet hedge.

The drone of an approaching car reached his ears. Pencil in hand, he sat listening. The sound grew louder, then ceased. Either the car had passed or had stopped somewhere near the house. Came a rap on the door.

"Yes," called Stuart and stood up, conscious of excitement.

Mrs. M'Gregor came in.

"There is nothing further you'll be wanting to-night?" she asked.

"No," said Stuart, strangely disappointed, but smiling at the old lady cheerfully. "I shall turn in very shortly."

"A keen east wind has arisen," she continued, severely eyeing the opened windows, "and even for a medical man you are strangely imprudent. Shall I shut the windows?"

"No, don't trouble, Mrs. M'Gregor. The room gets very stuffy with tobacco smoke, and really it is quite a warm night. I shall close them before I retire, of course."

"Ah well," sighed Mrs. M'Gregor, preparing to depart. "Good-night, Mr. Keppel."

"Good-night, Mrs. M'Gregor."

She retired, and Stuart sat staring out into the darkness. He was not prone to superstition, but it seemed like tempting providence to remain there with the windows open any longer. Yet paradoxically, he lacked the moral courage to close them—to admit to himself that he was afraid!

The telephone bell rang, and he started back in his chair as though to avoid a blow.

By doing so he avoided destruction.

At the very instant that the bell rang out sharply in the silence—so exact is the time-table of Kismet—a needle-like ray of blue light shot across the lawn from beyond and above the hedge and—but for that nervous start—must have struck fully upon the back of Stuart's skull. Instead, it shone past his head, which it missed only by inches, and he experienced a sensation as though some one had buffeted him upon the cheek furiously. He pitched out of his chair and on to the carpet.

The first object which the ray touched was the telephone; and next, beyond it, a medical dictionary; beyond that again, the grate, in which a fire was laid.

"My God!" groaned Stuart—"what is it!"

An intense crackling sound deafened him, and the air of the room seemed to have become hot as that of an oven. There came a series of dull reports—an uncanny wailing . . . and the needle-ray vanished. A monstrous shadow, moon-cast, which had lain across the carpet of the lawn—the shadow of a cowled man—vanished also.

Clutching the side of his head, which throbbed and tingled as though from the blow of an open hand, Stuart struggled to his feet. There was smoke in the room, a smell of burning and of fusing metal. He glared at the table madly.

The mouthpiece of the telephone had vanished!

"My God!" he groaned again, and clutched at the back of the chair.

His dictionary was smouldering slowly. It had a neat round hole some three inches in diameter, bored completely through, cover to cover! The fire in the grate was flaring up the chimney!

He heard the purr of a motor in the lane beside the house. The room was laden with suffocating fumes. Stuart stood clutching the chair and striving to retain composure—sanity. The car moved out of the lane.

Someone was running towards the back gate of the house . . . was scrambling over the hedge . . . was racing across the lawn!

A man burst into the study. He was a man of somewhat heavy build, clean-shaven and inclined to pallor. The hirsute blue tinge about his lips and jaw lent added vigour to a flexible but masterful mouth. His dark hair was tinged with grey, his dark eyes were brilliant with excitement. He was very smartly dressed and wore light tan gloves. He reeled suddenly, clutching at a chair for support.

"Quick! quick!" he cried—"the telephone! . . . *Ah!*"

Just inside the window he stood, swaying and breathing rapidly, his gaze upon the instrument.

"*Mon Dieu!*" he cried—"what has happened, then!"

Stuart stared at the new-comer dazedly.

"Hell has been in my room!" he replied. "That's all!"

"Ah!" said the stranger—"again he eludes me! The telephone was the only chance. *Pas d'blague!* we are finished!"

He dropped into a chair, removed his light grey hat and began to dry his moist brow with a fine silk handkerchief. Stuart stared at him like a man who is stupefied. The room was still laden with strange fumes.

"*Blimey!*" remarked the new-comer, and his Whitechapel was as perfect as his Montmartre. He was looking at the decapitated telephone. "This is a knock-out!"

"Might I ask," said Stuart, endeavouring to collect his scattered senses, "where you came from?"

"From up a tree!" was the astonishing reply. "It was the only way to get over!"

"Up a tree!"

"Exactly. Yes, I was foolish. I am too heavy. But what could I do! We must begin all over again."

Stuart began to doubt his sanity. This was no ordinary man.

"Might I ask," he said, "who you are and what you are doing in my house?"

"Ah!" The stranger laughed merrily. "You wonder about me—I can see it. Permit me to present myself—Gaston Max, at your service!"

"Gaston Max!" Stuart glared at the speaker incredulously. "Gaston Max! Why, I conduct a *post-mortem* examination upon Gaston Max tomorrow, in order to learn if he was poisoned!"

"Do not trouble, doctor. That poor fellow is not Gaston Max and he was not poisoned. You may accept my word for it. I had the misfortune to strangle him."

Part II

STATEMENT
OF M. GASTON MAX

I. THE DANCER OF MONTMARTRE

Chapter 1

## ZARA EL-KHALA

THE following statement which I, Gaston Max, am drawing up in duplicate for the guidance of whoever may in-
herit the task of tracing "The Scorpion"—a task which I
have begun—will be lodged—one copy at the Service de
Sûréte in Paris, and the other copy with the Commissioner
of Police, New Scotland Yard. As I apprehend that I may
be assassinated at any time, I propose to put upon record
all that I have learned concerning the series of murders
which I believe to be traceable to a certain person. In
the event of my death, my French colleagues will open
the sealed packet containing this statement and the English Assistant Commissioner of the Special Branch responsible for international affairs will receive instructions
to open that which I shall have lodged at Scotland Yard.

This matter properly commenced, then, with the visit

to Paris, incognito, of the Grand Duke Ivan, that famous soldier of whom so much was expected, and because I had made myself responsible for his safety during the time that he remained in the French capital, I (also incognito be it understood) struck up a friendship with one Casimir, the Grand Duke's valet. Nothing is sacred to a valet, and from Casimir I counted upon learning the real reason which had led this nobleman to visit Paris at so troublous a time. Knowing the Grand Duke to be a man of gallantry, I anticipated finding a woman in the case—and I was not wrong.

Yes, there was a woman, and *nom d'un nom!* she was beautiful.

Now in Paris we have many beautiful women, and in times of international strife it is true that we have had to shoot some of them. For my own part I say with joy that I have never been instrumental in bringing a woman to such an end. Perhaps I am sentimental; it is a French weakness; but on those few occasions when I have found a guilty woman in my power—and she has been pretty— *morbleu!* she has escaped! It may be that I have seen to it that she was kept out of further mischief, but nevertheless she has never met a firing-party because of me. Very well.

From the good fellow Casimir I learned that a certain dancer appearing at one of our Montmartre theatres had written to the Grand Duke craving the honour of his autograph—and enclosing her photograph.

Pf! it was enough. One week later the autograph arrived—attached to an invitation to dine with the Grand Duke at his hotel in Paris. Yes—he had come to Paris. I have said that he was susceptible and I have said that she was beautiful. I address myself to men of the world, and I shall not be in error if I assume that they will say, "A wealthy fool and a designing woman. It is an old story." Let us see.

The confidences of Casimir interested me in more ways than one. In the first place I had particular reasons for suspecting anyone who sought to obtain access to the Grand Duke. These were diplomatic. And in the second place I had suspicions of Zâra el-Khalâ. These were personal.

Yes—so she called herself—Zâra el Khalâ, which in Arabic is "Flower of the Desert." She professed to be an Egyptian, and certainly she had the long, almond-shaped eyes of the East, but her white skin betrayed her, and I knew that whilst she might possess Eastern blood, she was more nearly allied to Europe than to Africa. It is my business to note unusual matters, you understand, and I noticed that this beautiful and accomplished woman of whom all Paris was beginning to speak rapturously remained for many weeks at a small Montmartre theatre. Her performance, which was unusually decorous for the type of establishment at which she appeared, had not apparently led to an engagement elsewhere.

This aroused the suspicions to which I have referred. In the character of a vaudeville agent I called at the Montmartre theatre and was informed by the management that Zâra-el-Khalâ received no visitors, professional or otherwise. A small but expensive car awaited her at the stage door. My suspicions increased. I went away, but returned on the following night, otherwise attired, and from a hiding-place which I had selected on the previous evening I watched the dancer depart.

She came out so enveloped in furs and veils as to be unrecognizable, and a Hindu wearing a chauffeur's uniform opened the door of the car for her, and then, having arranged the rugs to her satisfaction, mounted to the wheel and drove away.

I traced the car. It had been hired for the purpose of taking Zâra el-Khalâ from her hotel—a small one in an unfashionable part of Paris—to the theatre and home nightly. I sent a man to call upon her at the hotel—in order to obtain press material, ostensibly. She declined to see him. I became really interested. I sent her a choice bouquet, having the card of a nobleman attached to it, together with a message of respectful admiration. It was returned. I prevailed upon one of the most handsome and gallant cavalry officers in Paris to endeavour to make her acquaintance. He was rebuffed.

. . *Eh bien!* I knew then that Mlle. Zâra of the Desert was unusual.

You will at once perceive that when I heard from the worthy Casimir how this unapproachable lady had actually written to the Grand Duke Ivan and had gone so far as to send him her photograph, I became excited. It appeared to me that I found myself upon the brink of an important discovery. I set six of my first-class men at work: three being detailed to watch the hotel of the Grand Duke Ivan and three to watch Zâra el-Khalâ. Two more were employed in watching the Hindu servant and one in watching my good friend Casimir. Thus, nine clever men and myself were immediately engaged upon the case.

Why do I speak of a "case" when thus far nothing of apparent importance had occurred? I will explain. Although the Grand Duke travelled incognito, his Government knew of the journey and wished to learn with what object it had been undertaken.

At the time that I made the acquaintance of Casimir the Grand Duke had been in Paris for three days, and he was —according to my informant—"like a raging lion." The charming dancer had vouchsafed no reply to his invitation and he had met with the same reception, on presenting himself in person, which had been accorded to myself and to those others who had sought to obtain an interview with Zâra el-Khalâ!

My state of mystification grew more and more profound. I studied the reports of my nine assistants.

It appeared that the girl had been in Paris for a period of two months. She occupied a suite of rooms in which all her meals were served. Except the Hindu who drove the hired car, she had no servant. She never appeared in the public part of the hotel unless veiled, and then merely in order to pass out to the car or in from it on returning. She drove out every day. She had been followed, of course, but her proceedings were unexceptionable. Leaving the car at a point in the Bois de Boulogne, she would take a short walk, if the day was fine enough, never proceeding out of sight of the Hindu, who followed with the automobile, and would then drive back to her hotel. She never received visits and never met any one during these daily excursions.

I turned to the report dealing with the Hindu.

He had hired a room high up under the roof of an apartment house where foreign waiters and others had their abodes. He bought and cooked his own food, which apparently consisted solely of rice, lentils and fruit. He went every morning to the garage and attended to the car, called for his mistress, and having returned remained until evening in his own apartment. At night, after returning from the theatre, he sometimes went out, and my agent had failed to keep track of him on every occasion that he had attempted pursuit. I detached the man who was watching Casimir and whose excellent reports revealed the fact that Casimir was an honest fellow—as valets go—and instructed him to assist in tracing the movements of the Hindu.

Two nights later they tracked him to a riverside café kept by a gigantic quadroon from Dominique and patronized by that type which forms a link between the lowest commercial and the criminal classes: itinerant vendors of Eastern rugs, street performers and Turkish cigarette makers.

At last I began to have hopes. The Grand Duke at this time was speaking of leaving Paris, but as he had found temporary consolation in the smiles of a lady engaged at the "Folies" I did not anticipate that he would depart for several days at any rate. Also he was the kind of man who is stimulated by obstacles.

The Hindu remained for an hour in the café, smoking and drinking some kind of syrup, and one of my fellows watched him. Presently the proprietor called him into a little room behind the counter and closed the door. The Hindu and the quadroon remained there for a few minutes, then the Hindu came out and left the café, returning to his abode. There was a telephone in this inner room, and my agent was of opinion that the Indian had entered either to make or to receive a call. I caused the line to be tapped.

On the following night the Hindu came back to the café, followed by one of my men. I posted myself at a selected point and listened for any message that might pass over the line to or from the café. At about the same hour as before—according to the report—someone called up the establishment, asking for "Miguel." This was the quadroon, and I heard his thick voice replying. The other voice—which had first spoken—was curiously sibilant but very distinct. Yet it did not sound like the voice of a Frenchman or of any European. This was the conversation:

"Miguel."

"Miguel speaks."

"*Scorpion*. A message for Chunda Lal."

"Very good."

Almost holding my breath, so intense was my excitement, I waited whilst Miguel went to bring the Hindu. Suddenly a new voice spoke—that of the Hindu.

"Chunda Lal speaks," it said.

I clenched my teeth; I knew that I must not miss a syllable.

"Scorpion" replied . . . in voluble *Hindustani*—a language of which I know less than a dozen words!

## Chapter 2

### CONCERNING THE GRAND DUKE

ALTHOUGH I had met with an unforeseen check, I had nevertheless learned three things. I had learned that Miguel the quadroon was possibly in league with the Hindu; that the Hindu was called Chunda Lal; and that Chunda Lal received messages, probably instructions, from a third party who announced his presence by the word *"Scorpion."*

One of my fellows, of course, had been in the café all the evening, and from him I obtained confirmation of the fact that it had been the Hindu who had been summoned to the telephone and whom I had heard speaking. Instant upon the man at the café replacing the telephone and disconnecting, I called up the exchange. They had been warned and were in readiness.

"From what subscriber did that call come?" I demanded.

Alas! another check awaited me. It had originated in a public call office, and "Scorpion" was untraceable by this means!

Despair is not permitted by the traditions of the Service de Sûrête. Therefore I returned to my flat and recorded the facts of the matter thus far established. I perceived that I had to deal, not with a designing woman, but with some shadowy being of whom she was an instrument. The anomaly of her life was in a measure explained. She sojourned in Paris for a purpose—a mysterious purpose which was concerned (I could not doubt it) with the Grand Duke Ivan. This was not an amorous but a political intrigue.

I communicated, at a late hour, with the senior of the three men watching the Grand Duke. The Grand Duke that evening had sent a handsome piece of jewellery purchased in Rue de la Paix to the dancer. It had been returned.

In the morning I met with the good Casimir at his

favorite café. He had just discovered that Zâra el-Khalâ drove daily to the Bois de Boulogne, alone, and that afternoon the Grand Duke had determined to accost her during her solitary walk. I prepared myself for this event. Arrayed in a workman's blouse and having a modest luncheon and a small bottle of wine in a basket, I concealed myself in that part of the Bois which was the favourite recreation ground of the dancer, and awaited her appearance.

The Grand Duke appeared first upon the scene, accompanied by Casimir. The latter pointed out to him a path through the trees along which Zâra el-Khalâ habitually strolled and showed him the point at which she usually rejoined the Hindu who followed along the road with the car. They retired. I seated myself beneath a tree from whence I could watch the path and the road and began to partake of the repast which I had brought with me.

At about three o'clock the dancer's car appeared, and the girl, veiled as usual, stepped out, and having exchanged a few words with the Indian, began to walk slowly towards me, sometimes pausing to watch a bird in the boughs above her and sometimes to examine some wild plant growing beside the way. I ate cheese from the point of a clasp-knife and drank wine out of the bottle.

Suddenly she saw me.

She had cast her veil aside in order to enjoy the cool and fragrant air, and as she stopped and regarded me doubtfully where I sat, I saw her beautiful face, undefiled, now, by make-up and unspoiled by the presence of garish Eastern ornaments. *Nom d'un nom!* but she was truly a lovely woman! My heart went out in sympathy to the poor Grand Duke. Had I received such a mark of favour from her as he had received, and had I then been scorned as now she scorned him, I should have been desperate indeed.

Coming around a bend in the path, then, she stood only a few paces away, looking at me. I touched the peak of my cap.

"Good-day, mademoiselle," I said. "The weather is very beautiful."

"Good-day," she replied.

I continued to eat cheese, and reassured she walked on past me. Twenty yards beyond, the Grand Duke was waiting. As I laid down my knife upon the paper which had been wrapped around the bread and cheese, and raised the bottle to my lips, the enamoured nobleman stepped out from the trees and bowed low before Zâra el-Khalâ.

She started back from him—a movement of inimitable grace, like that of a startled gazelle. And even before I had time to get upon my feet she had raised a little silver whistle to her lips and blown a short shrill note.

The Grand Duke, endeavouring to seize her hand, was pouring out voluble expressions of adoration in execrable French, and Zâra el-Khalâ was retreating step by step. She had quickly thrown the veil about her again. I heard the pad of swiftly running feet. If I was to intervene before the arrival of the Hindu, I must act rapidly. I raced along the path and thrust myself between the Grand Duke and the girl.

"Mademoiselle," I said, "is this gentleman annoying you?"

"How dare you, low pig!" cried the Grand Duke, and with a sweep of his powerful arm he hurled me aside.

"Thank you," replied Zâra el-Khalâ with great composure. "But my servant is here."

As I turned, Chunda Lal hurled himself upon the Grand Duke from behind. I had never seen an expression in a man's eyes like that in the eyes of the Hindu at this moment. They blazed like the eyes of a tiger, and his teeth were bared in a savage grin which I cannot hope to describe. His lean body seemed to shoot through the air, and he descended upon his burly adversary as a jungle beast falls upon its prey. Those long brown fingers clasping his neck, the Grand Duke fell forward upon his face.

"Chunda Lal!" said the dancer.

Kneeling, his right knee thrust between the shoulder blades of the prostrate man, the Hindu looked up—and I read murder in those glaring eyes. That he was an accomplished wrestler—or perhaps a strangler—I divined from the helplessness of the Grand Duke, who lay inert, robbed of every power except that of his tongue. He was swearing savagely.

"Chunda Lal!" said Zâra el-Khalâ again.

The Hindu shifted his grip from the neck to the arms of the Grand Duke. He pinioned him as is done in *jiu-jitsu* and forced him to stand upright. It was a curious spectacle—the impotency of this burly nobleman in the hands of his slight adversary. As they swayed to their feet, I thought I saw the glint of metal in the right hand of the Indian, but

I could not be sure, for my attention was diverted. At this moment Casimir appeared upon the scene, looking very frightened.

Suddenly releasing his hold altogether, the Hindu glaring into the empurpled face of the Grand Duke, shot out one arm and pointed with a quivering finger along the path.

"Go!" he said.

The Grand Duke clenched his fists, looked from face to face as if calculating his chances, then shrugged his shoulders, very deliberately wiped his neck and wrists, where the Indian had held him, with a large silk handkerchief and threw the handkerchief on the ground. I saw a speck of blood upon the silk. Without another glance he walked away, Casimir following sheepishly. It is needless, perhaps, to add that Casimir had not recognized me.

I turned to the dancer, touching the peak of my cap.

"Can I be of any assistance to mademoiselle?" I asked.

"Thank you—no," she replied.

She placed five francs in my hand and set off rapidly through the trees in the direction of the road, her bloodthirsty but faithful attendant at her heels!

I stood scratching my head and looking after her.

That afternoon I trusted a man acquainted with Hindustani to tap any message which might be sent to or from the café used by Chunda Lal. I learned that the Grand Duke had taken a stage box at the Montmartre theatre at which the dancer was appearing, and I decided that I would be present also.

A great surprise was in store for me.

Zâra el-Khalâ had at this time established a reputation which extended beyond those circles from which the regular patrons of this establishment were exclusively drawn and which had begun to penetrate to all parts of Paris. You will remember that it was the extraordinary circumstance of her remaining at this obscure place of entertainment so long which had first interested me in the lady. I had learned that she had rejected a number of professional offers, and, as I have already stated, I had assured myself of this unusual attitude by presenting the card of a well-known Paris agency—and being refused admittance.

Now, as I leaned upon the rail at the back of the auditorium and the time for the dancer's appearance grew near, I could not fail to observe that there was a sprinkling of evening-dress in the stalls and that the two boxes already occupied boasted the presence of parties of well-known men of fashion. Then the Grand Duke entered as a troupe of acrobats finished their performance. Zâra el-Khalâ was next upon the programme. I glanced at the Grand Duke and thought that he looked pale and unwell.

The tableau curtain fell and the manager appeared behind the footlights. He, also, seemed to be much perturbed.

"Ladies and gentlemen," he said, "I greatly regret to announce that Mlle. Zâra el-Khalâ is indisposed and unable to appear. We have succeeded in obtaining the services ——"

Of whom he had succeeded in obtaining the services I never heard, for the rougher section of the audience rose at him like a menacing wave! They had come to see the Egyptian dancer and they would have their money back! It was a swindle; they would smash the theatre!

If one had doubted the great and growing popularity of Zâra el-Khalâ, this demonstration must have proved convincing. Over the heads of the excited audience, I saw the Grand Duke rise as if to retire. The other box parties were also standing up and talking angrily.

"Why was it not announced outside the theatre?" someone shouted.

"We did not know until twenty minutes ago!" cried the manager in accents of despair.

I hurried from the theatre and took a taxicab to the hotel of the dancer. Running into the hall, I thrust a card in the hand of a concierge who stood there.

"Announce to Mlle. Zâra el-Khalâ that I must see her at once," I said.

The man smiled and returned the card to me.

"Mlle. Zâra el-Khalâ left Paris at seven o'clock, monsieur!"

"What!" I cried—"left Paris!"

"But certainly. Her baskets were taken to the Gare du Nord an hour earlier by her servant and she went off by the seven-fifty rapid for Calais. The theatre people were here asking for her an hour ago."

I hurried to my office to obtain the latest reports of my men. I had lost touch with them, you understand, during the latter part of the afternoon and evening. I found there the utmost confusion. They had been seeking me all over Paris to inform me that Zâra el-Khalâ had left. Two men had followed her and had telephoned from Calais for instructions. She had crossed by the night mail for Dover. It was already too late to instruct the English police.

For a few hours I had relaxed my usual vigilance—and this was the result. What could I do? Zâra el-Khalâ had committed no crime, but her sudden flight—for it looked like flight you will agree—was highly suspicious. And as I sat there in my office filled with all sorts of misgivings, in ran one of the men engaged in watching the Grand Duke.

The Grand Duke had been seized with illness as he left his box in the Montmartre theatre and had died before his car could reach the hotel!

## Chapter 3

## A STRANGE QUESTION

A CONVICTION burst upon my mind that a frightful crime had been committed. By whom and for what purpose I knew not. I hastened to the hotel of the Grand Duke. Tremendous excitement prevailed there, of course. There is no more certain way for a great personage to court publicity than to travel incognito. Everywhere that "M. de Stahler" had appeared all Paris had cried, "There goes the Grand Duke Ivan!" And now as I entered the hotel, press, police and public were demanding: "Is it true that the Grand Duke is dead?" Just emerging from the lift I saw Casimir. *In propria persona*—as M. Max—he failed to recognize me.

"My good man," I said—"are you a member of the suite of the late Grand Duke?"

"I am, or was, the valet of M. de Stahler, monsieur," he replied.

I showed him my card.

"To me 'M. de Stahler' is the Grand Duke Ivan. What other servants had he with him?" I asked, although I knew very well.

"None, monsieur."

"Where and when was he taken ill?"

"At the Theatre Coquerico, Montmartre, at about a quarter past ten o'clock to-night."

"Who was with him?"

"No one, monsieur. His Highness was alone in a box. I had instructions to call with the car at eleven o'clock."

"Well?"

"The theatre management telephoned at a quarter past ten to say that His Highness had been taken ill and that a physician had been sent for. I went in the car at once and found him lying in one of the dressing-rooms to which he had been carried. A medical man was in attendance. The Grand Duke was unconscious. We moved him to the car ——"

"*We?*"

"The doctor, the theatre manager, and myself. The Grand Duke was then alive, the physician declared, although he seemed to me to be already dead. But just before we reached the hotel, the physician, who was watching His Highness anxiously, cried, 'Ah, *mon Dieu!* It is finished. What a catastrophe!' "

"He was dead?"

"He was dead, monsieur."

"Who has seen him?"

"They have telephoned for half the doctors in Paris, monsieur, but it is too late."

He was affected, the good Casimir. Tears welled up in his eyes. I mounted in the lift to the apartment in which the Grand Duke lay. Three doctors were there, one of them being he of whom Casimir had spoken. Consternation was written on every face.

"It was his heart," I was assured by the doctor who had been summoned to the theatre. "We shall find that he suffered from heart trouble."

They were all agreed upon the point.

"He must have sustained a great emotional shock," said another.

"You are convinced that there was no foul play, gentlemen?" I asked.

They were quite unanimous on the point.

"Did the Grand Duke make any statement at the time of the seizure which would confirm the theory of a heart attack?"

No. He had fallen down unconscious outside the door of his box, and from this unconsciousness he had never recovered. (Depositions of witnesses, medical evidence and other documents are available for the guidance of whoever may care to see them, but, as is well known, the

death of the Grand Duke was ascribed to natural causes
and it seemed as though my trouble would after all prove
to be in vain.) Let us see what happened.

Leaving the hotel, on the night of the Grand Duke's
death, I joined the man who was watching the café telephone.

There had been a message during the course of the
evening, but it had been for a Greek cigarette-maker and
it referred to the theft of several bales of Turkish tobacco—useful information, of minor kind, but of little
interest to me. I knew that it would be useless to question
the man Miguel, although I strongly suspected him of being a member of "The Scorpion's" organization. Any
patron of the establishment enjoyed the privilege of re-
ceiving private telephone calls at the café on payment of
a small fee.

A man of less experience in obscure criminology might
now have assumed that he had been misled by a series of
striking coincidences. Remember, there was not a shadow
of doubt in the minds of the medical experts that the
Grand Duke had died from syncope. His own professional
adviser had sent written testimony to show that there was
hereditary heart trouble, although not of a character calculated to lead to a fatal termination except under extraordinary circumstances. His own Government, which had
every reason to suspect that the Grand Duke's assassination might be attempted, was satisfied. *Eh bien!* I was not.

I cross-examined the manager of the Theatre Coquerico.
He admitted that Mlle. Zâra el-Khalâ had been a mystery
throughout her engagement. Neither he nor anyone else
connected with the house had ever entered her dressing-
room or held any conversation with her, whatever, except
the stage-manager and the musical director. These had
spoken to her about her music and about lighting and
other stage effects. She spoke perfect French.

Such a state of affairs was almost incredible, but was
explained by the fact that the dancer, at a most modest
salary, had doubled the takings of the theatre in a few
days and had attracted capacity business throughout the
remainder of her engagement. She had written from Mar-
seilles, enclosing press notices and other usual matter
and had been booked direct for one week. She had remained for two months, and might have remained for-
ever, the poor manager assured me, at five times the
salary!

A curious fact now came to light. In all her photographs Zâra el-Khalâ appeared veiled, in the Eastern manner; that is to say, she wore a white silk *yashmak* which concealed all her face except her magnificent eyes! On the stage the veil was discarded; in the photographs it was always present.

And the famous picture which she had sent to the Grand Duke? He had destroyed it, in a fit of passion, on returning from the Bois de Boulogne after his encounter with Chunda Lal!

It is Fate after all—Kismet—and not the wit of man which leads to the apprehension of really great criminals —a tireless Fate which dogs their footsteps, a remorseless Fate from which they fly in vain. Long after the funeral of the Grand Duke, and at a time when I had almost forgotten Zâra el-Khalâ, I found myself one evening at the opera with a distinguished French scientist and he chanced to refer to the premature death (which had occured a few months earlier) of Henrik Ericksen, the Norwegian.

"A very great loss to the century, M. Max," he said. "Ericksen was as eminent in electrical science as the Grand Duke Ivan was eminent in the science of war. Both were stricken down in the prime of life—and under almost identical circumstances."

"That is true," I said thoughtfully.

"It would almost seem," he continued, "as if Nature had determined to foil any further attempts to rifle her secrets and Heaven to check mankind in the making of future wars. Only three months' after the Grand Duke's death, the American admiral, Mackney, died at sea—you will remember? Now, following Ericksen, Van Rembold, undoubtedly the greatest mining engineer of the century and the only man who has ever produced radium in workable quantities, is seized with illness at a friend's house and expires even before medical aid can be summoned."

"It is very strange."

"It is uncanny."

"Were you personally acquainted with the late Van Rembold?" I asked.

"I knew him intimately—a man of unusual charm, M. Max; and I have particular reason to remember his death, for I actually met him and spoke to him less than an hour before he died. We only exchanged a few words—we met on the street; but I shall never forget the subject of our chat."

"How is that?" I asked.

"Well, I presume Van Rembold's question was prompted by his knowledge of the fact that I had studied such subjects at one time; but he asked me if I knew of any race or sect in Africa or Asia who worshipped scorpions."

*"Scorpions!"* I cried. *"Ah, mon Dieu!* monsieur say it again—*scorpions?"*

"But yes, certainly. Does it surprise you?"

"Did it not surprise *you?"*

"Undoubtedly. I could not imagine what had occurred to account for his asking so strange a question. I replied that I knew of no such sect, and Van Rembold immediately changed the subject, nor did he revert to it. So that I never learned why he had made that singular inquiry."

You can imagine that this conversation afforded me much food for reflection. Whilst I could think of no reason why anyone should plot to assassinate Grand Dukes, admirals and mining engineers, the circumstances of the several cases were undoubtedly similar in a number of respects. But it was the remarkable question asked by Van Rembold which particularly aroused my interest.

Of course it might prove to be nothing more than a coincidence, but when one comes to consider how rarely the word "scorpion" is used, outside those countries in which these insects abound, it appears to be something more. Van Rembold, then, had had some occasion to feel curious about the scorpions; the name "Scorpion" was associated with the Hindu follower of Zâra el-Khalâ; and she it was who had brought the Grand Duke to Paris, where he had died.

Oh! it was a very fragile thread, but by following such a thread as this we are sometimes led to the heart of a labyrinth.

Beyond wondering if some sinister chain bound together this series of apparently natural deaths I might have made no move in the matter, but something occurred which spurred me to action. Sir Frank Narcombe, the great English surgeon, collapsed in the foyer of a London theatre and died shortly afterwards. Here again I perceived a case of a notable man succumbing unexpectedly in a public place—a case parallel to that of the Grand Duke, of Ericksen, of Van Rembold! It seemed as though some strange epidemic had attacked men of science—yes!

they were all men of science, even including the Grand Duke, who was said to be the most scientific soldier in Europe, and the admiral, who had perfected the science of submarine warfare.

"The Scorpion!" . . . that name haunted me persistently. So much so that at last I determined to find out for myself if Sir Frank Narcombe had ever spoken about a scorpion or if there was any evidence to show that he had been interested in the subject.

I could not fail to remember, too, that Zâra el-Khalâ had last been reported as crossing to England.

## Chapter 4

### THE FIGHT IN THE CAFE

NEW SCOTLAND YARD had been advised that any reference to a scorpion, in whatever form it occurred, should be noted and followed up, but nothing had resulted and as a matter of fact I was not surprised in the least. All that I had learned—and this was little enough—I had learned more or less by accident. But I came to the conclusion that a visit to London might be advisable.

I had caused a watch to be kept upon the man Miguel, whose establishment seemed to be a recognized resort of shady characters. I had no absolute proof, remember, that he knew anything of the private affairs of the Hindu, and no further reference to a scorpion had been made by anyone using the café telephone. Nevertheless I determined to give him a courtesy call before leaving for London . . . and to this determination I cannot doubt that once again I was led by providence.

Attired in a manner calculated to enable me to pass unnoticed among the patrons of the establishment, I entered the place and ordered cognac. Miguel having placed it before me, I lighted a cigarette and surveyed my surroundings.

Eight or nine men were in the café, and two women. Four of the men were playing cards at a corner table, and the others were distributed about the place, drinking and smoking. The women, who were flashily dressed but who belonged to that order of society which breeds the Apache, were deep in conversation with a handsome Algerian. I recognized only one face in the café—that of a dangerous character, Jean Sach, who had narrowly escaped the electric chair in the United States and who was well known to the Bureau. He was smiling at one of the two women —the woman to whom the Algerian seemed to be more particularly addressing himself.

Another there was in the café who interested me as a student of physiognomy—a dark, bearded man, one of the card-players. His face was disfigured by a purple scar extending from his brow to the left corner of his mouth, which it had drawn up into a permanent snarl, so that he resembled an enraged and dangerous wild animal. Mentally I classified this person as "Le Balafré."

I had just made up my mind to depart when the man Sach arose, crossed the café and seated himself insolently between the Algerian and the woman to whom the latter was talking. Turning his back upon the brown man, he addressed some remark to the woman, at the same time leering in her face.

Women of this class are difficult, you understand? Sach received from the lady a violent blow upon the face which rolled him on the floor! As he fell, the Algerian sprang up and drew a knife. Sach rolled away from him and also reached for the knife which he carried in a hip-pocket.

Before he could draw it, Miguel, the quadroon proprietor, threw himself upon him and tried to pitch him into the street. But Sach, although a small man, was both agile and ferocious. He twisted out of the grasp of the huge quadroon and turned, raising the knife. As he did so, the Algerian deftly kicked it from his grasp and left Sach to face Miguel unarmed. Screaming with rage, he sprang at Miguel's throat, and the two fell writhing upon the floor.

There could only be one end to such a struggle, of course, as the Algerian recognized by replacing his knife in his pocket and resuming his seat. Miguel obtained a firm hold upon Sach and raised him bodily above his head, as one has seen a professional weight-lifter raise a heavy dumb-bell. Thus he carried him, kicking and foaming at the mouth with passion, to the open door. From the step he threw him into the middle of the street.

At this moment I observed something glittering upon the floor close to the chair occupied by the Algerian.

Standing up—for I had determined to depart—I crossed in that direction, stooped and picked up this object which glittered. As my fingers touched it, so did my heart give a great leap.

The object was a *golden scorpion!*

Forgetful of my dangerous surroundings I stood looking at the golden ornament in my hand ... when suddenly and violently it was snatched from me! The Algerian, his brown face convulsed with rage, confronted me.

"Where did you find that charm?" he cried. "It belongs to me."

"Very well," I replied—"you have it."

He glared at me with a ferocity which the incident scarcely seemed to merit and exchanged a significant glance with someone who had approached and who now stood behind me. Turning, I met a second black gaze—that of the quadroon who having restored order had returned from the café door and now stood regarding me.

"Did you find it on the floor?" asked Miguel suspiciously.

"I did."

He turned to the Algerian.

"It fell when you kicked the knife from the hand of that pig," he said. "You should be more careful."

Again they exchanged significant glances, but the Algerian resumed his seat and Miguel went behind the counter. I left the café conscious of the fact that black looks pursued me.

The night was very dark, and as I came out on to the pavement someone touched me on the arm. I turned in a flash.

"Walk on, friend," said the voice of Jean Sach. "What was it that you picked up from the floor?"

"A golden scorpion," I answered quickly.

"Ah!" he whispered—"I thought so! It is enough. They shall pay for what they have done to me—those two. Hurry, friend, as I do."

Before I could say another word or strive to detain him, he turned and ran off along a narrow courtway which at this point branched from the street.

I stood for a moment, nonplussed, staring after him. By good fortune I had learned more in ten minutes than by the exercise of all my ingenuity and the resources of the Service I could have learned in ten months! *Par la barbe du prophète!* the Kismet which dogs the footsteps of malefactors assisted me!

Recollecting the advice of Jean Sach, I set off at a brisk pace along the street, which was dark and deserted and which passed through a district marked red on the Paris crimes-map. Arriving at the corner, above which projected a lamp, I paused and glanced back into the darkness. I could see no one, but I thought I could detect the sound of stealthy footsteps following me.

The suspicion was enough. I quickened my pace, anxious to reach the crowded boulevard upon which this second street opened. I reached it unmolested, but intending to throw any pursuer off the track, I dodged and doubled repeatedly on the way to my flat and arrived there about midnight, convinced that I had eluded pursuit—if indeed I had been pursued.

All my arrangements were made for leaving Paris, and now I telephoned to the assistant on duty in my office, instructing him to take certain steps in regard to the proprietor of the café and the Algerian and to find the hiding-place of the man Jean Sach. I counted it more than ever important that I should go to London at once.

In this belief I was confirmed at the very moment that I boarded the Channel steamer at Boulogne; for as I stepped upon the deck I found myself face to face with a man who was leaning upon the rail and apparently watching the passengers coming on board. He was a man of heavy build, dark and bearded, and his face was strangely familiar.

Turning, as I lighted a cigarette, I glanced back at him in order to obtain a view of his profile. I knew him instantly—for now the scar was visible. It was "Le Balafré" who had been playing cards in Miguel's café on the previous night!

I have sometimes been criticised, especially by my English confrères, for my faith in disguise. I have been told that no disguise is impenetrable to the trained eye. I reply that there are many disguises but few trained eyes! To my faith in disguise I owed the knowledge that a golden scorpion was the token of some sort of gang, society, or criminal group, and to this same faith which an English inspector of police once assured me to be a misplaced one I owed, on boarding the steamer, my escape from detection by this big bearded fellow who was possibly looking out for me!

Yet, I began to wonder if after all I had escaped the shadowy pursuer whose presence I had suspected in the dark street outside the café or if he had tracked me and learned my real identity. In any event, the rôles were about to be reversed! "Le Balafré" at Folkestone took a seat in a third-class carriage of the London train. I took one in the next compartment.

Arrived at Charing Cross, he stood for a time in the booking-hall, glanced at his watch, and then took up the handbag which he carried and walked out into the station yard. I walked out also.

"Le Balafré" accosted a cabman; and as he did so I passed close behind him and overheard a part of the conversation.

". . . Bow Road Station East! It's too far. What?"

I glanced back. The bearded man was holding up a note—a pound note apparently. I saw the cabman nod. Without an instant's delay I rushed up to another cabman who had just discharged a passenger.

"To Bow Road Station East!" I said to the man. "Double fare if you are quick!"

It would be a close race. But I counted on the aid of that Fate which dogs the steps of wrongdoers! My cab was off first and the driver had every reason for hurrying. From the moment that we turned out into the Strand until we arrived at our destination I saw no more of "Le Balafré." My extensive baggage I must hope to recover later.

At Bow Road Station I discovered a telephone box in a dark corner which commanded a view of the street. I entered this box and waited. It was important that I should remain invisible. Unless my bearded friend had been unusually fortunate he could not well have arrived before me.

As it chanced I had nearly six minutes to wait. Then, not ten yards away, I saw "Le Balafré" arrive and dismiss the cabman outside the station. There was nothing furtive in his manner; he was evidently satisfied that no one pursued him; and he stood in the station entrance almost outside my box and lighted a cigar!

Placing his bag upon the floor, he lingered, looking to left and right, when suddenly a big closed car painted dull yellow drew up beside the pavement. It was driven by a brown-faced chauffeur whose nationality I found difficulty in placing, for he wore large goggles. But before I could determine upon my plan of action, "Le Balafré" crossed the pavement and entered the car—and the car glided smoothly away, going East. A passing lorry obstructed my view and I even failed to obtain a glimpse of the number on the plate.

But I had seen something which had repaid me for my trouble. As the man of the scar had walked up to the car, he had exhibited to the brown-skinned chauffeur some object which he held in the palm of his hand . . . an object which glittered like gold!

## II. "LE BALAFRE"

### Chapter 1

## I BECOME CHARLES MALET

BEHOLD me established in rooms in Battersea and living retired during the day while I permitted my beard to grow. I had recognized that my mystery of "The Scorpion" was the biggest case which had ever engaged the attention of the Service de Sûréte, and I was prepared, if necessary, to devote my whole time for twelve months to its solution. I had placed myself in touch with Paris, and had had certain papers and licenses forwarded to me. A daily bulletin reached me, and one of these bulletins was sensational.

The body of Jean Sach had been recovered from the Seine. The man had been stabbed to the heart. Surveillance of Miguel and his associates continued unceasingly, but I had directed that no raids or arrests were to be made without direct orders from me.

I was now possessed of a French motor license and also that of a Paris taxi-driver, together with all the other documents necessary to establish the identity of one Charles Malet. Everything was in order. I presented myself—now handsomely bearded—at New Scotland Yard and applied for a license. The "knowledge of London" and other tests I passed successfully and emerged a fully-fledged cabman!

Already I had opened negotiations for the purchase of a dilapidated but serviceable cab which belonged to a small proprietor who had obtained a car of more up-to-date pattern to replace this obsolete one. I completed these negotiations by paying down a certain sum and arranged to garage my cab in the disused stable of a house near my rooms in Battersea.

Thus I now found myself in a position to appear anywhere at any time without exciting suspicion, enabled swiftly to proceed from point to point and to pursue anyone either walking or driving whom it might please me to pursue. It was a *modus operandi* which had served me well in Paris and which had led to one of my biggest successes (the capture of the French desperado known as "Mr. Q.") in New York.

I had obtained, *viâ* Paris, particulars of the recent death of Sir Frank Narcombe, and the circumstances attendant upon his end were so similar to those which had characterized the fate of the Grand Duke, of Van Rembold and the others, that I could not for a moment believe them to be due to mere coincidence. Acting upon my advice Paris advised Scotland Yard to press for a *post mortem* examination of the body, but the influence of Sir Frank's family was exercised to prevent this being carried out—and exercised successfully.

Meanwhile, I hovered around the houses, flats, clubs and offices of everyone who had been associated with the late surgeon, noting to what addresses they directed me to drive and who lived at those addresses. In this way I obtained evidence sufficient to secure three judicial separations, but not a single clue leading to "The Scorpion"! No matter.

At every available opportunity I haunted the East-End streets, hoping for a glimpse of the big car and the brown-skinned chauffeur or of my scarred man from Paris. I frequented all sorts of public bars and eating-houses used by foreign sailors and Asiatics. By day and by night I roamed about the dismal thoroughfares of that depressing district, usually with my flag down to imply that I was engaged.

Such diligence never goes long unrewarded. One evening, having discharged a passenger, a mercantile officer, at the East India Docks, as I was drifting, watchfully, back through Limehouse, I saw a large car pull up just ahead of me in the dark. A man got out and the car was driven off.

Two courses presented themselves. I was not sure that this was the car for which I sought, but it strangely re-

sembled it. Should I follow the car or the man? A rapid
decision was called for. I followed the man.

That I had not been mistaken in the identity of the car
shortly appeared. The man took out a cigar and standing
on the corner opposite the Town Hall, lighted it. I was
close to him at the time, and by the light of the match,
which he sheltered with his hands, I saw the scarred and
bearded face! *Triomphe!* it was he!

Having lighted his cigar, he crossed the road and entered
the saloon of a neighbouring public-house. Locking my
cab I, also, entered that saloon. I ordered a glass of bitter
beer and glanced around at the object of my interest. He
had obtained a glass of brandy and was contorting his
hideous face as he sipped the beverage. I laughed.

"Have they tried to poison you, mister!" I said.

"Ah, *pardieu!* poison—yes!" he replied.

"You want to have it out of a bottle," I continued confidentially—"Martell's Three Stars."

He stared at me uncomprehendingly.

"I don't know," he said haltingly. "I have very little
English."

"Oh, that's it!" I cried, speaking French with a barbarous accent. "You only speak French?"

"Yes, yes," he replied eagerly. "It is so difficult to make
oneself understood. This spirit is not cognac, it is some
kind of petrol!"

Finishing my bitter, I ordered two glasses of good
brandy and placed one before "Le Balafré."

"Try that," I said, continuing to speak in French. "You
will find it is better."

He sipped from his glass and agreed that I was right.
We chatted together for ten minutes and had another
drink, after which my dangerous-looking acquaintance
wished me good-night and went out. The car had come
from the West, and I strongly suspected that my man
either lived in the neighbourhood or had come there to
keep an appointment. Leaving my cab outside the public-
house, I followed him on foot, down Three Colt Street to
Ropemaker Street, where he turned into a narrow alley
leading to the riverside. It was straight and deserted, and
I dared not follow further until he had reached the corner.
I heard his footsteps pass right to the end. Then the sound
died away. I ran to the corner. The back of a wharf building—a high blank wall—faced a row of ramshackle tene-

ments, some of them built of wood; but not a soul was in sight.

I reluctantly returned to the spot at which I had left the cab—and found a constable there who wanted to know what I meant by leaving a vehicle in the street unattended. I managed to enlist his sympathy by telling him that I had been in pursuit of a "fare" who had swindled me with a bad half-crown. The ruse succeeded.

"Which street did he go down, mate?" asked the constable.

I described the street and described the scarred man. The constable shook his head.

"Sounds like one o' them foreign sailormen," he said. "But I don't know what he can have gone down there for. It's nearly all Chinese, that part."

His words came as a revelation; they changed the whole complexion of the case. It dawned upon me even as he spoke the word "Chinese" that the golden scorpion which I had seen in the Paris café was of Chinese workmanship! I started my engine and drove slowly to that street in which I had lost the track of "Le Balafré." I turned the cab so that I should be ready to drive off at a moment's notice, and sat there wondering what my next move should be. How long I had been there I cannot say, when suddenly it began to rain in torrents.

What I might have done or what I had hoped to do is of no importance; for as I sat there staring out at the dismal rain-swept street, a man came along, saw the head-lamps of the cab and stopped, peering in my direction. Evidently perceiving that I drove a cab and not a private car, he came towards me.

"Are you disengaged?" he asked.

Whether it was that I sympathized with him—he had no topcoat or umbrella—or whether I was guided by Fate I know not, but as he spoke I determined to give up my dreary vigil for that night. *Pardieu!* but certainly it was Fate again!

"Well, I suppose I am, sir," I said, and asked him where he wanted to go.

He gave an address not five hundred yards from my own rooms! I thought this so curious that I hesitated no longer.

"Jump in," I said; and still seeking in my mind for a link between the scorpion case and China, I drove off, and in less than half an hour, for the streets were nearly empty, arrived at my destination.

The passenger, whose name was Dr. Keppel Stuart, very kindly suggested a glass of hot grog, and I did not refuse his proferred hospitality. When I came out of his house again, the rain had almost ceased, and just as I stooped to crank the car I thought I saw a shadowy figure moving near the end of a lane which led to the trades-men's entrance of Dr. Stuart's house. A sudden suspicion laid hold upon me—a horrible doubt.

Having driven some twenty yards along the road, I leaned from my seat and looked back. A big man wearing a black waterproof overall was standing looking after me!

Remembering how cleverly I had been trailed from Miguel's café to my flat, in Paris (for I no longer doubted that someone had followed me on that occasion), I now perceived that I might again be the object of the same expert's attention. Stopping my engine half-way along the next road, I jumped out and ran back, hiding in the bushes which grew beside the gate of a large empty house. I had only a few seconds to wait.

A big closed car, running almost silently, passed before me . . . and "Le Balafré" was leaning out of the window!

At last I saw my chance of finding the headquarters of "The Scorpion." Alas! The man of the scar was as swift to recognize that possibility as I. A moment after he had passed my stationary cab, and found it to be deserted, his big car was off like the wind, and even before I could step out from the bushes the roar of the powerful engine was growing dim in the distance!

I was detected. I had to deal with dangerously clever people.

## Chapter 2

### BAITING THE TRAP

THE following morning I spent at home, in my modest rooms, reviewing my position and endeavouring to adjust my plans in accordance with the latest development. "The

Scorpion" had scored a point. What had aroused the suspicions of "Le Balafré," I knew not; but I was inclined to think that he had been looking from some window or peep-hole in the narrow street with the wooden houses when I had, injudiciously, followed him there.

On the other hand, the leakage might be in Paris—or in my correspondence system. The man of the scar might have been looking for me as I was looking for him. That he was looking for someone on the cross-channel boat I had not doubted.

He was aware, then, that Charles Malet, cabman, was watching him. But was he aware that Charles Malet was Gaston Max? And did he know where I lived? Also—did he perchance think that my meeting with Dr. Stuart in Limehouse had been prearranged? Clearly he had seen Dr. Stuart enter my cab, for he had pursued us to Battersea.

This course of reflection presently led me to a plan. It was a dangerous plan, but I doubted if I should ever find myself in greater danger than I was in already. *Nom d'un nom!* I had not forgotten the poor Jean Sach!

That night, well knowing that I carried my life in my hands, I drove again to Limehouse Town Hall, and again leaving my cab outside went into the bar where I had previously met "Le Balafré." If I had doubted that my movements were watched I must now have had such doubts dispelled; for two minutes later the man with the scar came in and greeted me affably!

I had learned something else. He did not know that I had recognized him as the person who had tracked me to Dr. Stuart's house!

He invited me to drink with him, and I did so. As we raised our glasses I made a move. Looking all about me suspiciously:

"Am I right in supposing that you have business in this part of London?" I asked.

"Yes," he replied. "My affairs bring me here sometimes."

"You are well acquainted with the neighbourhood?"

"Fairly well. But actually of course I am a stranger to London."

I tapped him confidentially upon the breast.

"Take my advice, as a friend," I said, "and visit these parts as rarely as possible."

"Why do you say that?"

"It is dangerous. From the friendly manner in which you entered into conversation with me, I perceived that you were of a genial and unsuspicious nature. Very well. I warn you. Last night I was followed from a certain street not far from here to the house of a medical man who is a specialist in certain kinds of criminology, you understand."

He stared at me very hard, his teeth bared by that fearful snarl. "You are a strange cabman."

"Perhaps I am. No matter. Take my advice. I have things written here"—I tapped the breast of my tunic—"which will astonish all the world shortly. I tell you, my friend, my fortune is made."

I finished my drink and ordered another for myself and one for my acquaintance. He was watching me doubtfully. Taking up my replenished glass, I emptied it at a draught and ordered a third. I leaned over towards the scarred man, resting my hand heavily upon his shoulder.

"Five thousand pounds," I whispered thickly, "has been offered for the information which I have here in my pocket. It is not yet complete, you understand, and because they may murder me before I obtain the rest of the facts, do you know what I am going to do with this?"

Again I tapped my tunic pocket. "Le Balafré" frowned perplexedly.

"I don't even know what you are talking about, my friend," he replied.

"*I* know what I am talking about," I assured him, speaking more and more huskily. "Listen, then: I am going to take all my notes to my friend, the doctor, and leave them with him, sealed—sealed, you follow me? If I do not come back for them, in a week, shall we say?—he sends them to the police. *I* do not profit, you think? No, *morbleu!* but there are some who hang!"

Emptying my third glass, I ordered a fourth and one for my companion. He checked me.

"No more for me, thank you," he said. "I have—business to attend to. I will wish you good-night."

"Good-night!" I cried boisterously—"good-night, friend! Take heed of my good advice!"

As he went out, the barman brought me my fourth glass of cognac, staring at me doubtfully. Our conversation had been conducted in French, but the tone of my voice had attracted attention.

"Had about enough, ain't you, mate?" he said. "Your ugly pal jibbed!"

"Quite enough!" I replied, in English now of course. "But I've had a stroke of luck to-night and I feel happy. Have one with me. This is a final."

On going out into the street I looked cautiously about me, for I did not expect to reach the house of Dr. Stuart unmolested. I credited "Le Balafré" with sufficient acumen to distrust the genuineness of my intoxication, even if he was unaware of my real identity. I never make the mistake of underestimating an opponent's wit, and whilst acting on the assumption that the scarred man knew me to be forcing his hand, I recognized that whether he believed me to be drunk or sober, Gaston Max or another, his line of conduct must be the same. He must take it for granted that I actually designed to lodge my notes with Dr. Stuart and endeavour to prevent me doing so.

I could detect no evidence of surveillance whatever and cranking the engine I mounted and drove off. More than once, as I passed along Commercial Road, I stopped and looked back. But so far as I could make out no one was following me. The greater part of my route lay along populous thoroughfares, and of this I was not sorry; but I did not relish the prospect of Thames Street, along which presently my course led me.

Leaving the city behind me, I turned into that thoroughfare, which at night is almost quite deserted, and there I pulled up. *Pardieu!* I was disappointed! It seemed as though my scheme had miscarried. I could not understand why I had been permitted to go unmolested, and I intended to walk back to the corner for a final survey before continuing my journey. This survey was never made.

As I stopped the cab and prepared to descend, a faint— a very faint—sound almost in my ear, set me keenly on the alert. Just in the nick of time I ducked . . . as the blade of a long knife flashed past my head, ripping its way through my cloth cap!

Yes! That movement had saved my life, for otherwise the knife must have entered my shoulder—and pierced to my heart!

Someone was hidden in the cab!

He had quietly opened one of the front windows and had awaited a suitable opportunity to stab me. Now, recognizing failure, he leapt out on the near side as I lurched and stumbled from my seat, and ran off like the wind. I never so much as glimpsed him.

*"Mon Dieu!"* I muttered, raising my hand to my head,

from which blood was trickling down my face, "the plan succeeds!"

I bound a handkerchief as tightly as possible around the wound in my scalp and put my cap on to keep the bandage in place. The wound was only a superficial one, and except for the bleeding I suffered no inconvenience from it. But I had now a legitimate reason for visiting Dr. Stuart, and as I drove on towards Battersea I was modifying my original plan in accordance with the unforeseen conditions.

It was long past Dr. Stuart's hours of consultation when I arrived at his house, and the servant showed me into a waiting-room, informing me that the doctor would join me in a few minutes. Directly she had gone out I took from the pocket of my tunic the sealed envelope which I had intended to lodge with the doctor. Pah! it was stained with blood which had trickled down from the wound in my scalp!

Actually, you will say, there was no reason why I should place a letter in the hands of Dr. Stuart; my purpose would equally well be served by *pretending* that I had done so. Ah, but I knew that I had to deal with clever people—with artists in crime—and it behooved me to be an artist also. I had good reason to know that their system of espionage was efficient; and the slipshod way is ever the wrong way.

The unpleasantly sticky letter I returned to my pocket, looking around me for some means of making up any kind of packet which could do duty as a substitute. Beyond a curtain draped over a recess at one end of the waiting-room I saw a row of boxes, a box of lint and other medical paraphernalia. It was the doctor's dispensary. Perhaps I might find there an envelope.

I crossed the room and looked. Immediately around the corner, on a level with my eyes, was a packet of foolscap envelopes and a stick of black sealing-wax! *Bien!* all that I now required was a stout sheet of paper to enclose in one of those envelopes. But not a scrap of paper could I find, except the blood-stained letter in my pocket—towards which I had formed a strong antipathy. I had not even a newspaper in my possession. I thought of folding three or four envelopes, but there were only six in all, and the absence of so many might be noted.

Drawing aside a baize curtain which hung from the bottom shelf, I discovered a number of old card-board boxes. It was sufficient. With a pair of surgical scissors I cut a piece from the lid of one and thrust it into an envelope, gumming down the lapel. At a little gas jet intended for the purpose I closed both ends with wax and—singular coincidence!—finding a Chinese coin fastened to a cork lying on the shelf, my sense of humour prompted me to use it as a seal! Finally, to add to the verisimilitude of the affair I borrowed a pen which rested in a bottle of red ink and wrote upon the envelope the number: 30, that day being the thirtieth day of the month.

It was well that the artist within me had dictated this careful elaboration, as became evident a few minutes later when the doctor appeared at the head of a short flight of stairs and requested me to step up into his consulting-room. It was a small room, so that the window, over which a linen blind was drawn, occupied nearly the whole of one wall. As Dr. Stuart, having examined the cut on my scalp, descended to the dispensary for lint, the habits of a lifetime asserted themselves.

I quickly switched off the light and peeped out of the window around the edge of the blind, which I drew slightly aside. In the shadow of the wall upon the opposite side of the narrow lane a man was standing! I turned on the light again. The watcher should not be disappointed!

My skull being dressed, I broached the subject of the letter, which I said I had found in my cab after the accident which had caused the injury.

"Someone left this behind to-day, sir," I said; "perhaps the gentleman who was with me when I had the accident; and I've got no means of tracing him. He may be able to trace *me*, though, or he may advertise. It evidently contains something valuable. I wonder if you would do me a small favour? Would you mind taking charge of it for a week or so, until it is claimed?"

He asked me why I did not take it to Scotland Yard.

"Because," said I, "if the owner claims it from Scotland Yard he is less likely to be generous than if he gets it direct from me!"

"But what is the point," asked Dr. Stuart, "in leaving it here?"

I explained that if *I* kept the letter I might be suspected of an intention of stealing it, whereas directly there was any inquiry, he could certify that I had left it in his charge. He seemed to be satisfied and asked me to come into his study for a moment. The man in the lane was probably satisfied, too. I had stood three paces from the table-lamp all the time, waving the letter about as I talked, and casting a bold shadow on the linen blind!

The first thing that struck me as I entered the doctor's study was that the French windows, which opened on a sheltered lawn, were open. I acted accordingly.

"You see," said Dr. Stuart, "I am enclosing your letter in this big envelope which I am sealing."

"Yes, sir," I replied, standing at some distance from him, so that he had to speak loudly. "And would you mind addressing it to the Lost Property Office."

"Not at all," said he, and did as I suggested. "If not reclaimed within a reasonable time, it will be sent to Scotland Yard."

I edged nearer to the open window.

"If it is not reclaimed," I said loudly, "it goes to Scotland Yard—yes."

"Meanwhile," concluded the doctor, "I am locking it in this private drawer in my bureau."

"It is locked in your bureau. Very good."

## Chapter 3

## DISAPPEARANCE OF CHARLES MALET

KNOWING, and I knew it well, that people of "The Scorpion" were watching, I do not pretend that I felt at my ease as I drove around to the empty house in which I garaged my cab. My inquiry had entered upon another stage, and Charles Malet was about to disappear from the case. I was well aware that if he failed in his vigilance for a single moment he might well disappear from the world!

The path which led to the stables was overgrown with weeds and flanked by ragged bushes; weeds and grass sprouted between the stones paving the little yard, also, although they were withered to a great extent by the petrol recently spilled there. Having run the cab into the yard, I alighted and looked around the deserted grounds, mysterious in the moonlight. Company would have been welcome, but excepting a constable who had stopped and chatted with me on one or two evenings I always had the stables to myself at night.

I determined to run the cab into the stable and lock it up without delay, for it was palpably dangerous in the circumstances to remain longer than necessary in that lonely spot. Hurriedly I began to put out the lamps. I unlocked the stable doors and stood looking all about me again. I was dreading the ordeal of driving the cab those last ten yards into the garage, for whilst I had my back to the wilderness of bushes it would be an easy matter for anyone in hiding there to come up behind me.

Nevertheless, it had to be done. Seating myself at the wheel I drove into the narrow building, stopped the engine and peered cautiously around towards the bright square formed by the open doors. Nothing was to be seen. No shadow moved.

A magazine pistol held in my hand, I crept, step by step, along the wall until I stood just within the opening. There I stopped.

I could hear a sound of quick breathing! There was someone waiting outside!

Dropping quietly down upon the pavement, I slowly protruded my head around the angle of the brick wall at a point not four inches above the ground. I knew that whoever waited would have his eyes fixed upon the doorway at the level of a man's head.

Close to the wall, a pistol in his left hand and an upraised sand-bag in his right, stood "Le Balafré!" His eyes gleamed savagely in the light of the moon and his teeth were bared in that fearful animal snarl. But he had not seen me.

Inch by inch I thrust my pistol forward, the barrel raised sharply. I could not be sure of my aim, of course, nor had I time to judge it carefully.

I fired.

The bullet was meant for his right wrist, but it struck him in the fleshy part of his arm. Uttering a ferocious cry he leapt back, dropped his pistol—and perceiving me as I sprang to my feet, lashed at my head with the sandbag. I raised my left arm to guard my skull and sustained the full force of the blow upon it.

I staggered back against the wall, and my own pistol was knocked from my grasp! My left arm was temporarily useless and the man of the scar was deprived of the use of his right. *Pardieu!* I had the better chance!

He hurled himself upon me.

Instantly he recovered the advantage, for he grasped me by the throat with his left hand—and, *nom d'un nom!* what a grip he had! Flat against the wall he held me, and began, his teeth bared in that fearful grin, to crush the life from me.

To such an attack there was only one counter. I kicked him savagely—and that death-grip relaxed. I writhed, twisted—and was free! As I regained my freedom I struck up at him, and by great good fortune caught him upon the point of the jaw. He staggered. I struck him over the heart, and he fell. I pounced upon him, exulting, for he had sought my life and I knew no pity.

Yet I had not thought so strong a man would choke so easily, and for some moments I stood looking down at him, believing that he sought to trick me. But it was not so. His affair was finished.

I listened. The situation in which I found myself was full of difficulty. An owl screeched somewhere in the trees, but nothing else stirred. The sound of the shot had not attracted attention, apparently. I stooped and examined the garments of the man who lay at my feet.

He carried a travel coupon to Paris bearing that day's date, together with some other papers, but, although I searched all his pockets, I could find nothing of real interest, until in an inside pocket of his coat I felt some hard, irregularly shaped object. I withdrew it, and in the moonlight it lay glittering in my palm . . . a *golden scorpion!*

It had apparently been broken in the struggle. The tail was missing, nor could I find it; but I must confess that I did not prolong the search.

Some chance effect produced by the shadow of the moonlight, and the presence of that recently purchased ticket, gave me the idea upon which without delay I proceeded to act. Satisfying myself that there was no mark upon any of his garments by which the man could be identified, I unlocked from my wrist an identification disk which I habitually wore there, and locked it upon the wrist of the man with the scar!

Clearly, I argued, he had been detailed to dispatch me and then to leave at once for France. I would make it appear that he had succeeded.

Behold me, ten minutes later, driving slowly along a part of the Thames Embankment which I chanced to remember, a gruesome passenger riding behind me in the cab. I was reflecting as I kept a sharp look-out for a spot which I had noted one day during my travels, how easily one could commit murder in London, when a constable ran out and intercepted me!

*Mon Dieu!* how my heart leapt!

"I'll trouble you for your name and number, my lad," he said.

"What for?" I asked, and remembering a rare fragment of idiom: "What's up with you?" I added.

"Your lamp's out!" he cried, "that's what's up with me!"

"Oh," said I, climbing from my seat—"very well. I'm sorry. I didn't know. But here is my license."

I handed him the little booklet and began to light my lamps, cursing myself for a dreadful artist because I had forgotten to do so.

"All right," he replied, and handed it back to me. "But how the devil you've managed to get *all* your lamps out, I can't imagine!"

"This is my first job since dusk," I explained, hurrying around to the tail-light.

"And *he* don't say much!" remarked the constable.

I replaced my matches in my pocket and returned to the front of the cab, making a gesture as of one raising a glass to his lips and jerking my thumb across my shoulder in the direction of my unseen fare.

"Oh, that's it!" said the constable, and moved off.

Never in my whole career have I been so glad to see the back of any man!

I drove on slowly. The point for which I was making was only some three hundred yards further along, but I had noted that the constable had walked off in the opposite direction. Therefore, arriving at my destination—a vacant wharf open to the road—I pulled up and listened.

Only the wash of the tide upon the piles of the wharf was audible, for the night was now far advanced.

I opened the door of the cab and dragged out "Le Balafré." Right and left I peered, truly like a stage villain, and then hauled my unpleasant burden along the irregularly paved path and on to the little wharf. Out in mid-stream a Thames Police patrol was passing, and I stood for a moment until the creak of the oars grew dim.

Then: there was dull splash far below . . . and silence again.

Gaston Max had been consigned to a watery grave!

Returning again to the garage, I wondered very much who he had been, this one, "Le Balafré." Could it be that he was "The Scorpion"? I could not tell, but I had hopes very shortly of finding out.

I had settled up my affairs with my landlady and had removed from my apartments all papers and other effects. In the garage I had placed a good suit of clothes and other necessities, and by telephone I had secured a room at a West-End hotel.

The cab returned to the stable, I locked the door, and by the light of one of the lamps, shaved off my beard and moustache. My uniform and cap I hung up on the hook where I usually left them after working hours, and changed into the suit which I had placed there in readiness. I next destroyed all evidences of identity and left the place in a neat condition. I extinguished the lamp, went out and locked the door behind me, and carrying a travelling-grip and a cane I set off for my new hotel.

Charles Malet had disappeared!

## Chapter 4

## I MEET AN OLD ACQUAINTANCE

ON the corner opposite Dr. Stuart's establishment stood a house which was "to be let or sold." From the estate-agent whose name appeared upon the notice-board I obtained the keys—and had a duplicate made of that which opened the front door. It was a simple matter, and the locksmith returned both keys to me within an hour. I informed the agent that the house would not suit me.

Nevertheless, having bolted the door, in order that prospective purchasers might not surprise me, I "camped out" in an upper room all day, watching from behind the screen of trees all who came to the house of Dr. Stuart. Dusk found me still at my post, armed with a pair of good binoculars. Every patient who presented himself I scrutinized carefully, and finding as the darkness grew that it became increasingly difficult to discern the features of visitors, I descended to the front garden and resumed my watch from the lower branches of a tree which stood some twenty feet from the roadway.

At selected intervals I crept from my post and surveyed the lane upon which the window of the consulting-room opened and also the path leading to the tradesmen's entrance, from which one might look across the lawn and in at the open study windows. It was during one of these tours of inspection and whilst I was actually peering through a gap in the hedge, that I heard the telephone bell. Dr. Stuart was in the study and I heard him speaking.

I gathered that his services were required immediately at some institution in the neighbourhood. I saw him take his hat, stick and bag from the sofa and go out of the room. Then I returned to the front garden of my vacant house.

No one appeared for some time. A policeman walked slowly up the road, and flashed his lantern in at the gate of the house I had commandeered. His footsteps died away. Then, faintly, I heard the hum of a powerful motor. I held my breath. The approaching car turned into the road at a point above me to the right, came nearer . . . and stopped before Dr. Stuart's door.

I focussed my binoculars upon the chauffeur.

It was the brown-skinned man! *Nom d'un nom!* a *woman* was descending from the car. She was enveloped in furs and I could not see her face. She walked up the steps to the door and was admitted.

The chauffeur backed the car into the lane beside the house.

My heart beating rapidly with excitement, I crept out by the further gate of the drive, crossed the road at a point fifty yards above the house and walking very quietly came back to the tradesmen's entrance. Into its enveloping darkness I glided and on until I could peep across the lawn.

The elegant visitor, as I hoped, had been shown, not into the ordinary waiting-room but into the doctor's study. She was seated with her back to the window, talking to a grey-haired old lady—probably the doctor's housekeeper. Impatiently I waited for this old lady to depart, and the moment that she did so, the visitor stood up, turned and . . . it was *Zâra el-Khalâ!*

It was only with difficulty that I restrained the cry of triumph which arose to my lips. On the instant that the study door closed, Zâra el-Khalâ began to try a number of keys which she took from her handbag upon the various drawers of the bureau!

"So!" I said—"they are uncertain of the drawer!"

Suddenly she desisted, looking nervously at the open windows; then, crossing the room, she drew the curtains. I crept out into the road again and by the same roundabout route came back to the empty house. Feeling my way in the darkness of the shrubbery, I found the motor bicycle which I had hidden there and I wheeled it down to the further gate of the drive and waited.

I could see the doctor's door, and I saw him returning along the road. As he appeared, from somewhere—I could not determine from where—came a strange and uncanny wailing sound, a sound that chilled me like an evil omen.

Even as it died away, and before Dr. Stuart had reached his door I knew what it portended—that horrible wail. Some one hidden I knew not where, had warned Zâra el-Khalâ that the doctor returned! But stay! Perhaps that some one was the dark-skinned chauffeur!

How I congratulated myself upon the precautions which I had taken to escape observation! Evidently the watcher had placed himself somewhere where he could command a view of the front door and the road.

Five minutes later the girl came out, the old housekeeper accompanying her to the door, the car emerged from the lane, Zâra el-Khalâ entered it and was driven away. I could see no third person inside the car, and no one was seated beside the chauffeur. I started my "Indian" and leapt in pursuit.

As I had anticipated, the route was Eastward, and I found myself traversing familiar ground. From the southwest to the east of London whirled the big car of mystery— and I was ever close behind it. Sometimes, in the crowded streets, I lost sight of my quarry for a time, but always I caught up again, and at last I found myself whirling along Commercial Road and not fifty yards behind the car.

Just by the canal bridge a drunken sailor lurched out in front of my wheel, and only by twisting perilously right into a turning called, I believe, Salmon Lane, did I avoid running him down.

*Sacre nom!* how I cursed him! The lane was too narrow for me to turn and I was compelled to dismount and to wheel my "Indian" back to the highroad. The yellow car had vanished, of course, but I took it for granted that it had followed the main road. At a dangerous speed, pursued by execrations from the sailor and all his friends, I set off east once more turning to the right down West India Dock Road.

Arriving at the dock, and seeing nothing ahead of me but desolation and ships' masts, I knew that that inebriated pig had spoiled everything! I could have sat down upon the dirty pavement and wept, so mortified was I! For if Zâra el-Khalâ had secured the envelope I had missed my only chance.

However, *pardieu!* I have said that despair is not permitted by the Bureau. I rode home to my hotel, deep in reflection. Whether the girl had the envelope or not, at least she had escaped detection by the doctor; therefore if she had failed she would try again. I could sleep in peace until the morrow.

Of the following day, which I spent as I had spent the preceding one, I have nothing to record. At about the same time in the evening the yellow car again rolled into view, and on this occasion I devoted all my attention to the dark-skinned chauffeur, upon whom I directed my glasses.

As the girl alighted and spoke to him for a moment, he raised the goggles which habitually he wore and I saw his face. A theory which I had formed on the previous night proved correct. The chauffeur was the Hindu, Chunda Lal! As Zâra el-Khalâ walked up the steps he backed the car into the narrow lane and I watched him constantly. Yet, watch as closely as I might, I could not see where he concealed himself in order to command a view of the road.

On this occasion, as I know, Dr. Stuart was at home. Nevertheless the girl stayed for close upon half an hour, and I began to wonder if some new move had been planned. Suddenly the door opened and she came out.

I crept through the bushes to my bicycle and wheeled it on to the drive. I saw the car start; but Madame Fortune being in playful mood, my own engine refused to start at all, and when ten minutes later I at last aroused a spark of life in the torpid machine I knew that pursuit would be futile.

Since this record is intended for the guidance of those who take up the quest of "The Scorpion" either in co-operation with myself or, in the event of my failure, alone, it would be profitless for me to record my disasters. Very well, I had one success. One night I pursued the yellow car from Dr. Stuart's house to the end of Limehouse Causeway without once losing sight of it.

A string of lorries from the docks, drawn by a traction engine, checked me at the corner for a time, although the yellow car passed. But I raced furiously on and by great good luck overtook it near the Dock Station. From thence onward pursuing a strangely tortuous route, I kept it in sight to Canning Town, when it turned into a public garage. I followed—to purchase petrol.

Chunda Lal was talking to the man in charge; he had not yet left his seat. But the car was empty!

At first I was stupid with astonishment. *Par la barbe du prophète!* I was astounded. Then I saw that I had really made a great discovery. The street into which I had injudiciously followed "Le Balafré" lay between Limehouse Causeway and Ropemaker Street, and it was at no great distance from this point that I had lost sight of the yellow car. In that street, which according to my friend the policeman was "nearly all Chinese," Zâra el-Khalâ had descended; in that street was "The Scorpion's" lair!

## Chapter 5

### CONCLUSION OF STATEMENT

I COME now to the conclusion of this statement and to the strange occurrence which led to my proclaiming myself. The fear of imminent assassination which first had prompted me to record what I knew of "The Scorpion" had left me since I had ceased to be Charles Malet. And that the disappearance of "Le Balafré" had been accepted by his unknown chief as evidence of his success in removing *me*, I did not doubt. Therefore I breathed more freely . . . and more freely still when my body was recovered!

Yes, my body was recovered from Hanover Hole; I read of it—a very short paragraph, but it is the short paragraphs that matter—in my morning paper. I knew then that I should very shortly be dead indeed—officially dead. I had counted on this happening before, you understand, for I more than ever suspected that "The Scorpion" knew me to be in England and I feared that he would "lie low" as the English say. However, since a fortunate thing happens better late than never, I saw in this paragraph two things: (1) that the enemy would cease to count upon Gaston Max; (2) that the Scotland Yard Commissioner would be authorised to open Part First of this Statement which had been lodged at his office two days after I landed in England—the portion dealing with my inquiries in Paris and with my tracking of "Le Balafré" to Bow Road Station and observing that he showed a golden scorpion to the chauffeur of the yellow car.

This would happen because Paris would wire that the identification disk found on the dead man was that of Gaston Max. Why would Paris do so? Because my reports had been discontinued since I had ceased to be Charles Malet and Paris would be seeking evidence of my whereabouts. My reports had discontinued because I had learned that I had to do with a criminal organization of whose ramifications I knew nothing. Therefore I took no more chances. I died.

I return to the night when Inspector Dunbar, the grim Dunbar of Scotland Yard, came to Dr. Stuart's house. His appearance there puzzled me. I could not fail to recognize him, for as dusk had fully come I had descended from my top window and was posted among the bushes of the empty house from whence I commanded a perfect view of the doctor's door. The night was unusually chilly—there had been some rain—and when I crept around to the lane bordering the lawn, hoping to see or hear something of what was taking place in the study, I found that the windows were closed and the blinds drawn.

Luck seemed to have turned against me; for that night, at dusk, when I had gone to a local garage where I kept my motor bicycle, I had discovered the back tire to be perfectly flat and had been forced to contain my soul in patience whilst the man repaired a serious puncture. The result was of course that for more than half an hour I had not had Dr. Stuart's house under observation. And a hundred and one things can happen in half an hour.

Had Dr. Stuart sent for the Inspector? If so, I feared that the envelope was missing, or at any rate that he had detected Zâra el-Khalâ in the act of stealing it and had determined to place the matter in the hands of the police. It was a maddening reflection. Again—I shrewdly suspected that I was not the only watcher of Dr. Stuart's house. The frequency with which the big yellow car drew up at the door a few moments after the doctor had gone out could not be due to accident. Yet I had been unable to detect the presence of this other watcher, nor had I any idea of the spot where the car remained hidden—if my theory was a correct one. Nevertheless I did not expect to see it come along whilst the Inspector remained at the house—always supposing that Zâra el-Khalâ had not yet succeeded. I wheeled out the "Indian" and rode to a certain tobacconist's shop at which I had sometimes purchased cigarettes.

He had a telephone in a room at the rear which customers were allowed to use on payment of a fee, and a public call-box would not serve my purpose, since the operator usually announces to a subscriber the fact that a call emanates from such an office. The shop was closed, but I rang the bell at the side door and obtained permission to use the telephone upon pleading urgency. I had assiduously cultivated a natural gift for mimicry, having found it of inestimable service in the practice of my profession. It served me now. I had worked in the past with Inspector Dunbar and his subordinate Sergeant Sowerby, and I determined to trust to my memory of the latter's mode of speech.

I rang up Dr. Stuart and asked for the Inspector, saying that Sergeant Sowerby spoke from Scotland Yard. "Hullo!" he cried, "is that you, Sowerby?"

"Yes," I replied in Sowerby's voice. "I thought I should find you there. About the body of Max . ."

"Eh!" said Dunbar—"what's that? Max?"

I knew immediately that Paris had not yet wired, therefore I told him that Paris *had* done so, and that the disk numbered 49685 was that of Gaston Max. He was inexpressibly shocked, deploring the rashness of Max in working alone.

"Come to Scotland Yard," I said, anxious to get him away from the house.

He said he would be with me in a few minutes, and I was racking my brains for some means of learning what business had taken him to Dr. Stuart when he gave me the desired information spontaneously.

"Sowerby, listen," said he: "It's 'The Scorpion' case right enough! That bit of gold found on the dead man is not a cactus stem; it's a scorpion's tail!"

So! they had found what I had failed to find! It must

have been attached, I concluded, to some inner part of
"Le Balafré's" clothing. There had been no mention of
Zâra el-Khalâ; therefore, as I rode back to my post I permitted myself to assume that she would come again, since
presumably she had thus far failed. I was right.

*Morbleu!* quick as I was the car was there before me!
But I had not overlooked this possibility and I had dis-
mounted at a good distance from the house and had left
the "Indian" in someone's front garden. As I had turned
out of the main road I had seen Dr. Stuart and Inspector
Dunbar approaching a rank upon which two or three cabs
usually stood.

I watched *la Belle* Zâra enter the house, a beautiful
woman most elegantly attired, and then, even before
Chunda Lal had backed the car into the lane I was off . . .
to the spot at which I had abandoned my motor bicycle.
In little more than half an hour I had traversed London,
and was standing in the shadow of that high, blank wall to
which I have referred as facing a row of wooden houses
in a certain street adjoining Limehouse Causeway.

You perceive my plan? I was practically sure of the
street; all I had to learn was which house sheltered "The
Scorpion"!

I had already suspected that this night was to be for
me an unlucky night. *Nom d'un p'tit bonhomme!* it was
so. Until an hour before dawn I crouched under that wall
and saw no living thing except a very old Chinaman who
came out of one of the houses and walked slowly away.
The other houses appeared to be empty. No vehicle of any
kind passed that way all night.

Turning over in my mind the details of this most per-
plexing case, it became evident to me that the advantages
of working alone were now outweighed by the disadvan-
tages. The affair had reached a stage at which ordinary
police methods should be put into operation. I had col-
lected some of the threads; the next thing was for Scotland Yard to weave these together whilst I sought for
more.

I determined to remain dead. It would afford me greater
freedom of action. The disappearance of "Le Balafré"
which must by this time have been noted by his associates,
might possibly lead to a suspicion that the dead man was
*not* Gaston Max; but providing no member of "The Scorpion" group obtained access to the body I failed to see

how this suspicion could be confirmed. I reviewed my position.

The sealed letter had achieved its purpose in part. Although I had failed to locate the house from which these people operated, I could draw a circle on the map within which I knew it to be; and I had learned that Zâra el-Khalâ and the Hindu were in London. What it all meant—to what end "The Scorpion" was working I did not know. But having learned so much, be sure I did not despair of learning more.

It was now imperative that I should get in touch with Dunbar and that I should find out exactly what had occurred at Dr. Stuart's house. Accordingly I determined to call upon the Inspector at Scotland Yard. I presented myself towards evening of the day following my vigil in Limehouse, sending up the card of a Bureau confrére, for I did not intend to let it be generally known that I was alive.

Presently I was shown up to that bare and shining room which I remembered having visited in the past. I stood just within the doorway, smiling. Inspector Dunbar rose, as the constable went out, and stood looking across at me.

I had counted on striking him dumb with astonishment. He was Scottishly unmoved.

"Well," he said, coming forward with outstretched hand, "I'm glad to see you. I knew you would have to come to us sooner or later!"

I felt that my eyes sparkled. There was no resentment within my heart. I rejoiced.

"Look," he continued, taking a slip of paper from his note-book. "This is a copy of a note I left with Dr. Stuart some time ago. Read it."

I did so, and this is what I read:

"*A*: the name of the man who cut out the lid of the cardboard box and sealed it in an envelope—Gaston Max!

"*B*: the name of the missing cabman—Gaston Max!

"*C*: The name of the man who rang me up at Dr. Stuart's and told me that Gaston Max was dead—Gaston Max!"

I returned the slip to Inspector Dunbar. I bowed.

"It is a pleasure and a privilege to work with you, Inspector," I said. . . .

This statement is nearly concluded. The whole of the

evening I spent in the room of the Assistant Commissioner discussing the matters herein set forth and comparing notes with Inspector Dunbar. One important thing I learned: that I had abandoned my nightly watches too early. For one morning just before dawn someone who was *not* Zâra had paid a visit to the house of Dr. Stuart! I determined to call upon the doctor.

As it chanced I was delayed and did not actually arrive until so late an hour that I had almost decided not to present myself . . . when a big yellow car flashed past the taxicab in which I was driving!

*Nom d'un nom!* I could not mistake it! This was within a few hundred yards of the house of Dr. Stuart, you understand, and I instantly dismissed my cabman and proceeded to advance cautiously on foot. I could not longer hear the engine of the car which had passed ahead of me, but then I knew that it could run almost noiselessly. As I crept along in that friendly shadow cast by a high hedge which had served me so well before, I saw the yellow car. It was standing on the opposite side of the road.

I reached the tradesmen's entrance.

From my left, in the direction of the back lawn of the house, came a sudden singular crackling noise and I discerned a flash of blue flame resembling faint "summer lightning." A series of muffled explosions followed . . . and in the darkness I tripped over something which lay along the ground at my feet—a length of cable it seemed to be.

Stumbling, I uttered a slight exclamation . . . and instantly received a blow on the head that knocked me flat upon the ground! Everything was swimming around me, but I realized that someone—Chunda Lal probably—had been hiding in the very passage which I had entered! I heard again that uncanny wailing, close beside me.

Vaguely I discerned an incredible figure—like that of a tall cowled monk, towering over me. I struggled to retain consciousness—there was a rush of feet . . . the throb of a motor. It stimulated me—that sound! I must get to the telephone and cause the yellow car to be intercepted.

I staggered to my feet and groped my way along the hedge to where I had observed a tree by means of which one might climb over. I was dizzy as a drunken man; but I half climbed and half fell on to the lawn. The windows were open. I rushed into the study of Dr. Stuart.

Pah! it was full of fumes. I looked around me. *Mon Dieu!* I staggered. For I knew that in this fume-laden room a thing more horrible and more strange than any within my experience had taken place that night.

Part III

## AT THE HOUSE OF AH-FANG-FU

## Chapter 1

### THE BRAIN THIEVES

THE Assistant Commissioner lighted a cigarette. "It would appear, then," he said, "that whilst some minor difficulties have been smoothed away, we remain face to face with the major problem: who is 'The Scorpion' and to what end are his activities directed?"

Gaston Max shrugged his shoulders and smiled at Dr. Stuart.

"Let us see," he suggested, "what we really know about this 'Scorpion.' Let us make a brief survey of our position in the matter. Let us take first what we have learned of him—if it is a 'him' with whom we have to deal—from the strange experiences of Dr. Stuart. Without attaching too much importance to that episode five years ago on the Wû-Men Bridge in China, we should remember, I think, that for any man to be known and, it would appear, to be

THE BRAIN THIEVES ● 103

*feared*, as 'The Scorpion,' is remarkable. Very well. Perhaps the one we seek is the man of the Wû-Men Bridge; perhaps he is not. We will talk about this one again presently.

"We come to the arrival on the scene of Zâra el-Khalâ, also called Mlle. Dorian. She comes because of what *I* have told to the scarred man from Paris, she comes to obtain that dangerous information which is to be sent to Scotland Yard, she comes, in a word, from 'The Scorpion.' We have two links binding the poor one 'Le Balafré' to 'The Scorpion': (1) his intimacy with Miguel and those others with whom 'Scorpion' communicated by telephone; (2) his possession of the golden ornament which lies there upon the table and which I took from his pocket. What can we gather from the statement made to Dr. Stuart by Mlle. Dorian? Let us study this point for a moment.

"In the first place we can only accept her words with a certain scepticism. Her story may be nothing but a fabrication. However, it is interesting because she claims to be the unwilling servant of a dreaded master. She lays stress upon the fact that she is an Oriental and does not enjoy the same freedom as a European woman. This is possible, up to a point. On the other hand she seems to enjoy not only freedom but every luxury. Therefore it may equally well be a lie. Some slight colour is lent to her story by the extraordinary mode of life which she followed in Paris. In the midst of Bohemianism she remained secluded as an odalisque in some *harêm* garden of Stambûl, whether by her own will or by will of another we do not know. One little point her existence seems to strengthen: that we are dealing with Easterns; for Zâra el-Khalâ is partly of Eastern blood and her follower Chunda Lal is a Hindu. *Eh bien.*

"Consider the cowled man whose shadow Dr. Stuart has seen on two occasions: once behind the curtain of his window and once cast by the moonlight across the lawn of his house. The man himself he has never seen. Now this hooded man cannot have been 'Le Balafré,' for 'Le Balafré' was already dead at the time of his first appearance. He may be 'The Scorpion'!"

Max paused impressively, looking around at those in the Commissioner's room.

"For a moment I return to the man of the Wû-Men Bridge. The man of the Wû-Men Bridge was veiled and this one is hooded! The man of the Wû-Men Bridge was known as 'The Scorpion,' and this one also is associated with a scorpion. We will return yet again to this point in a moment.

"Is there something else which we may learn from the experiences of Dr. Stuart? Yes! We learn that 'The Scorpion' suddenly decides that Dr. Stuart is dangerous, either because of his special knowledge (which would be interesting) or because the 'Scorpion' believes that he has become acquainted with the contents of the sealed envelope—which is not so interesting although equally dangerous for Dr. Stuart. 'The Scorpion' acts. He pays a second visit, again accompanied by Chunda Lal, who seems to be a kind of watch-dog who not only guards the person of Zâra el-Khalâ but who also howls when danger threatens the cowled man!

"And what is the weapon which the cowled man (who may be 'The Scorpion') uses to remove Dr. Stuart? It is a frightful weapon, my friends; it is a novel and deadly weapon. It is a weapon of which science knows nothing— a blue ray of the colour produced by a Mercury Vapour Lamp, according to Dr. Stuart who has seen it, and producing an odour like that of a blast furnace according to myself, who smelled it! Or this odour might have been caused by the fusing of the telephone; for the blue ray destroys such fragile things as telephones as easily as it destroys wood and paper! There is even a large round hole burned through the clay at the back of the study grate and through the brick wall behind it! Very well. 'The Scorpion' is a scientist and he is also the greatest menace to the world which the world has ever been called upon to deal with. You agree with me?"

Inspector Dunbar heaved a great sigh, Stuart silently accepted a cigarette from the Assistant Commissioner's box and the Assistant Commissioner spoke, slowly.

"I entirely agree with you, M. Max. Respecting this ray, as well as some one or two other *minutiae*, I have made a short note which we will discuss when you have completed your admirably lucid survey of the case."

Gaston Max bowed, and resumed.

"These are the things, then, which we learn from the terrible experiences of Dr. Stuart. Placing these experiences side by side with my own, in Paris and in London— which we have already discussed in detail—we find that we have to deal with an organisation—the object of which is unknown—comprising among its members both Europeans ('Le Balafré' was a Frenchman, I believe), crossbreeds such as Miguel and Zâra el-Khalâ" (Stuart winced), "one Algerian and a Hindu. It is then an organisation having ramifications throughout Europe, the East and, *mon Dieu!* where not? To continue. This little image"—he took up from the Commissioner's table the golden scorpion, and the broken fragment of tail—"is now definitely recognized by Dr. Stuart—who is familiar with the work of Oriental goldsmiths—to be of *Chinese* craftsmanship!"

"It may possibly be Tibetan," interrupted Stuart; "but it comes to the same thing."

"Very well," continued Max. "It is Chinese. We hope, very shortly, to identify a house situated somewhere within this red ink circle"—he placed his finger on a map of London which lay open on the table—"and which I know to be used as a meeting-place by members of this mysterious group. That circle, my friends, surrounds what is now known as 'Chinatown'! For the third time I return to the man of the Wû-Men Bridge; for the man of the Wû-Men Bridge was, apparently, a *Chinaman!* Do I make myself clear?"

"Remarkably so," declared the Assistant Commissioner, taking a fresh cigarette. "Pray continue, M. Max."

"I will do so. One of my most important investigations, in which I had the honour and the pleasure to be associated with Inspector Dunbar, led to the discovery of a dangerous group controlled by a certain 'Mr. King'——"

"Ah!" cried Dunbar, his tawny eyes sparkling with excitement, "I was waiting for that!"

"I knew you would be waiting for it, Inspector. Your powers of deductive reasoning more and more are earning my respect. You recall that singular case? The elaborate network extending from London to Buenos Ayres, from Peking to Petrograd? Ah! a wonderful system. It was an opium syndicate, you understand,"—turning again to the Assistant Commissioner.

"I recall the case," replied the Commissioner, "although I did not hold my present appointment at the time. I believe there were unsatisfactory features?"

"There were," agreed Max. "We never solved the mystery of the identity of 'Mr. King,' and although we succeeded in destroying the enterprise I have since thought that we acted with undue precipitation."

"Yes," said Dunbar rapidly; "but there was that poor girl to be rescued, you will remember? We couldn't waste time."

"I agree entirely, Inspector. Our hands were forced. Yet, I repeat, I have since thought that we acted with undue precipitation. I will tell you why. Do you recall the loss—not explained to this day—of the plans of the Haley torpedo?"

"Perfectly," replied the Commissioner; and Dunbar also nodded affirmatively.

"Very well. A similar national loss was sustained about the same time by my own Government. I am not at liberty to divulge its exact nature, as in the latter case the loss never became known to the public. But the only member of the French Chamber who had seen this document to which I refer was a certain 'M. Blank,' shall we say? I believe also that I am correct in stating that the late Sir Brian Malpas was a member of the British Cabinet at the time that the Haley plans were lost?"

"That is correct," said the Assistant Commissioner, "but surely the honour of the late Sir Brian was above suspicion?"

"Quite," agreed Max; "so also was that of 'M. Blank.' But my point is this: Both 'M. Blank' and the late Sir Brian were clients of the opium syndicate!"

Dunbar nodded again eagerly.

"Hard work I had to hush it up," he said. "It would have finished his political career."

The Assistant Commissioner looked politely puzzled.

"It was generally supposed that Sir Brian Malpas was addicted to drugs," he remarked; "and I am not surprised to learn that he patronised this syndicate to which you refer. But——" he paused, smiling satanically. "Ah!" he added—"I see! I see!"

"You perceive the drift of my argument?" cried Max. "You grasp what I mean when I say that we were too hasty? This syndicate existed for a more terrible purpose than the promulgating of a Chinese vice; it had in its clutches men entrusted with national secrets, men of genius but slaves of a horrible drug. Under the influence of that drug, my friends, how many of those secrets may they not have divulged?"

His words were received in hushed silence.

"What became of those stolen plans?" he continued, speaking now in a very low voice. "In the stress of recent

years has the Haley torpedo made its appearance so that
we might learn to which Government the plans had been
taken? No! the same mystery surrounds the fate of the
information filched from the drugged brain of 'M. Blank.'
In a word"—he raised a finger dramatically—"someone is
hoarding up those instruments of destruction! Who is it
that collects such things and for what purpose does he
collect them?"

Following another tense moment of silence:

"Let us have your own theory, M. Max," said the Assistant Commissioner.

Gaston Max shrugged his shoulders.

"It is not worthy of the name of a theory," he replied,
"the surmise which I have made. But recently I found
myself considering the fact that 'The Scorpion' might just
conceivably be a Chinaman. Now, 'Mr. King,' we believe,
was a Chinaman, and 'Mr. King,' as I am now convinced,
operated not for a personal but for a deeper, political
purpose. He stole the brains of genius and *accumulated*
that which he had stolen. 'The Scorpion' *destroys* genius.
Is it not possible that these contrary operations may be
part of a common plan?"

## Chapter 2

## THE RED CIRCLE

"You are not by any chance," suggested Stuart, smiling
slightly, "hinting at that defunct bogey, the 'Yellow
Peril'?"

"Ah!" cried Max, "but certainly I am not! Do not mis-
understand me. This group with which we are dealing is
shown to be not of a national but of an international character. The same applied to the organisation of 'Mr. King.'
But a Chinaman directed the one, and I begin to suspect
that a Chinaman directs the other. No, I speak of no
ridiculous 'Yellow Peril,' my friends. John Chinaman, as
I have known him, is the whitest man breathing; but can
you not imagine"—he dropped his voice again in that im-
pressive way which was yet so truly Gallic—"can you not

imagine a kind of Oriental society which like a great, a formidable serpent, lies hidden somewhere below that deceptive jungle of the East? These are troubled times. It is a wise state to-day that knows its own leaders. Can you not imagine a dreadful sudden menace, not of men and guns but of *brains* and *capital?*"

"You mean," said Dunbar slowly, "that 'The Scorpion' may be getting people out of the way who might interfere with this rising or invasion or whatever it is?"

"Just as 'Mr. King' accumulated material for it," interjected the Assistant Commissioner. "It is a bold conception, M. Max, and it raises the case out of the ordinary category and invests it with enormous international importance."

All were silent for a time, Stuart, Dunbar and the Commissioner watching the famous Frenchman as he sat there, arrayed in the latest fashion of Savile Row, yet Gallic to his finger-tips and in every gesture. It was almost impossible at times to credit the fact that a Parisian was speaking, for the English of Gaston Max was flawless except that he spoke with a faint American accent: Then, suddenly, a gesture, an expletive, would betray the Frenchman.

But such betrayals never escaped him when, in one of his inimitable disguises, he penetrated to the purlieus of Whitechapel, to the dens of Limehouse. Then he was the perfect Hooligan, as, mingling with the dangerous thieves of Paris, he was the perfect Apache. It was an innate gift of mimicry which had made him the greatest investigator of his day. He could have studied Chinese social life for six months and thereupon have become a mandarin whom his own servants would never have suspected to be a "foreign barbarian." It was pure genius, as opposed to the brilliant efficiency of Dunbar.

But in the heart of the latter, as he studied Gaston Max and realized the gulf that separated them, there was nothing but generous admiration of a master; yet Dunbar was no novice, for by a process of fine deductive reasoning he had come to the conclusion, as has appeared, that Gaston Max had been masquerading as a cabman and that the sealed letter left with Dr. Stuart had been left as a lure. By one of those tricks of fate which sometimes perfect the plans of men but more often destroy them, the body of "Le Balafré" had been so disfigured during the time that it had been buffeted about in the Thames that it was utterly unrecognizable and indescribable. But even the disk had not deceived Dunbar. He had seen in it another ruse of his brilliant confrére, and his orders to the keeper of the mortuary to admit no one without a written permit had been dictated by the conviction that Max wished the body to be mistaken for his own. In Inspector Dunbar, Gaston Max immediately had recognized an able colleague as Mrs. M'Gregor had recognized "a grand figure of a man."

The Assistant Commissioner broke the silence.

"There have been other cases," he said reflectively, "now that one considers the matter, which seemed to point to the existence of such a group or society as you indicate, M. Max, notably one with which, if I remember rightly, Inspector"—turning his dark eyes towards Dunbar—"Inspector Weymouth, late of this Branch, was associated?"

"Quite right, sir. It was his big case, and it got him a fine billet as Superintendent in Cairo if you remember?"

"Yes," mused the Assistant Commissioner—"he transferred to Egypt—a very good appointment, as you say. That, again, was before my term of office, but there were a number of very ghastly crimes connected with the case and it was more or less definitely established, I believe, that some extensive secret society did actually exist throughout the East, governed, I fancy, by a Chinaman."

"And from China," added Dunbar.

"Yes, yes, from China as you say, Inspector." He turned to Gaston Max. "Can it really be, M. Max, that we have to deal with an upcrop of some deeply-seated evil which resides in the Far East? Are all these cases, not the work of individual criminals but manisfestations of a more sinister, a darker force?"

Gaston Max met his glance and Max's mouth grew very grim.

"I honestly believe so," he answered. "I have believed it for nearly two years—ever since the Grand Duke died. And now, you said, I remember, that you had made a note the nature of which you would communicate."

"Yes," replied the Assistant Commissioner—"a small point, but one which may be worthy of attention. This ray, Dr. Stuart, which played such havoc in your study— do you know of anything approaching to it in more recent scientific devices?"

"Well," said Stuart, "it may be no more than a development of one of several systems, notably of that of the late Henrik Ericksen upon which he was at work at the time of his death."

"Exactly." The Assistant Commissioner smiled in his most Mephistophelean manner. "Of the late Henrik Ericksen, as you say."

He said no more for a moment and sat smoking and looking from face to face. Then:

"That is the subject of my note, gentlemen," he added. "The other *minutiæ* are of no immediate importance."

"*Nom d'un p'tit bonhomme!*" whispered Gaston Max. "I see! You think that Ericksen had completed his experiments before he died, but that he never lived to give them to the world?"

The Assistant Commissioner waved one hand in the air so that the discoloration of the first and second fingers was very noticeable.

"It is for you to ascertain these points, M. Max," he said—"I only suggest. But I begin to share your belief that a series of daring and unusual assassinations has been taking place under the eyes of the police authorities of Europe. It can only be poison—an unknown poison, perhaps. We shall be empowered to exhume the body of the late Sir Frank Narcombe in a few days' time, I hope. His case puzzles me hopelessly. What obstacle did a surgeon offer to this hypothetical Eastern movement? On the other hand, what can have been filched from him before his death? The death of an inventor, a statesman, a soldier, can be variously explained by your 'Yellow' hypothesis, M. Max, but what of the death of a surgeon?"

Gaston Max shrugged, and his mobile mouth softened in a quaint smile.

"We have learned a little," he said, "and guessed a lot. Let us hope to guess more—and learn everything!"

"May I suggest," added Dunbar, "that we hear Sowerby's report, sir?"

"Certainly," agreed the Assistant Commissioner—"call Sergeant Sowerby."

A moment later Sergeant Sowerby entered, his face very red and his hair bristling more persistently than usual.

"Anything to report, Sowerby?" asked Dunbar.

"Yes, Inspector," replied Sowerby, in his Police Court manner;—he faced the Assistant Commissioner, "with your permission, sir."

He took out a note-book which appeared to be the twin

of Dunbar's and consulted it, assuming an expression of profound reflection.

"In the first place, sir," he began, never raising his eyes from the page, "I have traced the cab sold on the hire-purchase system to a certain Charles *Mallet . . .*"

"Ha, ha!" laughed Max breezily—"he calls me a hammer! It is not Mallet, Sergeant Sowerby—you have got too many *l*'s in that name; it is Malet and is called like one from the Malay States!"

"Oh," commented Sowerby, glancing up—"indeed. Very good, sir. The owner claims the balance of purchase money!"

Every one laughed at that, even the satanic Assistant Commissioner.

"Pay your debts, M. Max," he said. "You will bring the Service de Sûréte into bad repute! Carry on, Sergeant."

"This cab," continued Sowerby, when Dunbar interrupted him.

"Cut out the part about the cab, Sowerby," he said. "We've found that out from M. Max. Have you anything to report about the yellow car?"

"Yes," replied Sowerby, unperturbed, and turning over to the next page. "It was hired from Messrs. Wickers' garage, at Canning Town, by the week. The lady who hired it was a Miss Dorian, a French lady. She gave no reference, except that of the Savoy Hotel, where she was stopping. She paid a big deposit and had her own chauffeur, a colored man of some kind."

"Is it still in use by her?" snapped Dunbar eagerly.

"No, Inspector. She claimed her deposit this morning and said she was leaving London."

"The cheque?" cried Dunbar.

"Was cashed half an hour later."

"At what bank?"

"London County & Birmingham, Canning Town. Her own account at a Strand bank was closed yesterday. The details all concern milliners, jewelers, hotels and so forth. There's nothing there. I've been to the Savoy, of course."

"Yes!"

"A lady named Dorian has had rooms there for six weeks, has dined there on several occasions, but was more often away than in the hotel."

"Visitors?"

"Never had any."

"She used to dine alone, then?"

"Always."

"In the public dining-room?"

"No. In her own room."

"*Morbleu!*" muttered Max. "It is she beyond doubt. I recognize her sociable habits!"

"Has she left now?" asked Dunbar.

"She left a week ago."

Sowerby closed his note-book and returned it to his pocket.

"Is that all you have to report, Sergeant?" asked the Assistant Commissioner.

"That's all, sir."

"Very good."

Sergeant Sowerby retired.

"Now, sir," said Dunbar, "I've got Inspector Kelly here. He looks after the Chinese quarter. Shall I call him?"

"Yes, Inspector."

Presently there entered a burly Irishman, bluff and good-humoured, a very typical example of the intelligent superior police officer, looking keenly around him.

"Ah, Inspector," the Assistant Commissioner greeted him—"we want your assistance in a little matter concerning the Chinese residential quarter. You know this district?"

"Certainly, sir. I know it very well."

"On this map"—the Assistant Commissioner laid a discoloured forefinger upon the map of London—"you will perceive that we have drawn a circle."

Inspector Kelly bent over the table.

"Yes, sir."

"Within that circle, which is no larger in circumference than a shilling as you observe, lies a house used by a certain group of people. It has been suggested to me that these people may be Chinese or associates of Chinese."

"Well, sir," said Inspector Kelly, smiling broadly, "considering the patch inside the circle I think it more than likely! Seventy-five or it may be eighty per cent of the rooms and cellars and attics in those three streets are occupied by Chinese."

"For your guidance, Inspector, we believe these people to be a dangerous gang of international criminals. Do you know of any particular house, or houses, likely to be used as a meeting-place by such a gang?"

Inspector Kelly scratched his close-cropped head.

"A woman was murdered just there, sir," he said, taking up a pen from the table and touching a point near the corner of Three Colt Street, "about a twelve-month ago. We traced the man—a Chinese sailor—to a house lying just about here." Again he touched the map. "It's a sort of little junk-shop with a ramshackle house attached, all cellars and rabbit-hutches, as you might say, overhanging a disused cutting which is filled at high tide. Opium is to be had there and card-playing goes on, and I won't swear that you couldn't get liquor. But it's well conducted as such dives go."

"Why is it not closed?" inquired the Assistant Commissioner, seizing an opportunity to air his departmental ignorance.

"Well, sir," replied Inspector Kelly, his eyes twinkling —"if we shut up all these places we should never know where to look for some of our regular customers! As I mentioned, we found the wanted Chinaman, three parts drunk, in one of the rooms."

"It's a sort of lodging house, then?"

"Exactly. There's a moderately big room just behind the shop, principally used by opium-smokers, and a whole nest of smaller rooms above and below. Mind you, sir, I don't say this is the place you're looking for, but it's the most likely inside your circle."

"Who is the proprietor?"

"A retired Chinese sailor called Ah-Fang-Fu, but better known as 'Pidgin.' His establishment is called locally 'The Pidgin House.' "

"Ah." The Commissioner lighted a cigarette. "And you know of no other house which might be selected for such a purpose as I have mentioned?"

"I can't say I do, sir. I know pretty well all the business affairs of that neighbourhood, and none of the houses inside your circle have changed hands during the past twelve months. Between ourselves, sir, nearly all the property in the district belongs to Ah-Fang-Fu, and anything that goes on in Chinatown *he* knows about!"

"Ah, I see. Then in any event he is the man we want to watch?"

"Well, sir, you ought to keep an eye on his visitors, I should say."

"I am obliged to you, Inspector," said the courteous Assistant Commissioner, "for your very exact information. If necessary I shall communicate with you again. Good-day."

"Good-day, sir," replied the Inspector. "Good-day, gentlemen."

He went out.

Gaston Max, who had diplomatically remained in the background throughout this interview, now spoke.

"*Pardieu!* but I have been thinking," he said. "Although 'The Scorpion,' as I hope, believes that that troublesome Charles Malet is dead, he may also wonder if Scotland Yard has secured from Dr. Stuart's fire any fragments of the information sealed in the envelope! What does it mean, this releasing of the yellow car, closing of the bank account and departure from the Savoy?"

"It means flight!" cried Dunbar, jumping violently to his feet. "By gad, sir!" he turned to the Assistant Commissioner—"the birds may have flown already!"

The Assistant Commissioner leaned back in his chair.

"I have sufficient confidence in M. Max," he said, "to believe that, having taken the responsibility of permitting this dangerous group to learn that they were under surveillance, he has good reason to suppose that they have not slipped through our fingers."

Gaston Max bowed.

"It is true," he replied, and from his pocket he took a slip of flimsy paper. "This code message reached me as I was about to leave my hotel. The quadroon, Miguel, left Paris last night and arrived in London this morning ——"

"He was followed?" cried Dunbar.

"But certainly. He was followed to Limehouse, and he was definitely seen to enter the establishment described to us by Inspector Kelly!"

"Gad!" said Dunbar—"then *someone* is still there?"

"Someone, as you say, is still there," replied Max. "But everything points to the imminent departure of this someone. Will you see to it, Inspector, that not a rat—*pardieu!* not a little mouse—is allowed to slip out of our red circle to-day. For to-night we shall pay a friendly visit to the house of Ah-Fang-Fu, and I should wish all the company to be present."

## Chapter 3

### MISKA'S STORY

STUART returned to his house in a troubled frame of mind. He had refrained so long from betraying the circumstances of his last meeting with Mlle. Dorian to the police authorities that this meeting now constituted a sort of guilty secret, a link binding him to the beautiful accomplice of "The Scorpion"—to the dark-eyed servant of the uncanny cowled thing which had sought his life by strange means. He hugged this secret to his breast, and the pain of it afforded him a kind of savage joy.

In his study he found a Post Office workman engaged in fitting a new telephone. As Stuart entered the man turned.

"Good-afternoon, sir," he said, taking up the destroyed instrument from the litter of flux, pincers and screw drivers lying upon the table. "If it's not a rude question, how on earth did *this* happen?"

Stuart laughed uneasily.

"It got mixed up with an experiment which I was conducting," he replied evasively.

The man inspected the headless trunk of the instrument.

"It seems to be fused, as though the top of it had been in a blast furnace," he continued. "Experiments of that sort are a bit dangerous outside a proper laboratory, I should think."

"They are," agreed Stuart. "But I have no facilities here, you see, and I was—er—compelled to attempt the experiment. I don't intend to repeat it."

"That's lucky," murmured the man, dropping the instrument into a carpet-bag. "If you do, it will cost you a tidy penny for telephones!"

Walking out towards the dispensary, Stuart met Mrs. M'Gregor.

"A Post Office messenger brought this letter for you, Mr. Keppel, just the now," she said, handing Stuart a sealed envelope.

He took the envelope from her hand, and turned quickly

away. He felt that he had changed colour. For it was addressed in the handwriting of . . . Mlle. Dorian!

"Thank you, Mrs. M'Gregor," he said, and turned into the dining-room.

Mrs. M'Gregor proceeded about her household duties, and as her footsteps receded, Stuart feverishly tore open the envelope. That elusive scent of jasmine crept to his nostrils. In the envelope was a sheet of thick note-paper (having the top cut off evidently in order to remove a printed address), upon which the following singular message was written:

"Before I go away there is something I want to say to you. You do not trust me. It is not wonderful that you do not. But I swear that I only want to save you from a *great* danger. If you will promise not to tell the police anything of it, I will meet you at six o'clock by the Book Stall at Victoria Station—on the Brighton side. If you agree you will wear something white in your button-hole. If not you cannot find me there. Nobody ever sees me again."

There was no signature, but no signature was necessary.

Stuart laid the letter on the table, and began to pace up and down the room. His heart was beating ridiculously. His self-contempt was profound. But he could not mistake his sentiments.

His duty was plain enough. But he had failed in it once, and even as he strode up and down the room, already he knew that he must fail again. He knew that, rightly or wrongly, he was incapable of placing this note in the hands of the police . . . and he knew that he should be at Victoria Station at six o'clock.

He would never have believed himself capable of becoming accessory to a series of crimes—for this was what his conduct amounted to; he had thought that sentiment no longer held any meaning for him. Yet the only excuse which he could find wherewith to solace himself was that this girl had endeavoured to save him from assassination. Weighed against the undoubted fact that she was a member of a dangerous criminal group what was it worth? If the supposition of Gaston Max was correct, "The Scorpion" had at least six successful murders to his credit, in addition to the attempt upon his (Stuart's) life and that of "Le Balafré" upon the life of Gaston Max. It was an accomplice of this nameless horror called the "The Scorpion" with whom at six o'clock he had a tryst, whom he was protecting from justice, by the suppression of whose messages to himself he was adding difficulties to the already difficult task of the authorities!

Up and down he paced, restlessly, every now and again glancing at a clock upon the mantelpiece. His behavior he told himself was contemptible.

Yet, at a quarter to six, he went out—and seeing a little cluster of daisies growing amongst the grass bordering the path, he plucked one and set it in his button-hole!

A few minutes before the hour he entered the station and glanced sharply around at the many groups scattered about in the neighbourhood of the bookstall. There was no sign of Mlle. Dorian. He walked around the booking office without seeing her and glanced into the waiting-room. Then, looking up at the station clock, he saw that the hour had come, and as he stood there staring upward he felt a timid touch upon his shoulder.

He turned—and she was standing by his side!

She was Parisian from head to foot, simply but perfectly gowned. A veil hung from her hat and half concealed her face, but could not hide her wonderful eyes nor disguise the delightful curves of her red lips. Stuart automatically raised his hat, and even as he did so wondered what she should have said and done had she suddenly found Gaston Max standing at his elbow! He laughed shortly.

"You are angry with me," said Mlle. Dorian, and Stuart thought that her quaint accent was adorable. "Or are you angry with yourself for seeing me?"

"I am angry with myself," he replied, "for being so weak."

"Is it so weak," she said, rather tremulously, "not to judge a woman by what she seems to be and not to condemn her before you hear what she has to say? If that is weak, I am glad; I think it is how a man should be."

Her voice and her eyes completed the spell, and Stuart resigned himself without another struggle to this insane infatuation.

"We cannot very well talk here," he said. "Suppose we go into the hotel and have late tea, Mlle. Dorian."

"Yes. Very well. But please do not call me that. It is not my name."

Stuart was on the point of saying, "Zâra el-Khalâ then," but checked himself in the nick of time. He might hold communication with the enemy, but at least he would give away no information.

"I am called Miska," she added. "Will you please call me Miska?"

"Of course, if you wish," said Stuart, looking down at her as she walked by his side and wondering what he would do when he had to stand up in Court, look at Miska in the felon's dock and speak words which would help to condemn her—perhaps to death, at least to penal servitude! He shuddered.

"Have I said something that displeases you?" she asked, resting a little white-gloved hand on his arm. "I am sorry."

"No, no," he assured her. "But I was thinking—I cannot help thinking . . ."

"How wicked I am?" she whispered.

"How lovely you are!" he said hotly, "and how maddening it is to remember that you are an accomplice of criminals!"

"Oh," she said, and removed her hand, but not before he had felt how it trembled. They were about to enter the tea-room when she added: "Please don't say that until I have told you why I do what I do."

Obeying a sudden impulse, he took her hand and drew it close under his arm.

"No," he said; "I won't. I was a brute, Miska. Miska means 'musk,' surely?"

"Yes." She glanced up at him timidly. "Do you think it a pretty name?"

"Very," he said, laughing.

Underlying the Western veneer was the fascinating naïveté of the Eastern woman, and Miska had all the suave grace, too, which belongs to the women of the Orient, so that many admiring glances followed her charming figure as she crossed the room to a vacant table.

"Now," said Stuart, when he had given an order to the waiter, "what do you want to tell me? Whatever it may be, I am all anxiety to hear it. I promise that I will only act upon anything you may tell me in the event of my life, or that of another, being palpably endangered by my silence."

"Very well. I want to tell you," replied Miska, "why I stay with Fo-Hi."

"Who is Fo-Hi?"

"I do not know!"

"What!" said Stuart. "I am afraid I don't understand you."

"If I speak in French will you be able to follow what I say?"

"Certainly. Are you more at ease with French?"

"Yes," replied Miska, beginning to speak in the latter language. "My mother was French, you see, and although I can speak in English fairly well I cannot yet *think* in English. Do you understand?"

"Perfectly. So perhaps you will now explain to whom you refer when you speak of Fo-Hi."

Miska glanced apprehensively around her, bending further forward over the table.

"Let me tell you from the beginning," she said in a low voice, "and then you will understand. It must not take me long. You see me as I am to-day because of a dreadful misfortune that befell me when I was fifteen years old.

"My father was *Wali* of Aleppo, and my mother, his third wife, was a Frenchwoman, a member of a theatrical company which had come to Cairo, where he had first seen her. She must have loved him, for she gave up the world, embraced Islam and entered his *harêm* in the great house on the outskirts of Aleppo. Perhaps it was because he, too, was half French, that they were mutually attracted. My father's mother was a Frenchwoman also, you understand.

"Until I was fifteen years of age, I never left the *harêm*, but my mother taught me French and also a little English; and she prevailed upon my father not to give me in marriage so early as is usual in the East. She taught me to understand the ways of European women, and we used to have Paris journals and many books come to us regularly. Then an awful pestilence visited Aleppo. People were dying in the mosques and in the streets, and my father decided to send my mother and myself and some others of the *harêm* to his brother's house in Damaskus.

"Perhaps you will think that such things do not happen in these days, and particularly to members of the household of a chief magistrate, but I can only tell you what is true. On the second night of our journey a band of Arabs swept down upon the caravan, overpowered the guards, killing them all, and carried off everything of value which we had. Me, also, they carried off—me and one other, a little Syrian girl, my cousin. Oh!" she shuddered violently—"even now I can sometimes hear the shrieks of my mother . . . and I can hear, also, the way they suddenly ceased, those cries . . ."

Stuart looked up with a start to find a Swiss waiter placing tea upon the table. He felt like rubbing his eyes. He had been dragged rudely back from the Syrian desert to the prosaic realities of a London hotel.

"Perhaps," continued Miska, "you will think that we were ill-treated, but it was not so. No one molested us. We were given every comfort which desert life can provide, servants to wait upon us and plenty of good food. After several weeks' journeying we came to a large city, having many minarets and domes glimmering in the moonlight; for we entered at night. Indeed, we always travelled at night. At the time I had no idea of the name of this city but I learned afterwards that it was Mecca.

"As we proceeded through the streets, the Assyrian girl and I peeped out through the little windows of the *shibrîyeh*—which is a kind of tent on the back of a camel —in which we travelled, hoping to see some familiar face or someone to whom we could appeal. But there seemed to be scarcely anyone visible in the streets, although lights shone out from many windows, and the few men we saw seemed anxious to avoid us. In fact, several ran down side turnings as the camels approached.

"We stopped before the gate of a large house which was presently opened, and the camels entered the courtyard. We descended, and I saw that a number of small apartments surrounded the courtyard in the manner of a *caravanserai*. Then, suddenly, I saw something else, and I knew why we had been treated with such consideration on the journey; I knew into what hands I had fallen—I knew that I was in the house of a *slave-dealer!*"

"Good heavens!" muttered Stuart—"this is almost incredible."

"I knew you would doubt what I had to tell you," declared Miska plaintively; "but I solemnly swear what I tell you is the truth. Yes, I was in the house of a slave-dealer, and on the very next day, because I was proficient in languages, in music and in dancing, and also because —according to their Eastern ideas—I was pretty, the dealer, Mohammed Abd-el-Bâli . . . offered me for sale."

She stopped, lowering her eyes and flushing hotly, then continued with hesitancy.

"In a small room which I can never forget I was offered the only indignity which I had been called upon to suffer since my abduction. I was *exhibited* to prospective purchasers."

As she spoke the words, Miska's eyes flashed passionately and her hand, which lay on the table, trembled. Stuart silently reached across and rested his own upon it.

"There were all kinds of girls," Miska continued, "black and brown and white, in the adjoining rooms, and some of them were singing and some dancing, whilst others wept. Four different visitors inspected me critically, two of them being agents for royal *harêms* and the other two —how shall I say it?—wealthy connoisseurs. But the price asked by Mohammed Abd-el-Bâli was beyond the purses of all except one of the agents. He had indeed settled the bargain, when the singing and dancing and shouting— every sound it seemed—ceased about me . . . and into the little room in which I crouched amongst perfumed cushions at the feet of the two men, walked Fo-Hi.

## Chapter 4

### MISKA'S STORY (concluded)

"Of course, I did not know that this was his name at the time; I only knew that a tall Chinaman had entered the room—and that his face was entirely covered by a green veil."

Stuart started, but did not interrupt Miska's story.

"This veil gave him in some way a frightfully malign and repellent appearance. As he stood in the doorway looking down I seemed to *feel* his gaze passing over me like a flame, although of course I could not see his eyes. For a moment he stood there looking at me; and much as his presence had affected me, its effect upon the slave-dealer and my purchaser was extraordinary. They seemed to be stricken dumb. Suddenly the Chinaman spoke, in perfect Arabic. 'Her price?' he said.

"Mohammed Abd-el-Bâli, standing trembling before him, replied:

" 'Miska is already sold, lord, but——'

" 'Her price?' repeated the Chinaman, in the same hard metallic voice and without the slightest change of intonation.

"The *harêm* agent who had bought me now said, his voice shaking so that the words were barely audible:

" 'I give her up, Mohammed—I give her up. Who am I to dispute with the Mandarin Fo-Hi;' and performing an abject obeisance he backed out of the room.

"At the same moment, Mohammed, whose knees were trembling so that they seemed no longer capable of supporting him, addressed the Chinaman.

" 'Accept the maiden as an unworthy gift,' he began—

" 'Her price?' repeated Fo-Hi.

"Mohammed, whose teeth had begun to chatter, asked him twice as much as he had agreed to accept from the other, Fo-Hi clapped his hands, and a fierce-eyed Hindu entered the room.

"Fo-Hi addressed him in a language which I did not understand, although I have since learned that it was Hindustanî, and the Indian from a purse which he carried counted out the amount demanded by the dealer and placed the money upon a little inlaid table which stood in the room. Fo-Hi gave him some brief order, turned and walked out of the room. I did not see him again for four years—that is to say until my nineteenth birthday.

"I know that you are wondering about many things and I will try to make some of them clear to you. You are wondering, no doubt, how such a trade as I have described is carried on in the East to-day almost under the eyes of European Governments. Now I shall surprise you. When I was taken from the house of the slave-dealer, in charge of Chunda Lal—for this was the name of the Hindu—do you know where I was carried to? I will tell you: to *Cairo!*"

"Cairo!" cried Stuart—then, perceiving that he had attracted attention by speaking so loudly, he lowered his voice. "Do you mean to tell me that you were taken as a *slave* to Cairo?"

Miska smiled—and her smile was the taunting smile of the East, which is at once a caress and an invitation.

"You think, no doubt, that there are no slaves in Cairo?" she said. "So do most people, and so did I—once. I learned better. There are palaces in Cairo, I assure you, in which there are many slaves. I myself lived in such a palace for four years, and I was not the only slave there. What do

British residents and French residents know of the inner domestic life of their Oriental neighbours? Are they ever admitted to the *harêm?* And the slaves—are they ever admitted outside the walls of the palace? Sometimes, yes, but never alone!

"By slow stages, following the ancient caravan routes, and accompanied by an extensive retinue of servants in charge of Chunda Lal, we came to Cairo; and one night approaching the city from the northeast and entering by the Bâb en-Nasr, I was taken to the old palace which was to be my prison for four years. How I passed those four years has no bearing upon the matters which I have to tell you, but I lived the useless, luxurious life of some Arabian princess, my lightest wish anticipated and gratified; nothing was denied me, except freedom.

"Then, one day—it was actually my nineteenth birthday —Chunda Lal presented himself and told me that I was to have an interview with Fo-Hi. Hearing these words, I nearly swooned, for a hundred times during the years of my strange luxurious captivity I had awakened trembling in the night, thinking that the figure of the awful veiled Chinaman had entered the room.

"You must understand that having spent my childhood in a *harêm,* the mode of life which I was compelled to follow in Cairo was not so insufferable as it must have been for a European woman. Neither was my captivity made unduly irksome. I often drove through the European quarters, always accompanied by Chunda Lal, and closely veiled, and I regularly went shopping in the bazaars—but never alone. The death of my mother—and later that of my father, of which Chunda Lal had told me —were griefs that time had dulled. But the horror of Fo-Hi was one which lived with me, day and night.

"To a wing of the palace kept closely locked, and which I had never seen opened, I was conducted by Chunda Lal. There, in a room of a kind with which I have since become painfully familiar, a room which was part library and part *mandarah,* part museum and part laboratory, I found the veiled man seated at a great littered table. As I stood trembling before him he raised a long yellow hand and waved to Chunda Lal to depart. When he obeyed and I heard the door close I could scarcely repress a shriek of terror.

"For what seemed an interminable time he sat watching me. I dared not look at him, but again I *felt* his gaze passing over me like a flame. Then he began to speak, in French, which he spoke without a trace of accent.

"He told me briefly that my life of idleness had ended and that a new life of activity in many parts of the world was about to commence. His manner was quite unemotional, neither harsh nor kindly, his metallic voice conveyed no more than the bare meaning of the words which he uttered. When, finally, he ceased speaking, he struck a gong which hung from a corner of the huge table, and Chunda Lal entered.

"Fo-Hi addressed a brief order to him in Hindustanî— and a few moments later a second Chinaman walked slowly into the room."

Miska paused, as if to collect her ideas, but continued almost immediately.

"He wore a plain yellow robe and had a little black cap on his head. His face, his wonderful evil face I can never forget, and his eyes—I fear you will think I exaggerate— but his eyes were green as emeralds! He fixed them upon me.

" 'This,' said Fo-Hi, 'is Miska.'

"The other Chinaman continued to regard me with those dreadful eyes; then:

" 'You have chosen well,' he said, turned and slowly went out again.

"I thank God that I have never seen him since, for his dreadful face haunted my dreams for long afterwards. But I have heard of him, and I know that next to Fo-Hi he is the most dangerous being in the known world. He has invented horrible things—poisons and instruments, which I cannot describe because I have never seen them; but I have seen . . . some of their effects."

She paused, overcome with the horror of her memories.

"What is the name of this other man?" asked Stuart eagerly. Miska glanced at him rapidly.

"Oh, do not ask me questions, please!" she pleaded. "I will tell you all I can, all I dare; what I do not tell you I cannot tell you—and this is one of the things I dare not tell. He is a Chinese scientist and, I have heard, the greatest genius in the whole world, but I can say no more— yet."

"Is he still alive—this man?"

"I do not know that. If he is alive, he is in China—at some secret palace in the province of Ho-Nan, which is the headquarters of what is called the 'Sublime Order.' I have never been there, but there are Europeans there, as well as Orientals."

"What! in the employ of these fiends!"

"It is useless to ask me—oh! indeed, I would tell you if I could, but I cannot! Let me go on from the time when I saw Fo-Hi in Cairo. He told me that I was a member of an organization dating back to remote antiquity which was destined to rule all the races of mankind—the Celestial Age he called their coming triumph. Something which they had lacked in order to achieve success had been supplied by the dreadful man who had entered the room and expressed his approval of me.

"For many years they had been at work in Europe, secretly, as well as in the East. I understood that they had acquired a quantity of valuable information of some kind by means of a system of opium-houses situated in the principal capitals of the world and directed by Fo-Hi and a number of Chinese assistants. Fo-Hi had remained in China most of the time, but had paid occasional visits to Europe. The other man—the monster with the black skull cap—had been responsible for the conduct of the European enterprises."

"Throughout this interview," interrupted Stuart, forgetful of the fact that Miska had warned him of the futility of asking questions, "and during others which you must have had with Fo-Hi, did you never obtain a glimpse of his face?"

"Never! No one has ever seen his face! I know that his eyes are a brilliant and unnatural yellow colour, but otherwise I should not know him if I saw him unveiled, to-morrow. Except," she added, "by a sense of loathing which his presence inspires in me. But I must hurry. If you interrupt me, I shall not have time.

"From that day in Cairo—oh! how can I tell you! I began the life of an adventuress! I do not deny it. I came here to confess it to you. I went to New York, to London, to Paris, to Petrograd; I went all over the world. I had beautiful dresses, jewels, admiration—all that women live for! And in the midst of it all mine was the life of the cloister; no nun could be more secluded!

"I see the question in your eyes—why did I do it? Why did I lure men into the clutches of Fo-Hi? For this is what I did; and when I have failed, I have been punished."

Stuart shrank from her.

"You confess," he said hoarsely, "that you knowingly lured men to *death?*"

"Ah, no!" she whispered, looking about her fearfully —"never! never! I swear it—never!"

"Then"—he stared at her blankly—"I do not understand you!"

"I dare not make it clearer—now: I dare not—dare not! But *believe* me! Oh, please, please," she pleaded, her soft voice dropping to a whisper—"believe me! If you knew what I risked to tell you so much, you would be more merciful. A horror which cannot be described"—again she shuddered—"will fall upon me if *he* ever suspects! You think me young and full of life, with all the world before me. You do not know. I am, literally, *already dead!* Oh! I have followed a strange career. I have danced in a Paris theatre and I have sold flowers in Rome; I have had my box at the Opera and I have filled opium pipes in a den at San Francisco! But never, never have I lured a man to his death. And through it all, from first to last, no man has so much as kissed my finger-tips!

"At a word, at a sign, I have been compelled to go from Monte Carlo to Buenos Ayres; at another sign from there to Tokio! Chunda Lal has guarded me as only the women of the East are guarded. Yet, in his fierce way, he has always tried to befriend me, he has always been faithful. But ah! I shrink from him many times, in horror, because I know *what* he is! But I may not tell you. Look! Chunda Lal has never been out of sound of this whistle"—she drew a little silver whistle from her dress—"for a moment since that day when he came into the house of the slave-dealer in Mecca, except——"

And now, suddenly, a wave of glorious colour flooded her beautiful face and swiftly she lowered her eyes, re-placing the little whistle. Stuart's rebellious heart leapt madly, for whatever he might think of her almost incred-ible story, that sweet blush was no subterfuge, no product of acting.

"You almost drive me mad," he said in a low voice, resembling the tones of repressed savagery. "You tell me so much, but withhold so much that I am more bewil-dered than ever. I can understand your helplessness in an Eastern household, but why should you obey the behests of this veiled monster in London, in New York, in Paris?"

She did not raise her eyes.

"I dare not tell you. But I dare not disobey him."

"Who is he?"

"No one knows, because no one has ever seen his face! Ah! you are laughing! But I swear before heaven I speak the truth! Indoors he wears a Chinese dress and a green veil. In passing from place to place, which he always does at night, he is attired in a kind of cowl which only exposes his eyes——"

"But how *can* such a fantastic being travel?"

"By road, on land, and in a steam yacht, at sea. Why should *you* doubt my honesty?" She suddenly raised her glance to Stuart's face and he saw that she had grown pale. "I have risked what I cannot tell you, and more than once—for you! I tried to call you on the telephone on the night that he set out from the house near Hampton Court to kill you, but I could get no reply, and——"

"Stop!" said Stuart, almost too excited to note at the time that she had betrayed a secret. "It was *you* who rang up that night?"

"Yes. Why did you not answer?"

"Never mind. Your call saved my life. I shall not forget." He looked into her eyes. "But can you not tell me what it all means? What or whom is 'The Scorpion'?"

She flinched.

"The Scorpion is—a passport. See." From a little pocket in the coat of her costume she drew out a golden scorpion! "I have one." She replaced it hurriedly. "I dare not, dare not tell you more. But this much I had to tell you, because . . . I shall never see you again!"

"What!"

"A French detective, a very clever man, learned a lot about 'The Scorpion' and he followed one of the members to England. This man killed him. Oh, I know I belong to a horrible organization!" she cried bitterly. "But I tell you I am helpless and *I* have never aided in such a thing. You should know that! But all he found out he left with you—and I do not know if I succeeded in destroying it. I do not ask you. I do not care. But I leave England to-night. Good-bye."

She suddenly stood up. Stuart rose also. He was about to speak when Miska's expression changed. A look of terror crept over her face, and hastily lowering her veil she walked rapidly away from the table and out of the room!

Many curious glances followed the elegant figure to the door. Then those glances were directed upon Stuart.

Flushing with embarrassment, he quickly settled the bill and hurried out of the hotel. Gaining the street, he looked eagerly right and left.

But Miska had disappeared!

## Chapter 5

## THE HEART OF CHUNDA LAL

DUSK had drawn a grey mantle over the East-End streets when Miska, discharging the cab in which she had come from Victoria, hurried furtively along a narrow alley tending Thamesward. Unconsciously she crossed a certain line—a line invisible except upon a map of London which lay upon the table of the Assistant Commissioner in New Scotland Yard—the line forming the "red circle" of M. Gaston Max. And, crossing this line, she became the focus upon which four pairs of watchful eyes were directed.

Arriving at the door of a mean house some little distance removed from that of Ah-Fang-Fu, Miska entered, for the door was open, and disappeared from the view of the four detectives who were watching the street. Her heart was beating rapidly. For she had thought, as she had stood up to leave the restaurant, that the fierce eyes of Chunda Lal had looked in through the glass panel of one of the doors.

This gloomy house seemed to swallow her up, and the men who watched wondered more and more what had become of the elegant figure, grotesque in such a setting, which had vanished into the narrow doorway—and which did not reappear. Even Inspector Kelly, who knew so much about Chinatown, did not know that the cellars of the three houses left and right of Ah-Fang-Fu's were connected by a series of doors planned and masked with Chinese cunning.

Half an hour after Miska had disappeared into the little house near the corner, the hidden door in the damp cellar below "The Pidgin House" opened and a bent old woman, a ragged, grey-haired and dirty figure, walked slowly up

the rickety wooden stair and entered a bare room behind
and below the shop and to the immediate left of the den of
the opium-smokers. This room, which was windowless,
was lighted by a tin paraffin lamp hung upon a nail in the
dirty plaster wall. The floor presented a litter of straw,
paper and broken packing-cases. Two steps led up to a
second door, a square heavy door of great strength. The
old woman, by means of a key which she carried, was
about to open this door when it was opened from the other
side.

Lowering his head as he came through, Chunda Lal
descended. He wore European clothes and a white turban.
Save for his ardent eyes and the handsome fanatical
face of the man, he might have passed for a lascar. He
turned and half closed the door. The woman shrank from
him, but extending a lean brown hand he gripped her arm.
His eyes glittered feverishly.

"So!" he said, "we are all leaving England? Five of the
Chinese sail with the P. and O. boat to-night. Ali Khân
goes to-morrow, and Râma Dass, with Miguel, and the
*Andaman*. I meet them at Singapore. But you?"

The woman raised her finger to her lips, glancing fearfully towards the open door. But the Hindu, drawing her
nearer, repeated with subdued fierceness:

"I ask it again—but *you?*"

"I do not know," muttered the woman, keeping her head
lowered and moving in the direction of the steps.

But Chunda Lal intercepted her.

"Stop!" he said—"not yet are you going. There is something I have to speak to you."

"Ssh!" she whispered, half turning and pointing up
toward the door.

"Those!" said the Hindu contemptuously—"the poor
slaves of the black smoke! Ah! they are floating in their
dream paradise; they have no ears to hear, no eyes to
see!" He grasped her wrist again. "They contest for
shadow smiles and dream kisses, but Chunda Lal have
eyes to see and ears to hear. He dream, too, but of lips
more sweet than honey, of a voice like the Song of the
Daood! *Inshalla!*"

Suddenly he clutched the grey hair of the bent old
woman and with one angry jerk snatched it from her head
—for it was a cunning wig. Disordered hair gleaming like
bronze waves in the dim lamplight was revealed and the

great dark eyes of Miska looked out from the artificially haggard face—eyes wide open and fearful.

"Bend not that beautiful body so," whispered Chunda Lal, "that is straight and supple as the willow branch. O, Miska"—his voice trembled emotionally and he that had been but a moment since so fierce stood abashed before her—"for you I become as the meanest and the lowest; for you I die!"

Miska started back from him as a muffled outcry sounded in the room beyond the half-open door. Chunda Lal started also, but almost immediately smiled—and his smile was tender as a woman's.

"It is the voice of the black smoke that speaks, Miska. We are alone. Those are dead men speaking from their tombs."

"Ah-Fang-Fu is in the shop," whispered Miska.

"And there he remain."

"But what of . . . *him?*"

Miska pointed toward the eastern wall of the room in which they stood.

Chunda Lal clenched his hands convulsively and turned his eyes in the same direction.

"It is of *him,*" he replied in a voice of suppressed vehemence, "it is of *him* I would speak." He bent close to Miska's ear. "In the creek, below the house, is lying the motor-boat. I go to-day to bring it down for him. He goes to-night to the other house up the river. To-morrow I am gone. Only you remaining."

"Yes, yes. He also leaves England to-morrow."

"And you?"

"I go with him," she whispered.

Chunda Lal glanced apprehensively toward the door. Then:

"Do not go with him!" he said, and sought to draw Miska into his arms. "O, light of my eyes, do not go with him!"

Miska repulsed him, but not harshly.

"No, no, it is no good, Chunda Lal. I cannot hear you."

"You think"—the Hindu's voice was hoarse with emotion—"that *he* will trace you—and kill you?"

"*Trace* me!" exclaimed Miska with sudden scorn. "Is it necessary for him to trace me? Am I not already dead except for *him!* Would I be his servant, his lure, his slave for one little hour, for one short minute, if my life was my own!"

Beads of perspiration gleamed upon the brown forehead of the Hindu, and his eyes turned from the door to the eastern wall and back again to Miska. He was torn by conflicting desires, but suddenly came resolution.

"Listen, then." His voice was barely audible. "If I tell you that your life *is* your own—if I reveal to you a secret which I learned in the house of Abdûl Rozân in Cairo——"

Miska watched him with eyes in which a new, a wild expression was dawning.

"If I tell you that life and not death awaits you, will you come away to-night, and we sail for India to-morrow! Ah! I have money! Perhaps I am rich as well as—someone; perhaps *I* can buy you the robes of a princess"—he drew her swiftly to him—"and cover those white arms with jewels."

Miska shrank from him.

"All this means nothing," she said. "How can the secret of Abdûl Rozân help me to live! And you—you will be dead before I die—yes! One little hour after *he* finds out that we go!"

"Listen again," hissed Chunda Lal intensely. "Promise me, and I will open for you a gate of life. For you, Miska, I will do it, and we shall be free. *He* will never find out. He shall not be living to find out!"

"No, no, Chunda Lal," she moaned. "You have been my only friend, and I have tried to forget . . ."

"I will forswear Kâli for ever," he said fervently, "and shed no blood for all my life! I will live for you alone and be your slave."

"It is no good. I cannot, Chunda Lal, I cannot."

"Miska!" he pleaded tenderly.

"No, no," she repeated, her voice quivering—"I cannot . . . Oh! do not ask it; I cannot!"

She picked up the hideous wig, moving towards the door. Chunda Lal watched her, clenching his hands; and his eyes, which had been so tender, grew fierce.

"Ah!" he cried—"and it may be I know a reason!"

She stopped, glancing back at him.

"It may be," he continued, and his repressed violence was terrible, "it may be that I, whose heart is never sleeping, have seen and heard! One night"—he crept towards her—"one night when I cry the warning that the Doctor Sahib returns to his house, you do not come! He goes in at the house, and you remain. But at last you come, and I see in your eyes——"

"Oh!" breathed Miska, watching him fearfully.

"Do I not see it in your eyes now! Never before have I thought so until you go to that house, never before have you escaped from my care as here in London. Twice again I have doubted, and because there was other work to do I have been helpless to find out. *To-night*"—he stood before her, glaring madly into her face—"I think so again—that you have gone to him. . . ."

"Oh, Chunda Lal!" cried Miska piteously and extended her hands towards him. "No, no—do not say it!"

"So!" he whispered—"I understand! You risk so much for him—for me you risk nothing! If he—the Doctor Sahib —say to you: 'Come with me, Miska——' "

"No, no! Can I never have one friend in all the world! I hear you call, Chunda Lal, but I am burning the envelope and—Doctor Stuart—finds me. I am trapped. You know it is so."

"I know you say so. And because he—Fo-Hi— is not sure and because of the piece of the scorpion which you find there, we go to that house—*he* and I—and we fail in what we go for." Chunda Lal's hands dropped limply to his sides. "Ah! I cannot understand, Miska. If we are not sure then, are we sure *now?* It may be"—he bent towards her—"we are trapped!"

"Oh, what do you mean?"

"We do not know how much the Frenchman learns. We do not know how much they read of what he had written. Why do we wait?"

"*He* has some plan, Chunda Lal," replied Miska wearily. "Does he ever fail?"

Her words rekindled the Hindu's ardour; his eyes lighted up anew.

"I tell you his plan," he whispered tensely. "Oh! you shall hear me! He watch you grow from a little lovely child, as he watch his death-spiders and his grey scorpions grow! He tend you and care for you and make you perfect, and he plan for you as he plan for his other creatures. Then, he see what I see, that you are not only his servant but also a woman and that you have a woman's heart. He learn—who think he knows all—that he, too, is not yet a spirit but only a man, and have a man's heart, a man's blood, a man's longings! It is because of the Doctor Sahib that he learn it——"

He grasped Miska again, but she struggled to elude

him. "Oh, let me go!" she pleaded. "It is madness you speak!"

"It is madness, yes—for *you!* Always I have watched, always I have waited; and I also have seen you bloom like *he* know it! To-morrow I am gone! Do you stay, for— *him?*"

"Oh," she whispered fearfully, "it cannot be."

"You say true when you say I have been your only friend, Miska. To-morrow *he* plan that you have no friend."

He released her, and slowly, from the sleeve of his coat, slipped into view the curved blade of a native knife.

"*Ali Khân Bhaî Salâm!*" he muttered—by which formula he proclaimed himself a *Thug!*

Rolling his eyes in the direction of the eastern wall, he concealed the knife.

"Chunda Lal!" Miska spoke wildly. "I am frightened! Please let me go, and to-morrow——"

"To-morrow!" Chunda Lal raised his eyes, which were alight with the awful light of fanaticism. "For me there may be no to-morrow! *Jey Bhowânî! Yah Allah!*"

"Oh, *he* may hear you!" whispered Miska pitifully. "Please go now. I shall know that you are near me, if ——"

"And then?"

"I will ask your aid."

Her voice was very low.

"And if it is written that I succeed?"

Miska averted her head.

"Oh, Chunda Lal . . . I cannot."

She hid her face in her hands.

Chunda Lal stood watching her for a moment in silence, then he turned toward the cellar door, and then again to Miska. Suddenly he dropped upon one knee before her, took her hand and kissed it, gently.

"I am your slave," he said, his voice shaken with emotion. "For myself I ask nothing—only your pity."

He rose, opened the door by which Miska had entered the room and went down into the cellars. She watched him silently, half fearfully, yet her eyes were filled with compassionate tears. Then, readjusting the hideous grey wig, she went up the steps and passed through the doorway into the den of the opium smokers.

## Chapter 6

## THE MAN WITH THE SCAR

STUART read through a paper, consisting of six closely
written pages, then he pinned the sheets together, folded
them and placed them in one of those long envelopes associated in his memory with the opening phase of "The
Scorpion" mystery. Smiling grimly, he descended to his
dispensary and returned with the Chinese coin attached
to the cork. With this he sealed the envelope.

He had volunteered that night for onerous service, and
his offer had been accepted. Gaston Max's knowledge of
Eastern languages was slight, whilst Stuart's was sound
and extensive, and the Frenchman had cordially wel-
comed the doctor's proposal that he should accompany
him to the house of Ah-Fang-Fu. Reviewing the facts
gleaned from Miska during the earlier part of the evening,
Stuart perceived that, apart from the additional light
which they shed upon her own relations with the group,
they could be of slight assistance to the immediate success
of the inquiry—unless the raid failed. Therefore he had
determined upon the course which now he was adopting.

As he completed the sealing of the envelope and laid it
down upon the table, he heard a cab drawn up in front of
the house, and presently Mrs. M'Gregor knocked and
entered the study.

"Inspector Dunbar to see you, Mr. Keppel," she said
—"and he has with him an awful-looking body, all cuts
and bandages. A patient, no doubt."

Stuart stood up, wondering what this could mean.

"Will you please show them in, Mrs. M'Gregor," he
replied.

A few moments later Dunbar entered, accompanied by
a bearded man whose head was bandaged so as partly
to cover one eye and who had an evil-looking scar running from his cheekbone, apparently—or at any rate from
the edge of the bandage—to the corner of his mouth, so

that the lip was drawn up in a fierce and permanent snarl.

At this person Stuart stared blankly, until Dunbar began to laugh.

"It's a wonderful make-up, isn't it?" he said. "I used to say that disguises were out of date, but M. Max has taught me I was wrong."

"Max!" cried Stuart.

"At your service," replied the apparition, "but for this evening only I am 'Le Balafré.' Yes, *pardieu!* I am a real dead man!"

The airy indifference with which he proclaimed himself to represent one whose awful body had but that day been removed from a mortuary, and one whom in his own words he had "had the misfortune to strangle," was rather ghastly and at the same time admirable. For "Le Balafré" had deliberately tried to murder him, and false sentiment should form no part of the complement of a criminal investigator.

"It is a daring idea," said Stuart, "and relies for its success upon the chance that 'The Scorpion' remains ignorant of the fate of his agent and continues to believe that the body found off Hanover Hole was yours."

"The admirable precautions of my clever colleague," replied Max, laying his hand upon Dunbar's shoulder, "in closing the mortuary and publishing particulars of the identification disk, made it perfectly safe. 'Le Balafré' has been in hiding. He emerges!"

Stuart had secret reasons for knowing that Max's logic was not at fault, and this brought him to the matter of the sealed paper. He took up the envelope.

"I have here," he said slowly, "a statement. Examine the seal."

He held it out, and Max and Dunbar looked at it. The latter laughed shortly.

"Oh, it is a real statement," continued Stuart, "the nature of which I am not at liberty to divulge. But as tonight we take risks, I propose to leave it in your charge, Inspector."

He handed the envelope to Dunbar, whose face was blank with astonishment.

"In the event of failure to-night," added Stuart, "or catastrophe, I authorise you to read this statement—and act upon it. If, however, I escape safely, I ask you to return it to me, unread."

"*Eh bien*," said Max, and fixed that eye the whole of which was visible upon Stuart. "Perhaps I understand, and certainly"—he removed his hand from Dunbar's shoulder and rested it upon that of Stuart—"but certainly, my friend, I sympathise!"

Stuart started guiltily, but Max immediately turned aside and began to speak about their plans.

"In a bag which Inspector Dunbar has thoughtfully left in the cab," he said——

Dunbar hastily retired and Max laughed.

"In that bag," he continued, "is a suit of clothes such as habitués of 'The Pidgin House' rejoice to wear. I, who have studied disguise almost as deeply as the great Willy Clarkson, will transform you into a perfect ruffian. It is important, you understand, that someone should be inside the house of Ah-Fang-Fu, as otherwise by means of some secret exit the man we seek may escape. I believe that he contemplates departing at any moment, and I believe that the visit of Miguel means that what I may term the masters of the minor lodges are coming to London for parting instructions—or, of course, Miguel may have come about the disappearance of 'Le Balafré.' "

"Suppose you meet Miguel!"

"My dear friend, I must trust to the Kismet who pursues evil-doers! The only reason which has led me to adopt this daring disguise is a simple one. Although I believe 'The Pidgin House' to be open to ordinary opium-smokers, it may not be open on 'lodge nights.' Do you follow me? Very well. I have the golden scorpion—which I suppose to be a sort of passport."

Stuart wondered more and more at the reasoning powers of this remarkable man, which could lead him to such an accurate conclusion.

"The existence of such a passport," continued Max, "would seem to point to the fact that all the members of this organisation are not known personally to one another. At the same time those invited or expected at present *may* be known to Ah-Fang-Fu or to whoever acts as concierge. You see? Expected or otherwise, I assume that 'Le Balafré' would be admitted—and at night I shall pass very well for 'Le Balafré'—somewhat damaged as a result of my encounter with the late Charles Malet, but still recognisable!"

"And I?"

"You will be 'franked' in. The word of 'Le Balafré'

should be sufficient for that! Of course I may be conducted immediately into the presence of the Chief—'The Scorpion' —and he may prove to be none other than Miguel, for instance—or my Algerian acquaintance—or may even be a 'she'—the fascinating Zâra el-Khalâ! We do not know. But I *think*—oh, decidedly I think—that the cowled one is a creature, and his habits and habitat suggests to me that he is a Chinaman."

"And in that event how shall you act?"

"At once! I shall hold him, if I can, or shoot him, if I cannot hold him! Both of us will blow police-whistles with which we shall be provided and Inspectors Dunbar and Kelly will raid the premises. But I am hoping for an interval. I do not like these inartistic scrimmages! The fact that these people foregather at an opium-house suggests to me that a certain procedure may be followed which I observed during the course of the celebrated 'Mr. Q.' case in New York. 'Mr. Q.' also had an audience-chamber adjoining an opium-den, and his visitors went there ostensibly to smoke opium. The opium-den was a sort of anteroom."

"Weymouth's big Chinese case had similar features," said Inspector Dunbar, who re-entered at that moment carrying a leathern grip. "If you are kept waiting and you keep your ears open, doctor, that's when your knowledge of the lingo will come in useful. We might rope in the whole gang and find we hadn't a scrap of evidence against them, for except the attempt on yourself, Dr. Stuart, there's nothing so far that I can see to connect 'The Scorpion' with Sir Frank Narcombe!"

"It is such a bungle that I fear!" cried Max. "Ah! how this looped-up lip annoys me!" He adjusted the bandage carefully.

"We've got the place comfortably surrounded," continued Dunbar, "and whoever may be inside is booked! A lady, answering to the description of Mlle. Dorian, went in this evening, so Sowerby reports."

Stuart felt that he was changing colour, and he stooped hastily to inspect the contents of the bag which Dunbar had opened.

"*Eh bien!*" said Gaston Max. "We shall not go empty-handed, then. And now to transfigure you, my friend!"

## Chapter 7

## IN THE OPIUM DEN

INTERRUPTING a spell of warm, fine weather the night had set in wet and stormy. The squalid streets through which Stuart and Gaston Max made their way looked more than normally deserted and uninviting. The wind moaned and the rain accompanied with a dreary tattoo. Sometimes a siren wailed out upon the river.

"We are nearly there," said Max. "*Pardieu!* they are well concealed, those fellows. I have not seen so much as an eyebrow."

"It would be encouraging to get a glimpse of some one!" replied Stuart.

"Ah, but bad—inartistic. It is the next door, I think . . . yes. I hope they have no special way of knocking."

Upon the door of a dark and apparently deserted shop he rapped.

Both had anticipated an interval of waiting, and both were astonished when the door opened almost at once, revealing a blackly cavernous interior.

"Go off! Too late! Shuttee shop!" chattered a voice out of the darkness.

Max thrust his way resolutely in, followed by Stuart. "Shut the door, Ah-Fang-Fu!" he said curtly, speaking with a laboured French accent. "*Scorpion!*"

The door was closed by the invisible Chinaman, there was a sound of soft movements and a hurricane-lantern suddenly made its appearance. Its light revealed the interior of a nondescript untidy little shop and revealed the presence of an old and very wrinkled Chinaman who held the lantern. He wore a blue smock and a bowler hat and his face possessed the absolute impassivity of an image. As he leaned over the counter, scrutinising his visitors, Max thrust forward the golden scorpion held in the palm of his hand.

"*Hoi, hoi!*" chattered the Chinaman, "Fo-Hi fellers, eh? You hab got plenty much late. Other fellers Fo-Hi pidgin plenty much sooner. You one time catchee allee same bhobbery, b'long number one joss-pidgin man!"

Being covertly nudged by Max:

"Cut the palaver, Pidgin," growled Stuart.

"Allee lightee," chattered Ah-Fang-Fu, for evidently this was he. "You play one piecee pipee till Fo-Hi got." Raising the lantern, he led the way through a door at the back of the shop. Descending four wooden steps, Stuart and Max found themselves in the opium-den.

"Full up. No loom," said the Chinaman.

It was a low-ceiled apartment, the beams of the roof sloping slightly upward from west to east. The centre part of the wall at the back was covered with matting hung from the rough cornice supporting the beams. To the right of the matting was the door communicating with the shop, and to the left were bunks. Other bunks lined the southerly wall, except where, set in the thickness of the bare brick and plaster, a second strong door was partly hidden by a pile of empty packing-cases and an untidy litter of straw and matting.

Along the northern wall were more bunks, and an open wooden stair, with a handrail, ascended to a small landing or platform before a third door high up in the wall. A few mats were strewn about the floor. The place was dimly lighted by a red-shaded lamp swung from the centre of the ceiling and near the foot of the stairs another lamp (of the common tin variety) stood upon a box near which was a broken cane chair. Opium-pipes, tins, and a pack of cards were on this box.

All the bunks appeared to be occupied. Most of the occupants were lying motionless, but one or two were noisily sucking at the opium-pipes. These had not yet attained to the opium-smokers' Nirvana. So much did Gaston Max, a trained observer, gather in one swift glance. Then Ah-Fang-Fu, leaving the lantern in the shop, descended the four steps and crossing the room began to arrange two mats with round head-cushions near to the empty packing-cases. Stuart and Max remained by the door.

"You see," whispered Max, "he has taken you on trust! And he did not appear to recognize me. It is as I thought. The place is 'open to the public' as usual, and Ah-Fang does a roaring trade, one would judge. For the benefit of patrons not affiliated to the order we have to pretend to smoke."

"Yes," replied Stuart with repressed excitement—"until

someone called Fo-Hi is at home, or visible; the word 'got'
may mean either of those things."

"Fo-Hi," whispered Max, "is 'The Scorpion'!"

"I believe you are right," said Stuart—who had good
reason to know it. "My God! what a foul den! The reek
is suffocating. Look at that yellow lifeless face yonder,
and see that other fellow whose hand hangs limply down
upon the floor. Those bunks might be occupied by corpses
for all the evidence of life that some of them show."

"*Morbleu!* do not raise your voice; for some of them are
occupied by 'Scorpions.' You noted the words of Ah-Fang?
*Ssh!*"

The old Chinaman returned with his curious shuffling
walk, raising his hand to beckon to them.

"Number one piece bunk, lo!" he chattered.

"Good enough," growled Stuart.

The two crossed and reclined upon the uncleanly mats.

"Make special loom," explained Ah-Fang-Fu. "Velly
special chop!"

He passed from bunk to bunk, and presently came to a
comatose Chinaman from whose limp hand, which hung
down upon the floor, the pipe had dropped. This pipe Ah-
Fang-Fu took from the smoker's fingers and returning to
the box upon which the tin lamp was standing began
calmly to load it.

"Good heavens!" muttered Stuart—"he is short of
pipes! Pah! how the place reeks!"

Ah-Fang-Fu busied himself with a tin of opium, the
pipe which he had taken from the sleeper, and another
pipe—apparently the last of his stock—which lay near the
lamp. Igniting the two, he crossed and handed them to
Stuart and Max.

"Velly soon—lo!" he said, and made a curious sign,
touching his brow, his lips and his breast in a manner
resembling that of a Moslem.

Max repeated the gesture and then lay back upon his
elbow, raising the mouthpiece of the little pipe to his lips
—but carefully avoiding contact.

Ah-Fang-Fu shuffled back to the broken cane chair,
from which he had evidently arisen to admit his late
visitors.

Inarticulate sounds proceeded from the bunks, breaking
the sinister silence which now descended upon the den.
Ah-Fang-Fu began to play Patience, constantly muttering
to himself. The occasional wash of tidal water became

audible, and once there came a scampering and squealing
of rats from beneath the floor.

"Do you notice the sound of lapping water" whispered
Stuart. "The place is evidently built upon a foundation of
piles and the cellars must actually be submerged at high-
tide."

"*Pardieu!* it is a death trap. What is this!"

A loud knocking sounded upon the street door. Ah-Fang-
Fu rose and shuffled up the steps into the shop. He could
be heard unbarring the outer door. Then:

"Too late! shuttee shop, shuttee shop!" sounded.

"I don't want nothin' out of your blasted shop, Pidgin!"
roared a loud and thick voice "I'm old Bill Bean, I am,
and I want a pipe, I do!"

"Hullo, Bill!" replied the invisible 'Pidgin,' "Allee
samee dlunk again!"

A red-bearded ship's fireman, wearing sea-boots, a
rough blue suit similar to that which Stuart wore, a muffler
and a peaked cap, lurched into view at the head of the
steps.

"Blimey!" he roared, over his shoulder. "Drunk! *Me*
drunk! An' all the pubs in these parts sell barley-water
coloured brown! Blimey! Chuck it, Pidgin!"

Ah-Fang-Fu reappeared behind him. "Catchee dlunk
ev'ly time for comee here," he chattered.

" 'Tain't 'umanly possible," declared the new arrival,
staggering down the steps, "fer a 'ealthy sailorman to git
drunk on coloured water just 'cause the publican calls it
beer! I ain't drunk; I'm only miserable. Gimme a pipe,
Pidgin."

Ah-Fang-Fu barred the door and ascended.

"Comee here," he muttered, "my placee, all full up
and no other placee b'long open."

Bill Bean slapped him boisterously on the back. "Cut
the palaver, Pidgin, and gimme a pipe. Piecee pipe, Pidgin!"

He lurched across the floor, nearly falling over Stuart's
legs, took up a mat and a cushion, lurched into the further
corner and cast himself down.

"Ain't I one o' yer oldest customers, Pidgin?" he inquired. "One o' yer oldest I am."

"Blight side twelve-time," muttered the Chinaman.
"Getchee me in tlouble, Bill. Number one police chop."

"Not the first time it wouldn't be!" retorted the fireman.
"Not the first time as you've been in trouble, Pidgin. An'

unless they 'ung yer—which it ain't 'umanly possible to 'ang a Chink—it wouldn't be the last—an' not by a damn long way . . . *an'* not by a damn long way!"

Ah-Fang-Fu, shrugging resignedly, shuffled from bunk to bunk in quest of a disused pipe, found one, and returning to the extemporised table, began to load it, muttering to himself.

"Don't like to 'ear about your wicked past, do you?" continued Bill. "Wicked old yellow-faced 'eathen! Remember the 'dive' in 'Frisco, Pidgin? *Wot* a rough 'ouse! Remember when I come in—full up I was: me back teeth well under water—an' you tried to Shanghai me?"

"You cutee palaber. All damn lie," muttered the Chinaman.

"Ho! a lie is it?" roared the other. "Wot about me wakin' up all of a tremble aboard o' the old *Nancy Lee*—aboard of a blasted wind-jammer! *Me*—a *fireman!* Wot about it? Wasn't that Shanghaiin'? Blighter! *An'* not a 'oat' in me pocket—not a 'bean'! Broke to the wide an' aboard of a old wind-jammer wot was a coffin-ship—a coffin-ship she was; an' 'er old man was the devil's father-in-law. Ho! lies! I *don't* think."

"You cutee palaber!" chattered Ah-Fang-Fu, busy with the pipe. "You likee too much chin-chin. You makee nice piecee bhobbery."

"Not a 'bean,' " continued Bill reminiscently—"not a 'oat.' " He sat up violently. "Even me pipe an' baccy was gone!" he shouted. "You'd even pinched me pipe an' baccy! You'd pinch the whiskers off a blind man, *you* would, Pidgin! 'And over the dope. Thank Gawd somebody's still the right stuff!"

Suddenly, from a bunk on the left of Gaston Max came a faint cry.

"Ah! He has bitten me!"

" 'Ullo!" said Bill—"wotcher bin given' *'im*, Pidgin? *Chandu* or hydrerphobia?"

Ah-Fang-Fu crossed and handed him the pipe.

"One piecee pipee. No more hab."

Bill grasped the pipe eagerly and raised it to his lips. Ah-Fang-Fu returned unmoved to his Patience and silence reclaimed the den, only broken by the inarticulate murmurings and the lapping of the tide.

"A genuine customer!" whispered Max.

"Ah!" came again, more faintly—"he . . . has . . . bitten . . . me."

"Blimey!" said Bill Bean in a drowsy voice—" 'eave the chair at 'im, Pidgin."

Stuart was about to speak when Gaston Max furtively grasped his arm. "Ssh!" he whispered. "Do not move, but look . . . at the top of the stair!"

Stuart turned his eyes. On the platform at the head of the stairs a Hindu was standing!

"Chunda Lal!" whispered Max. "Prepare for—anything!"

Chunda Lal descended slowly. Ah-Fang-Fu continued to play Patience. The Hindu stood behind him and began to speak in a voice of subdued fervour and with soft Hindu modulations.

"Why do you allow them, strangers, coming here tonight!"

Ah-Fang-Fu continued complacently to arrange the cards.

"S'pose hab gotchee pidgin allee samee Chunda Lal hab got? Fo-Hi no catchee buy bled and cheese for Ah-Fang-Fu. He"—nodding casually in the direction of Bill Bean—"plitty soon all blissful."

"Be very careful, Ah-Fang-Fu," said Chunda Lal tensely. He lowered his voice. "Do you forget so soon what happen last week?"

"No sabby."

"Some one comes here—we do not know how close he comes; perhaps he comes in—and he is of the *police*."

Ah-Fang-Fu shuffled uneasily in his chair.

"No p'lice chop for Pidgin!" he muttered. "Same feller tumble in liver?"

"He is killed—yes; but suppose they find the writing he has made! Suppose he has written that it is *here* people meet together?"

"Makee chit tella my name? Muchee hard luck! Number one police chop."

"You say Fo-Hi not buying you bread and cheese. Perhaps it is Fo-Hi that save you from hanging!"

Ah-Fang-Fu hugged himself.

"*Yak pozee!*" (Very good) he muttered.

Chunda Lal raised his finger.

"Be very careful, Ah-Fang-Fu!"

"Allee time velly careful."

"But admit no more of them to come in, these strangers."

"*Tchée, tchée!* Velly ploper. Sometime big feller come in if Pidgin palaber or not. Pidgin never lude to big feller."

"Your life may depend on it," said Chunda Lal impressively. "How many are here?"

Ah-Fang-Fu turned at last from his cards, pointing in three directions, and, finally, at Gaston Max.

"Four?" said the Hindu—"how can it be?"

He peered from bunk to bunk, muttering something—a name apparently—after scrutinising each. When his gaze rested upon Max he started, stared hard, and meeting the gaze of the one visible eye, made the strange sign.

Max repeated it; and Chunda Lal turned again to the Chinaman. "Because of that drunken pig," he said, pointing at Bill Bean—"we must wait. See to it that he is the last."

He walked slowly up the stairs, opened the door at the top and disappeared.

## Chapter 8

### THE GREEN-EYED JOSS

SINISTER silence reclaimed the house of Ah-Fang-Fu. And Ah-Fang-Fu resumed his solitary game.

"*He* recognised 'Le Balafré' " whispered Max—"and was surprised to see him! So there are three of the gang here! Did you particularly observe in which bunks they lay, doctor. *Ssh!*"

A voice from a bunk had commenced to sing monotonously.

"*Peyala peah,*" it sang, weird above the murmured accompaniment of the other dreaming smokers and the *wash-wash* of the tide—"*To mynna-peah-Phîr Kye ko kyah . . .*"

"He is speaking from an opium-trance," said Stuart softly. "A native song: 'If a cup of wine is drunk, and I have drunk it, what of that?' "

"*Mon Dieu!* it is uncanny!" whispered Max. "*Brr!* do

you hear those rats? I am wondering in what order we shall be admitted to the 'Scorpion's' presence, or if we shall all see him together."

"He may come in here."

"All the better."

"Gimme 'nother pipe, Pidgin," drawled a very drowsy voice from Bill Bean's corner.

Ah-Fang-Fu left his eternal arranging and rearranging of the cards and crossed the room. He took the opium-pipe from the fireman's limp fingers and returning to the box, refilled and lighted it. Max and Stuart watched him in silence until he had handed the second pipe to the man and returned to his chair.

"We must be very careful," said Stuart. "We do not know which are real smokers and which are not."

Again there was a weird interruption. A Chinaman lying in one of the bunks began to chant in a monotonous far-away voice:

"*Chong-liou-chouay*
*Om máni padmé hum.*"

"The Buddhist formula," whispered Stuart. "*He* is a real smoker. Heavens! the reek is choking me!"

The chant was repeated, the words dying away into a long murmur. Ah-Fang-Fu continued to shuffle the cards. And presently Bill Bean's second pipe dropped from his fingers. His husky voice spoke almost inaudibly.

"I'm . . . old . . . Bill . . . Bean. . . . I . . ."

A deep-noted siren hooted dimly.

"A steamer making for dock," whispered Max. "*Brr!* it is a nightmare, this! I think in a minute something will happen. *Ssh!*"

Ah-Fang-Fu glanced slowly around. Then he stood up, raised the lamp from the table and made a tour of the bunks, shining the light in upon the faces of the occupants. Max watched him closely, hoping to learn in which bunks the members of 'The Scorpion's' group lay. But he was disappointed. Ah-Fang-Fu examined *all* the bunks and even shone the light down upon Stuart and Max. He muttered to himself constantly, but seemed to address no one.

Replacing the lamp on the box, he whistled softly; and:——

"Look!" breathed Max. "The stair again!"

Stuart cautiously turned his eyes toward the open stair.

On the platform above stood a bent old hag whose witch-eyes were searching the place keenly! With a curiously lithe step, for all her age, she descended, and standing behind Ah-Fang-Fu tapped him on the shoulder and pointed to the outer door. He stood up and shuffled across, went up the four steps and unbarred the door.

"*Tchée, tchée,*" he chattered. "Pidgin make a lookout."

He went out and closed the door.

"Something happens!" whispered Max.

A gong sounded.

"Ah!"

The old woman approached the matting curtain hung over a portion of the wall, raised it slightly in the centre —where it opened—and disappeared beyond.

"You see!" said Stuart excitedly.

"Yes! it is the audience-chamber of 'The Scorpion'!"

The ancient hag came out again, crossed to a bunk and touched its occupant, a Chinaman, with her hand. He immediately got up and followed her. The two disappeared beyond the curtain.

"What shall we do," said Stuart, "if *you* are summoned?"

"I shall throw open those curtains the moment I reach them, and present my pistol at the head of whoever is on the other side. You—*ssh!*"

The old woman reappeared, looked slowly around and then held the curtains slightly apart to allow of the Chinaman's coming out. He saluted her by touching his head, lips and breast with his right hand, then passed up to the door communicating with the shop, which he opened, and went out.

His voice came, muffled:

"Fo-Hi!"

"Fo-Hi," returned the high voice of Ah-Fang-Fu.

The outer door was opened and shut. The old woman went up and barred the inner door, then returned and stood by the matting curtain. The sound of the water below alone broke the silence. It was the hour of high tide.

"There goes the first fish into Dunbar's net!" whispered Max.

The gong sounded again.

Thereupon the old woman crossed to another bunk and conducted a brown-skinned Eastern into the hidden room. Immediately they had disappeared:

"As I pull the curtains aside," continued Max rapidly,

"blow the whistle and run across and unbar the door. . . ."

So engrossed was he in giving these directions, and so engrossed was Stuart in listening to them, that neither detected a faint creak which proceeded from almost immediately behind them. This sound was occasioned by the slow and cautious opening of that sunken, heavy door near to which they lay—the door which communicated with the labyrinth of cellars. Inch by inch from the opening protruded the head of Ah-Fang-Fu!

"If the Chinaman offers any resistance," Max went on, speaking very rapidly—"*morbleu!* you have the means to deal with him! In a word, admit the police. *Ssh!* what is that!"

A moaning voice from one of the bunks came.

"*Cheal kegûr-men, mâs ká dheer!*"

"A native adage," whispered Stuart. "He is dreaming. 'There is always meat in a kite's nest.' "

"*Eh bien!* very true—and I think the kite is at home!"

The head of Ah-Fang-Fu vanished. A moment later the curtains opened again slightly and the old woman came out, ushering the brown man. He saluted her and unbarred the door, going out.

"Fo-Hi," came dimly.

There was no definite answer—only the sound of a muttered colloquy; and suddenly the brown man returned and spoke to the old woman in a voice so low that his words were inaudible to the two attentive listeners in the distant corner.

"Ah!" whispered Max—"what now?"

"Shall we rush the curtain!" said Stuart.

"No!" Max grasped his arm—"wait! wait! See! he is going out. He has perhaps forgotten something. A second fish in the net."

The Oriental went up the steps into the shop. The old woman closed and barred the door, then opened the matting curtain and disappeared within.

"I was right," said Max.

But for once in his career he was wrong.

She was out again almost immediately and bending over a bunk close to the left of the masked opening. The occupant concealed in its shadow did not rise and follow her, however. She seemed to be speaking to him. Stuart and Max watched intently.

The head of Ah-Fang-Fu reappeared in the doorway behind them.

"Now is our time!" whispered Max tensely. "As I rush for the curtains, you run to the shop door and get it unbolted, whistling for Dunbar——"

Ah-Fang-Fu, fully opening the door behind them, crept out stealthily.

"Have your pistol ready," continued Max, "and first put the whistle between your teeth——"

Ah-Fang-Fu silently placed his bowler hat upon the floor, shook down his long pigtail, and moving with catlike tread, stooping, drew nearer.

*"Now, doctor!"* cried Max.

Both sprang to their feet. Max leapt clear of the matting and other litter and dashed for the curtain. He reached it, seized it and tore it bodily from its fastenings. Behind him the long flat note of a police whistle sounded—and ended abruptly.

*"Ah! Nom d'un nom!"* cried Max.

A cunningly devised door—looking like a section of solid brick and plaster wall—was closing slowly—heavily. Through the opening which yet remained he caught a glimpse of a small room, draped with Chinese dragon tapestry and having upon a raised, carpeted dais a number of cushions forming a *dîwan* and an inlaid table bearing a silver snuff vase. A cowled figure was seated upon the dais. The door closed completely. Within a niche in its centre sat a yellow leering idol, green eyed and complacent.

Wild, gurgling cries brought Max sharply about.

An answering whistle sounded from the street outside . . . a second . . . a third.

Ah-Fang-Fu, stooping ever lower, at the instant that Stuart had sprung to his feet had seized his ankle from behind, pitching him on to his face. It was then that the note of the whistle had ceased. Now, the Chinaman had his long pigtail about Stuart's neck, at which Stuart, prone with the other kneeling upon his body, plucked vainly.

Max raised his pistol . . . and from the bunk almost at his elbow leapt Miguel the quadroon, a sand-bag raised. It descended upon the Frenchman's skull . . . and he crumbled up limply and collapsed upon the floor. There came a crash of broken glass from the shop.

Uttering a piercing cry, the old woman staggered from the door near which she had been standing as if stricken helpless, during the lightning moments in which these things had happened—and advanced in the direction of Ah-Fang-Fu.

"Ah, God! You kill him! You *kill* him?" she moaned.

"Through the window, Sowerby! This way!" came Dunbar's voice. "Max! Max!"

The sustained note of a whistle, a confusion of voices and a sound of heavy steps proclaimed the entrance of the police into the shop and the summoning of reinforcements.

Ah-Fang-Fu rose. Stuart had ceased to struggle. The Chinaman replaced his hat and looked up at the woman, whose eyes glared madly into his own.

"*Tchée, tchée,*" he said sibilantly—"*Tchon-dzee-ti Fan-Fu.*"*

"Down with the door!" roared Dunbar.

The woman threw herself, with a wild sob, upon the motionless body of Stuart.

Ensued a series of splintering crashes, and finally the head of an axe appeared through the panels of the door. Ah-Fang-Fu tried to drag the woman away, but she clung to Stuart desperately and was immovable. Thereupon the huge quadroon, running across the room, swept them both up into his giant embrace, man and woman together, and bore them down by the sunken doorway into the cellars below!

The shop door fell inwards, crashing down the four steps, and Dunbar sprang into the place, revolver in hand, followed by Inspector Kelly and four men of the River Police, one of whom carried a hurricane lantern. Ah-Fang-Fu had just descended after Miguel and closed the heavy door.

"Try this way, boys!" cried Kelly, and rushed up the stair. The four men followed him. The lantern was left on the floor. Dunbar stared about him. Sowerby and several other men entered. Suddenly Dunbar saw Gaston Max lying on the floor.

"My God!" he cried—"they have killed him!"

He ran across, knelt and examined Max, pressing his ear against his breast.

Inspector Kelly reaching the top of the stairs and finding the door locked, hurled his great bulk against it and burst it open.

*"Yes, yes. It is the will of the Master."

"Follow me, boys!" he cried. "Take care! Bring the lantern, somebody."

The fourth man grasped the lantern and all followed the Inspector up the stair and out through the doorway. His voice came dimly:

"Mind the beam! Pass the light forward. . . ."

Sowerby was struggling with the door by which Miguel and Ah-Fang-Fu unseen had made their escape and Dunbar, having rested Max's head upon a pillow, was glaring all about him, his square jaw set grimly and his eyes fierce with anger.

A voice droned from a bunk:

*"Cheal kegûr men mâs kâ-dheer!"*

The police were moving from bunk to bunk, scrutinising the occupants. The uproar had penetrated to them even in their drugged slumbers. There were stirrings and mutterings and movements of yellow hands.

"But where," muttered Dunbar, "is Dr. Stuart? And where is 'The Scorpion?'"

He turned and stared at the wall from which the matting had been torn. And out of the little niche in the cunningly masked door the green-eyed joss leered at him complacently.

Part IV

THE LAIR OF THE SCORPION

Chapter 1

## THE SUBLIME ORDER

STUART awoke to a discovery so strange that for some
time he found himself unable to accept its reality. He
passed his hands over his face and eyes and looked about
him dazedly. He experienced great pain in his throat, and
he could feel that his neck was swollen. He stared down
at his ankles, which also were throbbing agonisingly—to
learn that they were confined in gyves attached by a short
chain to a ring in the floor!

He was lying upon a deep *dīwan*, which was covered
with leopard-skins and which occupied one corner of the
most extraordinary room he had ever seen or ever could
have imagined. He sat up, but was immediately overcome
with faintness which he conquered with difficulty.

The apartment, then, was one of extraordinary Oriental elegance, having two entrances closed with lacquer

sliding doors. Chinese lamps swung from the ceiling, illuminated it warmly, and a great number of large and
bright silk cushions were strewn about the floor. There
were tapestries in black and gold, rich carpets and
couches, several handsome cabinets and a number of tall
cases of Oriental workmanship containing large and
strangely bound books, scientific paraphernalia, curios
and ornaments.

At the further end of the room was a deep tiled hearth
in which stood a kind of chemical furnace which hissed
constantly. Upon ornate small tables and pedestals were
vases and cases—one of the latter containing a number of
orchids, in flower.

Preserved lizards, snakes, and other creatures were in
a row of jars upon a shelf, together with small skeletons
of animals in frames. There was also a perfect human
skeleton. Near the centre of the room was a canopied
chair, of grotesque Chinese design, upon a dais, a big
bronze bell hanging from it; and near to the *diwan* upon
which Stuart was lying stood a large, very finely carved
table upon which were some open faded volumes and a
litter of scientific implements. Near the table stood a very
large bowl of what looked like platinum, upon a tripod,
and several volumes lay scattered near it upon the carpet.
From a silver incense-burner arose a pencilling of blue
smoke.

One of the lacquer doors slid noiselessly open and a
man entered. Stuart inhaled sibilantly and clenched his
fists.

The new-comer wore a cowled garment of some dark
blue material which enveloped him from head to feet. It
possessed oval eye-holes, and through these apertures
gleamed two eyes which looked scarcely like the eyes of
a human being. They were of that brilliant yellow colour
sometimes seen in the eyes of tigers, and their most
marked and awful peculiarity was their unblinking regard. They seemed always to be open to their fullest extent, and Stuart realised with anger that it was impossible
to sustain for long the piercing unmoved gaze of Fo-Hi
. . . for he knew that he was in the presence of "The Scorpion"!

Walking with a slow and curious dignity, the cowled
figure came across to the table, first closing the lacquer
door. Stuart's hands convulsively clutched the covering
of the *diwan* as the sinister figure approached. The intoler-

able gaze of those weird eyes had awakened a horror, a loathing horror, within him, such as he never remembered to have experienced in regard to any human being. It was the sort of horror which the proximity of a poisonous serpent occasions—or the nearness of a scorpion. . . .

Fo-Hi seated himself at the table.

Absolute silence reigned in the big room, except for the hissing of the furnace. No sound penetrated from the outer world. Having no means of judging how long he had been insensible, Stuart found himself wondering if the raid on the den of Ah-Fang-Fu had taken place hours before, days earlier, or weeks ago.

Taking up a test-tube from a rack on the table, Fo-Hi held it near a lamp and examined the contents—a few drops of colourless fluid. These he poured into a curious long-necked yellow bottle. He began to speak, but without looking at Stuart.

His diction was characteristic, resembling his carriage in that it was slow and distinctive. He seemed deliberately to choose each word and to give to it all its value, syllable by syllable. His English was perfect to the verge of the pedantic; and his voice was metallic and harsh, touching at times, when his words were vested with some subtle or hidden significance, guttural depths which betrayed the Chinaman. He possessed uncanny dignity as of tremendous intellect and conscious power.

"I regret that you were so rash as to take part in last night's abortive raid, Dr. Stuart," he said.

Stuart started. So he had been unconscious for many hours!

"Because of your professional acquirements at one time I had contemplated removing you," continued the unemotional voice. "But I rejoice to think that I failed. It would have been an error of judgment. I have useful work for such men. You shall assist in the extensive laboratories of my distinguished predecessor."

"Never!" snapped Stuart.

The man's callousness was so purposeful and deliberate that it awed. He seemed like one who stands above all ordinary human frailties and emotions.

"Your prejudice is natural," rejoined Fo-Hi calmly. "You are ignorant of our sublime motives. But you shall nevertheless assist us to establish that intellectual control which is destined to be the new World Force. No doubt you are conscious of a mental hiatus extending from the moment when you found the pigtail of the worthy Ah-Fang-Fu about your throat until that when you recovered consciousness in this room. It has covered a period roughly of twenty-four hours, Dr. Stuart."

"I don't believe it," muttered Stuart—and found his own voice to seem as unreal as everything else in the nightmare apartment. "If I had not revived earlier, I should never have revived at all."

He raised his hand to his swollen throat, touching it gingerly.

"Your unconsciousness was prolonged," explained Fo-Hi, consulting an open book written in Chinese characters, "by an injection which I found it necessary to make. Otherwise, as you remark, it would have been prolonged indefinitely. Your clever but rash companion was less happy."

"What!" cried Stuart—"he is dead? You fiend! You damned yellow fiend!" Emotion shook him and he sat clutching the leopard-skins and glaring madly at the cowled figure.

"Fortunately," resumed Fo-Hi, "my people—with one exception—succeeded in making their escape. I may add that the needless scuffling attendant upon arresting this unfortunate follower of mine, immediately outside the door of the house, led to the discovery of your own presence. Nevertheless, the others departed safely. My own departure is imminent; it has been delayed because of certain domestic details and by the necessity of awaiting nightfall. You see, I am frank with you."

"Because the grave is silent!"

"The grave, and . . . China. There is no other alternative in your case."

"Are you sure that there is no other in your own?" asked Stuart huskily.

"An alternative to my returning to China? Can you suggest one?"

"The scaffold!" cried Stuart furiously, "for you and the scum who follow you!"

Fo-Hi lighted a Bunsen burner.

"I trust not," he rejoined placidly. "With two exceptions, all my people are now out of England."

Stuart's heart began to throb painfully. With two exceptions! Did Miska still remain? He conquered his anger and tried to speak calmly, recognising how he lay utterly in the power of this uncanny being and how closely his happiness was involved even if he escaped with life.

"And you?" he said.

"In these matters, Dr. Stuart," replied Fo-Hi, "I have always modelled my behavior upon that of the brilliant scientist who preceded me as European representative of our movement. Your beautiful Thames is my highway as it was his highway. No one of my immediate neighbours has ever seen me or my once extensive following enter this house." He selected an empty test-tube. "No one shall see me leave."

The unreality of it all threatened to swamp Stuart's mind again, but he forced himself to speak calmly.

"Your own escape is just possible, if some vessel awaits you; but do you imagine for a moment that you can carry me to China and elude pursuit?"

Fo-Hi, again consulting the huge book with its yellow faded characters, answered him absently.

"Do you recall the death of the Grand Duke Ivan?" he said. "Does your memory retain the name of Van Rembold and has your Scotland Yard yet satisfied itself that Sir Frank Narcombe died from 'natural causes'? Then, there was Ericksen, the most brilliant European electrical expert of the century, who died quite suddenly last year. I honor you, Dr. Stuart, by inviting you to join a company so distinguished."

"You are raving! What have these men in common with me?"

Stuart found himself holding his breath as he awaited a reply—for he knew that he was on the verge of learning that which poor Gaston Max had given his life to learn. A moment Fo-Hi hesitated—and in that moment his captive recognised, and shuddered to recognise that he won this secret too late. Then:

"The Grand Duke is a tactician who, had he remained in Europe, might well have readjusted the frontiers of his country. Van Rembold, as a mining engineer, stands alone, as does Henrik Ericksen in the electrical world. As for Sir Frank Narcombe, he is beyond doubt the most brilliant surgeon of today, and I, a judge of men, count you his peer in the realm of pure therapeutics. Whilst your studies in snake-poisons (which were narrowly watched for us in India) give you an unique place in toxicology. These great men will be some of your companions in China."

"In China!"

"In China, Dr. Stuart, where I hope you will join them. You misapprehend the purpose of my mission. It is not destructive, although neither I nor my enlightened predecessor have ever scrupled to remove any obstacle from the path of that world-change which no human power can check or hinder; it is primarily constructive. No state or group of states can hope to resist the progress of a movement guided and upheld by a monopoly of the world's genius. The Sublime Order, of which I am an unworthy member, stands for such a movement."

"Rest assured it will be crushed."

"Van Rembold is preparing radium in quantities hitherto unknown from the vast pitchblend deposits of Ho-Nan —which industry we control. He visited China arrayed in his shroud, and he travelled in a handsome Egyptian sarcophagus purchased at Sotherby's on behalf of a Chinese collector."

Fo-Hi stood up and crossed to the hissing furnace. He busied himself with some obscure experiment which proceeded there, and:

"Your own state-room will be less romantic, Dr. Stuart," he said, speaking without turning his head; "possibly a packing-case. In brief, that intellectual giant who achieved so much for the Sublime Order—my immediate predecessor in office—devised a means of inducing artificial catalepsy——"

"My God!" muttered Stuart, as the incredible, the appalling truth burst upon his mind.

"My own rather hazardous delay," continued Fo-Hi, "is occasioned in some measure by my anxiety to complete the present experiment. Its product will be your passport to China."

Carrying a tiny crucible, he returned to the table.

Stuart felt that his self-possession was deserting him. Madness threatened . . . if he was not already mad. He forced himself to speak.

"You taunt me because I am helpless. I do not believe that those men have been spirited into China. Even if it were so, they would die, as I would die, rather than prostitute their talents to such mad infamy."

Fo-Hi carefully poured the contents of the crucible into a flat platinum pan.

"In China, Dr. Stuart," he said, "we know how to *make* men work! I myself am the deviser of a variant of the

unduly notorious *kite* device and the scarcely less celebrated 'Six Gates of Wisdom.' I term it The Feast of a
Thousand Ants. It is performed with the aid of African
driver ants, a pair of surgical scissors and a pot of honey.
I have observed you studying with interest the human
skeleton yonder. It is that of one of my followers—a Nubian
mute—who met with an untimely end quite recently. You
are wondering, no doubt, how I obtained the frame in so
short a time? My African driver ants, Dr. Stuart, of which
I have three large cases in a cellar below this room, performed the task for me in exactly sixty-nine minutes."

Stuart strained frenziedly at his gyves.

"My God!" he groaned. "All I have heard of you was
the merest flattery. You are either a fiend or a madman!"

"When you are enlisted as a member of the Sublime
Order," said Fo-Hi softly, "and you awaken in China, Dr.
Stuart—you will work. We have no unwilling recruits."

"Stop your accursed talk. I have heard enough."

But the metallic voice continued smoothly:

"I appreciate the difficulty which you must experience in
grasping the true significance of this movement. You have
seen mighty nations, armed with every known resource of
science, at a deadlock on the battlefield. You naturally fail
to perceive how a group of Oriental philosophers can
achieve what the might of Europe failed to achieve. You
will remember, in favour of my claims, that we command
the service of the world's genius, and have a financial
backing which could settle the national loans of the
world! In other words, exhumation of a large percentage
of the great men who have died in recent years would be
impossible. Their tombs are empty."

"I have heard enough. Drug me, kill me; but spare me
your confidences."

"In the crowded foyer of a hotel," continued Fo-Hi im-
perturbably, "of a theatre, of a concert-room; in the pri-
vacy of their home, of their office; wherever opportunity
offered, I caused them to be touched with the point of a
hypodermic needle such as this." He held up a small
hypodermic syringe.

"It contained a minute quantity of the serum which I
am now preparing—the serum whose discovery was the
crowning achievement of a great scientist's career (I refer, Dr. Stuart, to my brilliant predecessor). They were
buried alive; but no surgeon in Europe or America would
have hesitated to certify them dead. Aided by a group of

six Hindu fanatics, trained as *Lughaîs* (grave-diggers), it was easy to gain access to their resting-places. One had the misfortune to be cremated by his family—a great loss to my Council. But the others are now in China, at our headquarters. They are labouring day and night to bring this war-scarred world under the sceptre of an Eastern Emperor."

"Faugh!" cried Stuart. "The whole of that war-scarred world will stand armed before you!"

"We realise that, doctor; therefore we are prepared for it. We spoke of the Norwegian Henrik Ericksen. This is his most recent contribution to our armament."

Fo-Hi rested one long yellow hand upon a kind of model searchlight.

"I nearly committed the clumsy indiscretion of removing you with this little instrument," he said. "You recall the episode? Ericksen's Disintegrating Ray, Dr. Stuart. The model, here, possesses a limited range, of course, but the actual instrument has a compass of seven and a half miles. It can readily be carried by a heavy plane! One such plane in a flight from Suez to Port Said, could destroy all the shipping in the Canal and explode every grain of ammunition on either shore! Since I must leave England to-night, the model must be destroyed, and unfortunately a good collection of bacilli has already suffered the same fate."

Placidly, slowly, and unmoved from his habit of un-ruffled dignity, Fo-Hi placed the model in a deep mortar, whilst Stuart watched him speechless and aghast. He poured the contents of a large pan into the mortar, where-upon a loud hissing sound broke the awesome silence of the room and a cloud of fumes arose.

"Not a trace, doctor!" said the cowled man. "A little preparation of my own. It destroys the hardest known substance—with the solitary exception of a certain clay—in the same way that nitric acid would destroy tissue paper. You see I might have aspired to become famous among safe-breakers."

"You have preferred to become infamous among mur-derers!" snapped Stuart.

"To murder, Dr. Stuart, I have never stooped. I am a specialist in selective warfare. When you visit the labora-tory of our chief chemist in Kiangsu you will be shown the whole of the armory of the Sublime Order. I regret that the activities of your zealous and painfully inquisitive friend, M. Gaston Max, have forced me to depart from England before I had completed my work here."

"I pray you may never depart," murmured Stuart.

Fo-Hi having added some bright green fluid to that in the flat pan, had now poured the whole into a large test-tube, and was holding it in the flame of the burner. At the moment that it reached the boiling point it became colourless. He carefully placed the whole of the liquid in a retort to which he attached a condenser. He stood up.

Crossing to a glass case which rested upon a table near the *diwan* he struck it lightly with his hand. The case contained sand and fragments of rock, but as Fo-Hi struck it, out from beneath the pieces of rock darted black active creatures.

"The common black scorpion of Southern India," he said softly. "Its venom is the basis of the priceless formula, *F. Katalepsis*, upon which the structure of our Sublime Order rests, Dr. Stuart; hence the adoption of a scorpion as our device."

He took up a long slender flask.

"This virus prepared from a glandular secretion of the Chinese swamp-adder is also beyond price. Again—the case upon the pedestal yonder contains five perfect bulbs, three already in flower, as you observe, of an orchid discovered by our chief chemist in certain forests of Burma. It only occurs at extremely rare intervals—eighty years or more—and under highly special conditions. If the other two bulbs flower, I shall be enabled to obtain from the blooms a minimum quantity of an essential oil for which the nations of the earth, if they knew its properties, would gladly empty their treasuries. This case must at all costs accompany me."

"Yet because you are still in England," said Stuart huskily, "I venture to hope that your devil dreams may end on the scaffold."

"That can never be, Dr. Stuart," returned Fo-Hi placidly. "The scaffold is not for such as I. Moreover, it is a crude and barbaric institution which I deplore. Do you see that somewhat peculiarly constructed chair, yonder? It is an adaptation, by a brilliant young chemist of Canton, of Ericksen's Disintegrating Ray. A bell hangs beside it. If you were seated in that chair and I desired to dismiss you, it would merely be necessary for me to strike the bell once with the hammer. Before the vibration of the note had become inaudible you would be seeking your ancestors among the shades. It is the throne of the gods. Such a death is poetic."

He returned to the table and, observing meticulous care, emptied the few drops of colourless liquid from the condenser into a test-tube. Holding the tube near a lamp, he examined the contents, then poured the liquid into the curious yellow bottle. A faint vapor arose from it.

"You would scarcely suppose," he said, "that yonder window opens upon an ivy-grown balcony commanding an excellent view of that picturesque Tudor survival, Hampton Court? I apprehend, however, that the researches of your late friend, M. Gaston Max, may ere long lead Scotland Yard to my doors, although there has been nothing in the outward seeming of this house, in the circumstances of my tenancy, or in my behaviour since I have—secretly —resided here, to excite local suspicion."

"Scotland Yard men may surround the house now!" said Stuart viciously.

"One of the two followers I have retained here with me, watches at the gate," replied Fo-Hi. "An intruder seeking to enter by any other route, through the hedge, over the wall, or from the river, would cause electric bells to ring loudly in this room, the note of the bell signifying the point of entry. Finally, in the event of such a surprise, I have an exit whereby one emerges at a secret spot on the river bank. A motor-boat, suitably concealed, awaits me there."

He placed a thermometer in the neck of the yellow bottle and the bottle in a rack. He directed the intolerable gaze of his awful eyes upon the man who sat, teeth tightly clenched, watching him from the *diwan*.

"Ten minutes of life—in England—yet remain to you, Dr. Stuart. In ten minutes this fluid will have cooled to a temperature of 99 degrees, when I shall be enabled safely to make an injection. You will be reborn in Kiangsu."

Fo-Hi walked slowly to the door whereby he had entered, opened it and went out. The door closed.

## Chapter 2

## THE LIVING DEATH

THE little furnace hissed continuously. A wisp of smoke floated up from the incense-burner.

Stuart sat with his hands locked between his knees, and his gaze set upon the yellow flask.

Even now he found it difficult to credit the verity of his case. He found it almost impossible to believe that such a being as Fo-Hi existed, that such deeds had been done, were being done, in England, as those of which he had heard from the sinister cowled man. Save for the hissing of the furnace and the clanking of the chain as he strove with all his strength to win freedom, that wonderful evil room was silent as the King's Chamber at the heart of the Great Pyramid.

His gaze reverted to the yellow flask.

"Oh, my God!" he groaned.

Terror claimed him—the terror which he had with difficulty been fending off throughout that nightmare interview with Fo-Hi. Madness threatened him, and he was seized by an almost incontrollable desire to shout execrations—prayers—he knew not what. He clenched his teeth grimly and tried to think, to plan.

He had two chances:

The statement left with Inspector Dunbar, in which he had mentioned the existence of a house "near Hampton Court," and . . . Miska.

That she was one of the two exceptions mentioned by Fo-Hi he felt assured. But was she in this house, and did she know of his presence there? Even so, had she access to that room of mysteries—of horrors?

And who was the other who remained? Almost certainly it was the fanatical Hindu, Chunda Lal, of whom she had spoken with such palpable terror and who watched her unceasingly, untiringly. *He* would prevent her intervening even if she had power to intervene.

His great hope, then, was in Dunbar . . . for Gaston Max was dead.

At the coming of that thought, the foul doing to death of the fearless Frenchman, he gnashed his teeth savagely and strained at the gyves until the pain in his ankles brought out beads of perspiration upon his forehead.

He dropped his head into his hands and frenziedly clutched at his hair with twitching fingers.

The faint sound occasioned by the opening of one of the sliding doors brought him sharply upright.

Miska entered!

She looked so bewilderingly beautiful that terror and sorrow fled, leaving Stuart filled only with passionate admiration. She wore an Eastern dress of gauzy shimmering silk and high-heeled gilt Turkish slippers upon her stockingless feet. About her left ankle was a gold bangle, and there was barbaric jewellery upon her arms. She was a figure unreal as all else in that house of dreams, but a figure so lovely that Stuart forgot the yellow flask . . . forgot that less than ten minutes of life remained to him.

"Miska!" he whispered—"Miska!"

She exhibited intense but repressed excitement and fear. Creeping to the second door—that by which Fo-Hi had gone out—she pressed her ear to the lacquered panel and listened intently. Then coming swiftly to the table, she took up a bunch of keys, approached Stuart and, kneeling, unlocked the gyves. The scent of jasmine stole to his nostrils.

"God bless you!" he said with stifled ardour.

She rose quickly to her feet, standing before him with head downcast. Stuart rose with difficulty. His legs were cramped and aching. He grasped Miska's hand and endeavoured to induce her to look up. One swift glance she gave him and looked away again.

"You must go—this instant," she said. "I show you the way. There is not a moment to lose. . . ."

"Miska!"

She glanced at him again.

"You must come with me!"

"Ah!" she whispered—"that is impossible! Have I not told you so?"

"You have told me, but I cannot understand. Here, in England, you are free. Why should you remain with that cowled monster?"

"Shall I tell you?" she asked, and he could feel how she

trembled. "If I tell you, will you promise to believe me—and to go?"

"Not without you!"

"Ah, no, no! If I tell you that my only chance of life—such a little, little chance—is to stay, will you go?"

Stuart secured her other hand and drew her towards him, half resisting.

"Tell me," he said softly. "I will believe you—and if it can spare you one moment of pain or sorrow, I will go as you ask me."

"Listen," she whispered, glancing fearfully back toward the closed door—"Fo-Hi has something that makes people to die; and only he can bring them to life again. Do you believe this?"

She looked up at him rapidly, her wonderful eyes wide and fearful. He nodded.

"Ah! you know! Very well. On that day in Cairo, which I am taken before him—you remember, I tell you?—he ... oh!"

She shuddered wildly and hid her beautiful face against Stuart's breast. He threw his arms about her.

"Tell me," he said.

"With the needle, he ... inject ..."

"Miska!"

Stuart felt the blood rushing to his heart and knew that he had paled.

"There is something else," she went on, almost inaudibly, "with which he gives life again to those he has made dead with the needle. It is a light green liquid tasting like bitter apples; and once each week for six months it must be drunk or else ... the living death comes. Sometimes I have not seen Fo-Hi for six months at a time, but a tiny flask, one draught, of the green liquid, always comes to me wherever I am, every week ... and twice each year I see him—Fo-Hi ... and he ..."

Her voice quivered and ceased. Moving back, she slipped a soft shoulder free of its flimsy covering.

Stuart looked—and suppressed a groan.

Her arm was dotted with the tiny marks made by a hypodermic syringe!

"You see?" she whispered tremulously. "If I go, I die, and I am buried alive ... or else I live until my body ..."

"Oh, God!" moaned Stuart—"the fiend! the merciless, cunning fiend! Is there *nothing* ..."

"Yes, yes!" said Miska, looking up. "If I can get enough

of the green fluid and escape. But he tell me once—it was in
America—that he only prepares one tiny draught at a time!
Listen! I must stay, and if he can be captured he must be
forced to make this antidote . . . Ah! go! go!"

Her words ended in a sob, and Stuart held her to him
convulsively, his heart filled with such helpless, fierce
misery and bitterness as he had never known.

"Go, please go!" she whispered. "It is my only chance
—there is no other. There is not a moment to wait. Listen
to me! You will go by that door by which I come in. There
is a better way, through a tunnel he has made to the
river bank; but I cannot open the door. Only *he* has the
key. At the end of the passage some one is waiting———"

"Chunda Lal!"

Miska glanced up rapidly and then drooped her eyes
again.

"Yes—poor Chunda Lal. He is my only friend. Give him
this."

She removed an amulet upon a gold chain from about
her neck and thrust it into Stuart's hand.

"It seems to you silly, but Chunda Lal is of the East;
and he has promised. Oh! be quick! I am afraid. I tell you
something. Fo-Hi does not know, but the police Inspector
and many men search the river bank for the house! I see
them from a window———"

"What!" cried Stuart—"Dunbar is here!"

"*Shh! ssh!*" Miska clutched him wildly. "*He* is not far
away. You will go and bring him here. No! for me do not
fear. I put the keys back and he will think you have opened
the lock by some trick———"

"Miska!"

"Oh, no more!"

She slipped from his arms, crossed and reopened the
lacquered door, revealing a corridor dimly lighted. Stuart
followed and looked along the corridor.

"Right to the end," she whispered, "and down the steps.
You know"—touching the amulet which Stuart carried—
"how to deal with—Chunda Lal."

But still he hesitated; until she seized his hand and
urged him. Thereupon he swept her wildly into his arms.

"Miska! how can I leave you! It is maddening!"

"You must! you must!"

He looked into her eyes, stooped and kissed her upon
the lips. Then, with no other word, he tore himself away
and walked quickly along the corridor. Miska watched

him until he was out of sight, then re-entered the great
room and closed the door. She turned, and:

"Oh, God of mercy" she whispered.

Just within the second doorway stood Fo-Hi watching
her.

## Chapter 3

## THE FIFTH SECRET OF RACHE CHURAN

STRICKEN silent with fear, Miska staggered back against
the lacquered door, dropping the keys which she held in
her hand. Fo-Hi had removed the cowled garment and was
now arrayed in a rich mandarin robe. Through the grotesque green veil which obscured his features the brilliant
eyes shone catlike.

"So," he said softly, "you speed the parting guest.
And did I not hear the sound of a chaste salute?"

Miska watched him, wild-eyed.

"And he knows," continued the metallic voice, " 'how to
deal with Chunda Lal'? But it may be that Chunda Lal will
know how to deal with *him!* I had suspected that Dr.
Keppel Stuart entertained an unprofessional interest in
his charming patient. Your failure to force the bureau
drawer in his study excited my suspicion—unjustly, I admit; for did not I fail also when I paid the doctor a personal
visit? True, I was disturbed. But this suspicion later returned. It was in order that some lingering doubt might
be removed that I afforded you the opportunity of inter-
viewing my guest. But whatever surprise his ingenuity,
aided by your woman's wit, has planned for Chunda Lal,
I dare to believe that Chunda Lal, being forewarned, will
meet successfully. He is expecting an attempt, by Dr.
Stuart, to leave this house. He has my orders to detain
him."

At that, anger conquered terror in the heart of Miska,
and:

"You mean he has your orders to kill him!" she cried
desperately.

Fo-Hi closed the door.

"On the contrary, he has my orders to take every possible care of him. Those blind, tempestuous passions which merely make a woman more desirable find no place in the trained mind of the scientist. That Dr. Stuart covets my choicest possession in no way detracts from his value to my Council."

Miska had never moved from the doorway by which Stuart had gone out; and now, having listened covertly and heard no outcry, her faith in Chunda Lal was restored. Her wonderful eyes narrowed momentarily, and she spoke with the guile, which seems so naïve, of the Oriental woman.

"I care nothing for him—this Dr. Stuart. But he had done you no wrong——"

"Beyond seeking my death—none. I have already said"—the eyes of Fo-Hi gleamed through the hideous veil—"that I bear him no ill will."

"But you plan to carry him to China—like those others."

"I assign him a part in the New Renaissance—yes. In the Deluge that shall engulf the world, his place is in the Ark. I honor him."

"Perhaps he rather remain a—nobody—than be so honored."

"In his present state of imperfect understanding it is quite possible," said Fo-Hi smoothly. "But if he refuses to achieve greatness he must have greatness thrust upon him. Van Rembold, I seem to recall, hesitated for some time to direct his genius to the problem of producing radium in workable quantities from the pitchblend deposits of Ho-Nan. But the *split rod* had not been applied to the soles of his feet more than five times ere he reviewed his prejudices and found them to be surmountable."

Miska, knowing well the moods of the monstrous being whose unveiled face she had never seen, was not deceived by the suavity of his manner. Nevertheless, she fought down her terror, knowing how much might depend upon her retaining her presence of mind. How much of her interview with Stuart he had overheard she did not know, nor how much he had witnessed.

"But," she said, moving away from him, "he does not matter—this one. Forgive me if I think to let him go; but I am afraid——"

Fo-Hi crossed slowly, intercepting her.

"Ah!" said Miska, her eyes opening widely—"you are going to punish me again! For why? Because I am a woman and cannot always be cruel?"

From its place on the wall Fo-Hi took a whip. At that:

"Ah! no, no!" she cried. "You drive me mad! I am only in part of the East and I cannot bear it—I cannot bear it! You teach me to be like the women of England, who are free, and you treat me like the women of China, who are slaves. Once, it did not matter. I thought it was part of a woman's life to be treated so. But now I cannot bear it!" She stamped her foot fiercely upon the floor. "I tell you I cannot bear it!"

Whip in hand, Fo-Hi stood watching her.

"You release that man—for whom you 'care nothing'—in order that he may bring my enemies about me, in order that he may hand me over to the barbarous law of England. Now, you 'cannot bear' so light a rebuke as the whip. Here, I perceive, is some deep psychological change. Such protests do not belong to the women of my country; they are never heard in the *zenana,* and would provoke derision in the *harêms* of Stambûl."

"You have trained me to know that life in a *harêm* is not life, but only the existence of an animal."

"I have trained you—yes. What fate was before you when I intervened in that Mecca slave-market? You who are 'only in part of the East.' Do you forget so soon how you cowered there amongst the others, Arabs, Circassians, Georgians, Nubians, striving to veil your beauty from those ravenous eyes? From *what* did I rescue you?"

"And *for* what?" cried Miska bitterly. "To use me as a lure—and beat me if I failed."

Fo-Hi stood watching her, and slowly, as he watched, terror grew upon her and she retreated before him, step by step. He made no attempt to follow her, but continued to watch. Then, raising the whip he broke it across his knee and dropped the pieces on the floor.

At that she extended her hands towards him pitifully.

"Oh! what are you going to do to me!" she said. "Let me go! let me go! I can no more be of use to you. Give me back my life and let me go—let me go and hide away from them all—from all . . . the world. . . ."

Her words died away and ceased upon a supprest hysterical sob. For, in silence, Fo-Hi stood watching her, unmoved.

"Oh!" she moaned, and sank cowering upon a dîwan—
"why do you watch me so!"

"Because," came the metallic voice, softly—"you are
beautiful with a beauty given but rarely to the daughters
of men. The Sublime Order has acquired many pretty
women—for they are potent weapons—but none so fair as
you. Miska, I would make life sweet for you."

"Ah! you do not mean that!" she whispered fearfully.

"Have I not clothed you in the raiment of a princess!"
continued Fo-Hi. "To-night, at my urgent request, you
wear the charming national costume in which I delight to
see you. But is there a woman of Paris, of London, of New
York, who has such robes, such jewels, such apartments
as you possess? Perhaps the peculiar duties which I have
required you to perform, the hideous disguises which you
have sometimes been called upon to adopt, have dis-
gusted you."

Her heart beating wildly, for she did not know this mood
but divined it to portend some unique horror, Miska
crouched, head averted.

"To-night the hour has come to break the whip. To-night
the master in me dies. My cloak of wise authority has
fallen from me and I offer myself in bondage to *you*—my
slave!"

"This is some trap you set for me!" she whispered.

But Fo-Hi, paying no heed to her words, continued in
the same rapt voice:

"Truly have you observed that the Chinese wife is but a
slave to her lord. I have said that the relation of master
and slave is ended between us. I offer you a companionship
that signifies absolute freedom and perfect understanding. Half of all I have—and the world lies in my grasp—is
yours. I offer a throne set upon the Seven Mountains of
the Universe. Look into my eyes and read the truth."

But lower and lower she cowered upon the *dîwan*.

"No, no! I am afraid!"

Fo-Hi approached her closely and abject terror now
had robbed her of strength. Her limbs seemed to have
become numbed, her tongue clave to the roof of her mouth.

"Fear me no more, Miska," said Fo-Hi. "I *will* you
nothing but joy. The man who has learned the Fifth Secret
of Rachê Churân—who has learned how to control his will
—holds a power absolute and beyond perfectability. You
know, who have dwelt beneath my roof, that there is no

escape from my will." His calm was terrible, and his glance, through the green veil, was like a ray of scorching heat. His voice sank lower and lower.

"There is one frailty, Miska, that even the Adept cannot conquer. It is inherent in every man. Miska, I would not *force* you to grasp the joy I offer; I would have you *accept* it willingly. No! do not turn from me! No woman in all the world has every heard me plead, as I plead to you. Never before have I *sued* for favours. Do not turn from me, Miska."

Slightly, the metallic voice vibrated, and the ruffling of that giant calm was a thing horrible to witness. Fo-Hi extended his long yellow hands, advancing step by step until he stood over the cowering girl. Irresistibly her glance was drawn to those blazing eyes which the veil could not hide, and as she met that unblinking gaze her own eyes dilated and grew fixed as those of a sleep walker. A moment Fo-Hi stood so. Then passion swept him from his feet and he seized her fiercely.

"Your eyes drive me mad!" he hissed. "Your lips taunt me, and I know all earthly greatness to be a mirage, its conquests visions, and its fairness dust. I would rather be a captive in your white arms than the emperor of heaven! Your sweetness intoxicates me, Miska. A fever burns me up!"

Helpless, enmeshed in the toils of that mighty will, Miska raised her head; and gradually her expression changed. Fear was smoothed away from her lovely face as by some magic brush. She grew placid; and finally she smiled—the luresome, caressing smile of the East. Nearer and nearer drew the green veil. Then, uttering a sudden fierce exclamation, Fo-Hi thrust her from him.

"That smile is not for *me*, the man!" he cried gutturally. "Ah! I could curse the power that I coveted and set above all earthly joys! I who boasted that he could control his will—I read in your eyes that I am *willing* you to love me! I seek a gift and can obtain but a tribute!"

Miska, with a sobbing moan, sank upon the *dïwan*. Fo-Hi stood motionless, looking straight before him. His terrible calm was restored.

"It is a bitter truth," he said—"that to win the world I have bartered the birthright of men: the art of winning a woman's heart. There is much in our Chinese wisdom. I erred in breaking the whip. I erred in doubting my own prescience, which told me that the smiles I could not woo were given freely to another . . . and perhaps the kisses. At least I can set these poor frail human doubts at rest."

He crossed and struck a gong which hung midway between the two doors.

## Chapter 4

## THE GUILE OF THE EAST

HER beautiful face a mask of anguish, Miska cowered upon the *dîwan,* watching the closed doors. Fo-Hi stood in the centre of the great room with his back to the entrance. Silently one of the lacquered panels slid open and Chunda Lal entered. He saluted the figure of the veiled Chinaman but never once glanced in the direction of the *dîwan* from which Miska wildly was watching him.

Without turning his head, Fo-Hi, who seemed to detect the presence of the silent Hindu by means of some fifth sense, pointed to a bundle of long rods stacked in a corner of the room.

His brown face expressionless as that of a bronze statue, Chunda Lal crossed and took the rods from their place.

*"Tûm samajhte ho?"* (Do you understand?) said Fo-Hi. Chunda Lal inclined his head.

*"Mâin tûmhâri bat manûnga"* (Your orders shall be obeyed), he replied.

"Ah, God! no!" whispered Miska—"what are you going to do?"

"Your Hindustani was ever poor, Miska," said Fo-Hi.

He turned to Chunda Lal.

"Until you hear the gong," he said in English.

Miska leapt to her feet, as Chunda Lal, never once glancing at her, went out bearing the rods, and closed the door behind him. Fo-Hi turned and confronted her.

*"Ta'ala hîna* (come hither), Miska!" he said softly. "Shall I speak to you in the soft Arab tongue? Come to me, lovely Miska. Let me feel how that sorrowful heart will leap like a captive gazelle."

But Miska shrank back from him, pale to the lips.

"Very well." His metallic voice sank to a hiss. "I employ no force. You shall yield me your heart as a love offering. Of such motives as jealousy and revenge you know me to be incapable. What I do, I do with a purpose. That compassion of yours shall be a lever to cast you into my arms. Your hatred you shall conquer."

"Oh, have you no mercy? Is there *nothing* human in your heart? Did I say I hate you!"

"Your eyes are eloquent, Miska. I cherish two memories of those beautiful eyes. One is of their fear and loathing—of *me;* the other is of their sweet softness when they watched the departure of my guest. Listen! Do you hear nothing?"

In an attitude of alert and fearful attention Miska stood listening. Fo-Hi watched her through the veil with those remorseless blazing eyes.

"I will open the door," he said smoothly, "that we may more fully enjoy the protests of one for whom you 'care nothing'—of one whose lips have pressed—your hand."

He opened the door by which Chunda Lal had gone out and turned again to Miska. Her eyes looked unnaturally dark by contrast with the pallor of her face.

Chunda Lal had betrayed her. She no longer doubted it. For he had not dared to meet her glance. His fear of Fo-Hi had overcome his love for her . . . and Stuart had been treacherously seized somewhere in the corridors and rendered helpless by the awful art of the thug.

"There is a brief interval," hissed the evil voice. "Chunda Lal is securing him to the frame and baring the soles of his feet for the caresses of the rod."

Suddenly, from somewhere outside the room, came a sound of dull, regular blows . . . then, a smothered moan!

Miska sprang forward and threw herself upon her knees before Fo-Hi, clutching at his robe frantically.

"Ah! merciful God! he is there! Spare him! spare him! No more—no more!"

"He is there?" repeated Fo-Hi suavely. "Assuredly he is there, Miska. I know not by what trick he hoped to 'deal with' Chunda Lal. But, as I informed you, Chunda Lal was forewarned."

The sound of blows continued, followed by that of another, louder groan.

"Stop him! Stop him!" shrieked Miska.

"You 'care nothing' for this man. Why do you tremble?"

"Oh!" she wailed piteously. "I cannot bear it . . . oh, I cannot bear it! Do what you like with me, but spare him. Ah! you have no mercy."

Fo-Hi handed her the hammer for striking the gong.

"It is *you* who have no mercy," he replied. "I have asked but one gift. The sound of the gong will end Dr. Stuart's discomfort . . . and will mean that you *voluntarily* accept my offer. What! you hesitate?" A stifled scream rang out sharply.

"Ah, yes! yes!"

Miska ran and struck the gong, then staggered back to the *dîwan* and fell upon it, hiding her face in her hands. The sounds of torture ceased.

Fo-Hi closed the door and stood looking at her where she lay.

"I permit you some moments of reflection," he said, "in order that you may compose yourself to receive the addresses which I shall presently have the honour, and joy, of making to you. Yes—this door is unlocked." He threw the keys on the table. "I respect your promise . . . and Chunda Lal guards the *outer* exits."

He opened the further door, by which he had entered, and went out.

Miska, through the fingers of her shielding hands, watched him go.

When he had disappeared she sprang up, clenching her teeth, and her face was contorted with anguish. She began to move aimlessly about the room, glancing at the many strange objects on the big table and looking long and fearfully at the canopied chair beside which hung the bronze bell. Finally:

"Oh, Chunda Lal! Chunda Lal!" she moaned, and threw herself face downward on the *dîwan*, sobbing wildly.

So she lay, her whole body quivering with the frenzy of her emotions, and as she lay there, inch by inch, cautiously, the nearer door began to open.

Chunda Lal looked in.

Finding the room to be occupied only by Miska, he crossed rapidly to the *dîwan*, bending over her with infinite pity and tenderness.

"Miska!" he whispered softly.

As though an adder had touched her, Miska sprang to her feet—and back from the Hindu. Her eyes flashed fiercely.

"Ah! *you! you!*" she cried at him, with a repressed

savagery that spoke of the Oriental blood in her veins. "Do not speak to me—look at me! Do not come near me! I hate you! God! how I hate you!"

"Miska! Miska!" he said beseechingly—"you pierce my heart! you kill me! Can you not understand——"

"Go! go!"

She drew back from him, clenching and unclenching her jewelled fingers and glaring madly into his eyes.

"Look, Miska!" He took the gold chain and amulet from his bosom. "Your token! Can you not understand! *Yah Allah!* how little you trust me—and I would die for one glance of your eyes! *He*—Stuart Sahib—has gone, gone long since!"

"Ah! Chunda Lal!"

Miska swayed dizzily and extended her hands towards him. Chunda Lal glanced fearfully about him.

"Did I not," he whispered, with an intense ardour in his soft voice,—"did I not lay my life, my service, all I have, at your feet? Did I not vow to serve you in the name of *Bhowânî!* He is long since gone to bring his friends— who are searching from house to house along the river. At any moment they may be here!"

Miska dropped weakly upon her knees before him and clasped his hand.

"Chunda Lal, my friend! Oh, forgive me!" Her voice broke. "Forgive . . ."

Chunda Lal raised her gently.

"Not upon your knees to *me*, Miska. It was a little thing to do—for you. Did I not tell you that—*he*—had cast his eyes upon you? Mine was the voice you heard to cry out. Ah! you do not know; it is to gain *time* that I seem to serve *him!* Only this, Miska"—he revealed the blade of a concealed knife—"stand between Fo-Hi and— you! Had I not read it in his eyes!"

He raised his glance upward frantically.

"*Jey Bhowânî!* give me strength, give me courage! For if I fail . . ."

He glared at her passionately, clutching his bosom; then, pressing the necklet to his lips, he concealed it again, and bent, whispering urgently:

"Listen again—I reveal it to you without price or hope of reward, for I know there is no love in your heart to give, Miska; I know that it takes you out of my sight for always. But I tell you what I learn in the house of Abdûl Rozân. Your life is your own, Miska! With the needle"—

yet closer he bent to her ear and even softer he spoke—"he pricks your white skin—no more! The vial he sends contains a harmless cordial!"

"Chunda Lal!"

Miska swayed again dizzily, clutching at the Hindu for support.

"Quick! fly!" he said, leading her to the door. "I will see *he* does not pursue!"

"No, no! you shall shed no blood for me! Not even . . . *his.* You come also!"

"And if he escape, and know that I was false to him, he will *call me back,* and I shall be dragged to those yellow eyes, though I am a thousand miles away! *Inshalla!* those eyes! No—I must strike swift, or he robs me of my strength."

For a long moment Miska hesitated.

"Then, I also remain, Chunda Lal, my friend! We will wait—and watch—and listen for the bells—here—that tell they are in the grounds of the house."

"Ah, Miska!"—the glance of the Hindu grew fearful— "you are clever—but *he* is the Evil One! I fear for you. Fly now. There is yet time . . ."

A faint sound attracted Miska's attention. Placing a quivering finger to her lips, she gently thrust Chunda Lal out into the corridor.

"He returns!" she whispered: "If I call—come to me, my friend. But we have not long to wait!"

She closed the door.

## Chapter 5

### WHAT HAPPENED TO STUART

STUART had gained the end of the corridor, unmolested. There he found a short flight of steps, which he descended and came to a second corridor forming a right angle with the first. A lamp was hung at the foot of the steps, and by its light he discerned a shadowy figure standing at the further end of this second passage.

A moment he hesitated, peering eagerly along the corridor. The man who waited was Chunda Lal. Stuart approached him and silently placed in his hand the gold amulet.

Chunda Lal took it as one touching something holy, and raising it he kissed it with reverence. His dark eyes were sorrowful. Long and ardently he pressed the little trinket to his lips, then concealed it under the white robe which he wore and turned to Stuart. His eyes were sorrowful no more, but fierce as the eyes of a tiger.

"Follow!" he said.

He unlocked a door and stepped out into a neglected garden, Stuart close at his heels. The sky was cloudy, and the moon obscured. Never glancing back, Chunda Lal led the way along a path skirting a high wall upon which climbing fruit trees were growing until they came to a second door and this also the Hindu unlocked. He stood aside.

"To the end of this lane," he said, in his soft queerly modulated voice, "and along the turning to the left to the river bank. Follow the bank towards the palace and you will meet them."

"I owe you my life," said Stuart.

"Go! you owe me nothing," returned the Hindu fiercely.

Stuart turned and walked rapidly along the lane. Once he glanced back. Chunda Lal was looking after him . . . and he detected something that gleamed in his hand, gleamed not like gold but like the blade of a knife!

Turning the corner, Stuart began to run. For he was unarmed and still weak, and there had been that in the fierce black eyes of the Hindu when he had scorned Stuart's thanks which had bred suspicion and distrust.

From the position of the moon, Stuart judged the hour to be something after midnight. No living thing stirred about him. The lane in which now he found himself was skirted on one side by a hedge beyond which was open country and on the other by a continuation of the high wall which evidently enclosed the grounds of the house that he had just quitted. A cool breeze fanned his face, and he knew that he was approaching the Thames. Ten more paces and he came to the bank.

In his weak condition the short run had exhausted him. His bruised throat was throbbing painfully, and he experienced some difficulty in breathing. He leaned up against the moss-grown wall, looking back into the darkness of the lane.

No one was in sight. There was no sound save the gentle lapping of the water upon the bank.

He would have liked to bathe his throat and to quench his feverish thirst, but a mingled hope and despair spurred him and he set off along the narrow path towards where dimly above some trees he could discern in the distance a group of red-roofed buildings. Having proceeded for a considerable distance, he stood still, listening for any sound that might guide him to the search-party—or warn him that he was followed. But he could hear nothing.

Onward he pressed, not daring to think of what the future held for him, not daring to dwell upon the memory, the maddening sweetness, of that parting kiss. His eyes grew misty, he stumbled as he walked, and became oblivious of his surroundings. His awakening was a rude one.

Suddenly a man, concealed behind a bush, sprang out upon him and bore him irresistibly to the ground!

"Not a word!" rapped his assailant, "or I'll knock you out!"

Stuart glared into the red face lowered so threateningly over his own, and:

"Sergeant Sowerby!" he gasped.

The grip upon his shoulders relaxed.

"Damn!" cried Sowerby—"if it isn't Dr. Stuart?"

"What is that!" cried another voice from the shelter of the bush. *"Pardieu!* say it again! . . . Dr. Stuart!"

And Gaston Max sprang out!

"Max!" murmured Stuart, staggering to his feet—"Max!"

*"Nom d'un nom!* Two dead men meet!" exclaimed Gaston Max. "But indeed"—he grasped Stuart by both hands and his voice shook with emotion—"I thank God that I see you!"

Stuart was dazed. Words failed him, and he swayed dizzily.

"I thought *you* were murdered," said Max, still grasping his hand, "and I perceive that you had made the same mistake about me! Do you know what saved me, my friend, from the consequences of that frightful blow? It was the bandage of 'Le Balafré'!"

"You must possess a skull like a negro's!" said Stuart feebly.

"I believe I have a skull like a baboon!" returned Max, laughing with joyous excitement. "And you, doctor, you must possess a steel wind-pipe; for flesh and blood could never have survived the pressure of that horrible pigtail. You will rejoice to learn that Miguel was arrested on the Dover boat-train this morning and Ah-Fang-Fu at Tilbury Dock some four hours ago. So we are both avenged! But we waste time!"

He unscrewed a flask and handed it to Stuart.

"A terrible experience has befallen you," he said. "But tell me—do you know where it is—the lair of 'The Scorpion'?"

"I do!" replied Stuart, having taken a welcome draught from the flask. "Where is Dunbar? We must carefully surround the place or he will elude us."

"Ah! as he eluded us at 'The Pidgin House'!" cried Max. "Do you know what happened? They had a motor-boat in the very cellar of that warren. At high tide they could creep out into the cutting, drawing their craft along from pile to pile, and reach the open river at a point fifty yards above the house! In the damnable darkness they escaped. But we have two of them."

"It was all my fault," said Sowerby guiltily. "I missed my spring when I went for the Chinaman who came out first, and he gave one yell. The old fox in the shop heard it and the fat was in the fire."

"You didn't miss your spring at me!" retorted Stuart ruefully.

"No," agreed Sowerby. "I didn't mean to miss a second time!"

"What's all this row," came a gruff voice.

"Ah! Inspector Dunbar!" said Max.

Dunbar walked up the path, followed by a number of men. At first he did not observe Stuart, and:

"You'll be waking all the neighborhood," he said. "It's the next big house, Sowerby, the one we thought, surrounded by the brick wall. There's no doubt, I think. . . . Why!"

He had seen Stuart, and he sprang forward with outstretched hand.

"Thank God!" he cried, disregarding his own counsel about creating a disturbance. "This is fine! Eh, man! but I'm glad to see you!"

"And *I* am glad to be here!" Stuart assured him.

They shook hands warmly.

"You have read my statement, of course?" asked Stuart.

"I have," replied the Inspector, and gave him a swift glance of the tawny eyes. "And considering that you've nearly been strangled, I'll forgive you. But I wish we'd known about this house——"

"Ah! Inspector," interrupted Gaston Max, "but you have never seen Zâra el-Khalâ! I have seen her—and *I* forgive him, also!"

Stuart continued rapidly:

"We have little time to waste. There are only three people in the house, so far as I am aware: Miska—known to you, M. Max, as Zâra el Khalâ—the Hindu, Chunda Lal, and—Fo-Hi——"

"Ah!" cried Max—" 'The Scorpion'!"

"Exactly, 'The Scorpion.' Chunda Lal, for some obscure personal reason, not entirely unconnected with Miska, enabled me to make my escape in order that I might lead you to the house. Therefore we may look upon Chunda Lal, as well as Miska, in the light of an accomplice——"

*"Eh bien!* a spy in the camp! This is where we see how fatal to the success of any enterprise, criminal or otherwise, is the presence of a pretty woman! Proceed, my friend!"

"There are three entrances to the apartment in which Fo-Hi apparently spends the greater part of his time. Two of these I know, although I am unaware where one of them leads to. But the third, of which he alone holds the key, communicates with a tunnel leading to the river bank, where a motor-boat is concealed."

"Ah, that motor-boat!" cried Max. "He travels at night, you understand——"

"Always, I am told."

"Yes, always. Therefore, once he is out on the river, he is moderately secure between the first lock and the Nore! When a police patrol is near he can shut off his engine and lie under the bank. Last night he crept away from us in that fashion. To-night is not so dark, and the River Police are watching all the way down."

"Furthermore," replied Stuart, "Chunda Lal, who acts as engineer, has it in his power to prevent Fo-Hi's escape by that route! But we must count upon the possibility of his attempting to leave by water. Therefore, in disposing your forces, place a certain number of men along the bank and below the house. Is there a River Police boat near?"

"Not nearer than Putney Bridge," answered Dunbar. "We shall have to try and block that exit."

"There's no time to waste," continued Stuart excitedly —"and I have a very particular request to make: that you will take Fo-Hi *alive.*"

"But of course," said Gaston Max, "if it is humanly possible."

Stuart repressed a groan; for even so he had little hope of inducing the awful veiled man to give back life to the woman who would have been instrumental in bringing him to the scaffold . . . and no compromise was possible!

"If you will muster your men, Inspector," he said, "I will lead you to the spot. Once we have affected an entrance we must proceed with dispatch. He has alarm bells connected with every possible point of entry."

"Lead on, my friend," cried Gaston Max. "I perceive that time is precious."

## Chapter 6

### "JEY BHOWANI!"

As the door closed upon Chunda Lal, Miska stepped back from it and stood, unconsciously, in a curiously rigid and statuesque attitude, her arms pressed to her sides and her hands directed outward. It was the physical expression of an intense mental effort to gain control of herself. Her heart was leaping wildly in her breast—for the future that had held only horror and a living tomb, now opened out sweetly before her. She had only to ply her native wiles for a few precious moments . . . and *someone* would have her in his arms, to hold her safe from harm! If the will of the awful Chinaman threatened to swamp her individuality, then—there was Chunda Lal.

But because of his helpless, unselfish love, she hesitated even at the price of remaining alone again with Fo-Hi, to demand any further sacrifice of the Hindu. Furthermore —he might fail!

The lacquer door slid noiselessly open and Fo-Hi entered. He paused, watching her.

"Ah," he said, in that low-pitched voice which was so terrifying—"a *ghazîyeh* of Ancient Egypt! How beautiful

you are, Miska! You transport me to the court of golden
Pharaoh. Miska! daughter of the moon-magic of Isis—
Zâra el-Khalâ! At any hour my enemies may be clamoring
at my doors. But *this* hour is mine!"

He moved at his customary slow gait to the table, took
up the keys . . . and locked both doors!

Miska, perceiving in this her chance of aid from Chunda
Lal utterly destroyed, sank slowly upon the *dîwan*, her
pale face expressing the utmost consternation. Suppose
the police did not come!

Fo-Hi dropped the keys on the table again and approached her. She stood up, retreating before him. He inhaled sibilantly and paused.

"So your 'acceptance' was only a trick," he said. "Your
loathing of my presence is as strong as ever. Well!" At
the word, as a volcano leaps into life, the hidden fires
which burned within this terrible man leapt up consum-
ingly—"if the gift of the flower is withheld, at least I will
grasp the Dead Sea Fruit!"

He leapt toward Miska—and she fled shrieking before
him. Running around a couch which stood near the centre
of the room, she sprang to the door and beat upon it madly.

"Chunda Lal!" she cried—"Chunda Lal!"

Fo-Hi was close upon her, and she turned striving to
elude him.

"Oh, merciful God! *Chunda Lal!*"

The name burst from her lips in a long frenzied scream.
Fo-Hi had seized her!

Grasping her shoulders, he twisted her about so that he
could look into her eyes. A low, shuddering cry died away,
and her gaze became set, hypnotically, upon Fo-Hi. He
raised one hand, fingers outstretched before her. She
swayed slightly.

"Forget!" he said in a deep, guttural voice of command
—"forget. I *will* it. We stand in an empty world, you and
I; you, Miska, and I, Fo-Hi, your master."

"My master," she whispered mechanically.

"Your lover."

"My lover."

"You give me your life, to do with as I will."

"As you will."

Fo-Hi momentarily raised the blazing eyes.

"Oh, empty shell of a vanished joy!" he cried.

Then, frenziedly grasping Miska by her arms, he glared
into her impassive face.

"Your heart leaps wildly in your breast!" he whispered tenderly. "Look into my eyes. . . ."

Miska sighed and opened her eyes yet more widely. She shuddered and a slow smile appeared upon her lips.

The lacquer screen making the window was pushed open and Chunda Lal leapt in over the edge. As Fo-Hi drew the yielding, hypnotised girl towards him, Chunda-Lal, a gleaming *kûkri* held aloft, ran with a silent panther step across the floor.

He reached Fo-Hi, drew himself upright; the glittering blade quivered . . . and Fo-Hi divined his presence.

Uttering a short, guttural exclamation, he thrust Miska aside. She staggered dazedly and fell prone upon the floor. The quivering blade did not descend.

Fo-Hi drew himself rigidly upright, extending his hands, palms downward, before him. He was exerting a super-human effort. The breath whistled through his nostrils. Chunda Lal, knife upraised, endeavored to strike; but his arm seemed to have become incapable of movement and to be held, helpless, aloft.

Staring at the rigid figure before him, he began to pant like a man engaged in a wrestle for life.

Fo-Hi stretched his right arm outward, and with a gesture of hand and fingers beckoned to Chunda Lal to come before him.

And now, Miska, awakening as from a fevered dream, looked wildly about her, and then, serpentine, began to creep to the table upon which the keys were lying. Always watching the awful group of two, she rose slowly, snatched the keys and leapt across to the open window. . . .

Chunda Lal, swollen veins standing out cord-like on his brow, his gaze set hypnotically upon the moving hand, dropped his knife and began to move in obedience to the will of Fo-Hi.

As he came finally face to face with the terrible Adept of Rachê Churân, Miska disappeared into the shadow of the balcony. Fo-Hi by an imperious gesture commanded Chunda Lal to kneel and bow his head. The Hindu, gasping, obeyed.

Thereupon Fo-Hi momentarily relaxed his giant concentration and almost staggered as he glared down at the kneeling man. But never was that dreadful gaze removed from Chunda Lal. And now the veiled man drew himself rigidly upright again and stepped backward until the fallen *kûkri* lay at his feet. He spoke, "Chunda Lal!"

The Hindu rose, gazing before him with unseeing eyes. His forehead was wet with perspiration.

Fo-Hi pointed to the knife.

Chunda Lal, without removing his sightless gaze from the veiled face, stooped, groped until he found the knife and rose with it in his hand.

Back stepped Fo-Hi, and back, until he could touch the big table. He moved a brass switch—and a trap opened in the floor behind Chunda Lal. Fo-Hi raised his right hand, having the fingers tightly closed as if grasping the hilt of a knife. With his left hand he pointed to the trap. Again he spoke.

*"Tûm samajhe ho?"*

Mechanically Chunda Lal replied:

*"Ah, Sahib, tûmhara hûken jaldi: kiyâ jaegâ."* (Yes, I hear and obey.)

As Fo-Hi raised his clenched right hand, so did Chunda Lal raise the *kûkri*. Fo-Hi extended his left hand rigidly towards the Hindu and seemed to force him, step by step, back towards the open trap. Almost at the brink, Chunda Lal paused, swayed, and began to utter short, agonised cries. Froth appeared upon his lips.

Raising his right hand yet further aloft, Fo-Hi swiftly brought it down, performing the gesture of stabbing himself to the heart. His ghastly reserve deserted him.

*"Jey Bhowâna!"* he screamed—*"Yah Allah!"*

Chunda Lal, uttering a loud groan, stabbed himself and fell backward into the opening. Ensued a monstrous crash of broken glass.

As he fell, Fo-Hi leapt to the brink of the trap, glaring down madly into the cellar below. His yellow fingers opened and closed spasmodically.

"Lie there," he shrieked—"my 'faithful' servant! The ants shall pick your bones!"

He grasped the upstanding door of the trap and closed it. It descended with a reverberating boom. Fo-Hi raised his clenched fists and stepped to the door. Finding it locked, he stood looking toward the open screen before the window.

"Miska!" he whispered despairingly.

He crossed to the window and was about to look out, when a high-pitched electric bell began to ring in the room.

Instantly Fo-Hi closed the screen and turned, looking in the direction from whence the sound of ringing pro-

ceeded. As he did so, a second bell, in another key, began
to ring—a third—a fourth.

Momentarily the veiled man exhibited evidence of indecision. Then, from beneath his robe he took a small key.
Approaching an ornate cabinet set against the wall to the
left of one of the lacquer doors, he inserted the key in a
hidden lock, and slid the entire cabinet partly aside revealing an opening.

Fo-Hi bent, peering down into the darkness of the passage below. A muffled report came, a flash out of the blackness of the river tunnel, and a bullet passed through the
end of the cabinet upon which his hand was resting,
smashing an ivory statuette and shattering the glass.

Hurriedly he slid the cabinet into place again and
stood with his back to it, arms outstretched.

"Miska!" he said—and a note of yet deeper despair had
crept into the harsh voice.

Awhile he stood thus; then he drew himself up with dignity. The bells had ceased.

Methodically Fo-Hi began to take certain books from the
shelves and to cast them into the great metal bowl which
stood upon the tripod. Into the bowl he poured the contents of a large glass jar. Flames and clouds of smoke
arose. He paused, listening.

Confused voices were audible, seemingly from all
around him, together with a sound of vague movements.

Fo-Hi took up vials and jars and dashed them to pieces
upon the tiled hearth in which the furnace rested. Test-
tubes, flasks and retorts he shattered, and finally, raising the large glass case of orchids he dashed it down amid
the debris of the other nameless and priceless monstrosi-
ties unknown to Western science.

## Chapter 7

## THE WAY OF A SCORPION

A BLACK cloud swept past the face of the moon and cold illumination flooded the narrow lane and patched with light the drive leading up to the front of the isolated mansion. Wrought-iron gates closed both entrances and a high wall, surmounted by broken glass and barbed wire, entirely surrounded the grounds.

"This one also is locked," said Gaston Max, trying the gate and then peering through the bars in the direction of the gloomy house.

All the visible windows were shuttered. No ray of light showed anywhere. The house must have been pronounced deserted by anyone contemplating it.

"Upon which side do you suppose the big room to be?" asked Max.

"It is difficult to judge," replied Stuart. "But I am disposed to believe that it is in the front of the house and on the first floor, for I traversed a long corridor, descended several stairs, turned to the right and emerged in a part of the garden bordering the lane in which Inspector Kelly is posted."

"I was thinking of the window and the balcony which 'The Scorpion' informed you commanded a view of Hampton Court. Hampton Court," he turned half-left, "lies about yonder. Therefore you are probably right, doctor; the room as you say should be in front of the house. Since we do not know how to disconnect the alarms, once we have entered the grounds it is important that we should gain access to the house immediately. Ah! *morbleu!* the moon disappears again!"

Darkness crept over the countryside.

"There is an iron balcony jutting out amongst the ivy just above and to the right of the porch!" cried Stuart, who had also been peering up the moon-patched drive. "I would wager that that is the room!"

"Ah!" replied Max, "I believe you are right. This, then,

184

is how we shall proceed: Inspector Kelly, with the aid of
two men, can get over the wall near that garden door by
which you came out. If they cannot force it from inside,
you also must get over and lead the way to the entrance
you know of. Sowerby and two more men will remain to
watch the lane. The river front is well guarded. We will
post a man here at this gate and one at the other. Dunbar
and I will climb this one and rush straight for that balcony which we must hope to reach by climbing up the
ivy. Ah! here comes Inspector Dunbar . . . and *someone* is
with him!"

Dunbar appeared at the double around the corner of the
lane which led riverward, and beside him ran a girl who
presented a bizarre figure beside the gaunt Scotsman and
a figure wildly out of place in that English riverside setting.

It was Miska, arrayed in her flimsy *harêm* dress!

"Miska!" cried Stuart, and sprang towards her, sweep-
ing her hungrily into his arms—forgetful of, indifferent to,
the presence of Max and Dunbar.

"Ah!" sighed the Frenchman—"yes, she is beautiful!"

Trembling wildly, Miska clung to Stuart and began to
speak, her English more broken than ever, because of her
emotion.

"Listen—quick!" she panted. "Oh! do not hold me so
tight. I have all the house-keys—look!"—she held up a
bunch of keys—"but not the keys of the gates. Two men
have gone to the end of the tunnel where the boat is hid beside the river. Someone—he better climb this gate and by
the ivy he can reach the room in which Fo-Hi is! I come
down so. You do not see me because the moon goes out
and I run to the side-door. It is open. *You* come with me!"

She clung to Stuart, looking up into his eyes.

"Yes, yes, Miska!"

"Oh! Chunda Lal!"—she choked down a sob. "Be quick!
be quick! *He* will kill him! he will kill him!"

"Off you go, doctor!" cried Max. "Come along, Dunbar!"

He began to climb the ironwork of the gate.

"This way!" said Miska, dragging Stuart by the arm.
"Oh! I am wild with fear and sorrow and joy!"

"With joy, dear little Miska!" whispered Stuart, as he
followed her.

They passed around the bend into the narrower lane
which led towards the river and upon which the garden-

door opened. Stuart detained her. If the fate of the whole world had hung in the balance—as, indeed, perhaps it did— he could not have acted otherwise. He raised her bewitching face and kissed her ardently.

She trembled and clung to him rapturously.

"I *live!*" she whispered. "Oh! I am mad with happiness! It is Chunda Lal that gives me life—for he tells me the truth. It is not with the living-death that *he* touches me; it is a trick, it is all a trick to bind me to him! Oh, Chunda Lal! Hurry! he is going to kill him!"

But supreme above all the other truths in the world, the joyous truth that Miska was to live set Stuart's heart on fire.

"Thank God!" he said fervently—"oh, thank God! Miska!"

At the garden-door a group of men awaited them. Sergeant Sowerby and two assistants remaining to watch the entrance and the lane, Miska led Stuart and the burly Inspector Kelly along that path beside the wall which Stuart so well remembered.

"Hurry!" she whispered urgently. "We must try to reach him before . . ."

"You fear for Chunda Lal?" said Stuart.

"Oh, yes! He has a terrible power—Fo-Hi—which he never employs with me, until to-night. Ah! it is only Chunda Lal, who saved me! But Chunda Lal he can command with his *Will*. From it, once he has made anyone a slave to it, there is no escape. I have seen one in the city of Quebec, in Canada, forget all else and begin to act in obedience to the will of Fo-Hi who is thousands of miles away!"

"My God!" murmured Stuart, "what a horrible monster!"

They had reached the open door beyond which showed the dimly lighted passage. Miska hesitated.

"Oh! I am afraid!" she whispered.

She thrust the keys into the hand of Inspector Kelly, pointing to one of them, and:

"That is the key!" she said. "Have your pistol ready. Do not touch anything in the room and do not go in if I tell you not to. Come!"

They pressed along the passage, came to the stair and were about to ascend, when there ensued a dull reverberating boom, and Miska shrank back into Stuart's arms with a stifled shriek.

"Oh, Chunda Lal!" she moaned—"Chunda Lal! It is the trap!"

"The trap!" said Inspector Kelly.

"The cellar trap. He has thrown him down . . . to the ants!"

Inspector Kelly uttered a short laugh; but Stuart repressed a shudder. He was never likely to forget the skeleton of the Nubian mute which had been stripped by the ants in sixty-nine minutes!

"We are too late!" whispered Miska. "Oh! listen! listen!"

Bells began to ring somewhere above them.

"Max and Dunbar are in!" said Kelly. "Come on, sir! Follow closely, boys!"

He ran up the stairs and along the corridor to the door at the end.

A muffled shot sounded from somewhere in the depths of the house.

"That's Harvey!" said one of the men who followed— "Our man must have tried to escape by the tunnel to the river bank!"

Inspector Kelly placed the key in the lock of the door.

It was at this moment that Gaston Max, climbing up to the front balcony by means of the natural ladder afforded by the ancient ivy, grasped the iron railing and drew himself up to the level of the room. By this same stairway Chunda Lal had ascended to death and Miska had climbed down to life.

"Mind the ironwork doesn't give way, sir!" called Dunbar from below.

"It is strong," replied Max. "Join me here, my friend."

Max, taking a magazine pistol from his pocket, stepped warily over the ledge into the mysterious half-light behind the great screen. As he did so, one of the lacquer doors was unlocked from the outside, and across the extraordinary, smoke-laden room he saw Inspector Kelly enter. He saw something else.

Seated in a strangely-shaped canopied chair was a figure wearing a rich mandarin robe, but having its face covered with a green veil.

"*Mon Dieu!* at last!" he cried, and leapt into the room. " 'The Scorpion'!"

Even as he leapt, and as the Scotland Yard men closed in upon the chair also, all of them armed and all half fear-

ful, a thing happened which struck awe to every heart—
for it seemed to be supernatural.

Raising a metal hammer which he held in his hand, Fo-
Hi struck the bronze bell hung beside the chair. It emitted
a deep, loud note. . . .

There came a flash of blinding light, an intense crackling sound, the crash of broken glass, and a dense cloud of
pungent fumes rose in the heated air.

Dunbar had just climbed in behind Gaston Max. Both
were all but hurled from their feet by the force of the ex-
plosion. Then:

"Oh, my God!" cried Dunbar, staggering, half blinded,
*"look—look!"*

A deathly silence claimed them all. Just within the doorway Stuart appeared, having his arm about the shoulders
of Miska.

The Throne of the Gods was empty! A thin coating of
grey dust was settling upon it and upon the dais which
supported it.

They had witnessed a scientific miracle . . . the complete and instantaneous disintegration of a human body.
Gaston Max was the first to recover speech.

"We are defeated," he said. " 'The Scorpion,' surrounded, destroys himself. It is the way of a scorpion."